D0266741

Prisons of Glass

I watch her. Did I love her? She looks boyish, flat-faced, boring really, breezy.

The strong silent type. She's so like a man – and yet she isn't a man. Is that what turned me on? That magic combination of masculine and feminine – was that her power? Am I outside it now? Have I escaped it?

Does love transform the ordinary, like they say? What is love anyway, just an idea. Those evenings in the dark room, when I drew the photographic paper through its bath of chemicals, then watched it floating in the water in the sink: at first there's nothing, then imperceptibly the image begins to faint in onto the page, it steals on so gently at first, then slowly, slowly deepens and strengthens until its finally indelibly *there*. The dark room of love in the mind – at first when she looked at me it meant really nothing. Only gradually the image of her stole across the blank sheet, so gradually at first, until it took possession of me, and now she's all over me, stamped all over my body, never to be got rid of again.

I'm lost without you –

SHEFFIELD HALLAM UNIVERSITY
LEARNING CENTRE
WITHDRAWN FROM STOCK

Also by Elizabeth Wilson

Women and the Welfare State

Only Halfway to Paradise

Mirror Writing

What is to be done about
Violence Towards Women?

Adorned in Dreams:
Fashion and Modernity

Hidden Agendas

Elizabeth Wilson

Prisons of Glass

A Methuen Paperback

SHEFFIELD CITY POLYTECHNIC LIBRARY

WL
828
Wilson

COLLEGIATE CRESCENT

A Methuen Paperback

PRISONS OF GLASS

British Library Cataloguing in Publication Data

Wilson, Elizabeth, *1936–*
   Prisons of glass.
   I. Title
   823′.914[F]   PR6073.I464/

   ISBN 0-413-41830-8

First published in 1986
by Methuen London Ltd
This edition published 1987
by Methuen London Ltd
11 New Fetter Lane, London EC4P 4EE
Copyright © 1986 by Elizabeth Wilson

Printed and bound in Great Britain
by Richard Clay Ltd, Bungay, Suffolk

(I CAN'T GET NO) SATISFACTION:
Words & Music by Mick Jagger/Keith Richard © 1965.
Used by permission of ABKCO Music Inc/
Westminster Music Limited

This book is sold subject to the condition
that it shall not, by way of trade or otherwise,
be lent, resold, hired out, or otherwise circulated
without the publisher's prior consent in any form
of binding or cover other than that in which it is
published and without a similar condition
including this condition being imposed
on the subsequent purchaser.

For Angie, in Powis Square

'Henceforth there would be no discontinuity, no gap, no dead time, no remission.'

(Pauline Réage: *The Story of O*)

'A few minutes later, when there was no reason to expect such a thing, the noise was heard, in many streets, of wholesale window smashing.'

(Emmeline Pankhurst: *My Own Story*)

'A living mirror, thus, am I (to) your resemblance as you are mine . . . glasses, and mirrors . . . this burning glass . . .'

(Luce Irigaray: *Speculum of the other Woman*)

PART ONE: 1981

Gone West

The scorched land is empty and silent. Above them the bare slopes are burnt yellow, like the flanks of an old lioness, almost bald. The three women are coming down the long lawns, and as they descend towards the shade of the black oaks, the redwoods, and the madrone trees with leaves like rhododendrons, their footsteps begin to crack through dry twigs and leaf mould. The cabins built in secluded spots are invisible, the whole ravine might be deserted. Willow sighs at the heat.

Crystal speeds ahead, longing to be in the water.

'Don't go so fast – and watch out for rattlesnakes.'

Eileen and Willow pick their way more carefully down the steep incline. Willow has her weight, Eileen her baby, asleep in its basket, which swings slightly as Eileen carries it along.

'And this is really all your land, you and the other women,' says Eileen.

'The community's self-sufficient' – Willow's proud of it – 'We even make a profit from the sprouts and the goats' milk. That way we finance the summer camps for girls.'

'I thought you meant *Brussels* sprouts at first. I couldn't think how you grew them in that dark shed. But then Crystal said it's that stuff you get in sandwiches, health food stuff.'

At the bottom of the ravine the creek's dammed up to form a pool. The women, Willow's friends, made that too. Crystal wobbles on the edge, pulls off her shorts, one foot in the air. It feels strange to be naked in this hot open space. A duck watches from the flat stones of the ford further along.

Eileen finds a shady spot for the baby, the basket carefully wedged so that it can't slip down towards the stream. Crystal steps into the water. The soft velvet mud sinks, gives way, clouds the whisky-brown pool.

'It's lovely!'

Undressed, Willow is monumental. She walks with a

stately rolling motion, with overlapping flesh. Eileen is skimpy, shrimpy, shy, hugs herself as she runs and slips down the bank with a backward glance at the baby's basket.

The duck aqua-planes, quacking, towards the three women, in search of company. Crystal swims round and round like a dog, Eileen splashes near the edge, Willow floats on a rubber lorry tyre. They bob in the sun, under the blue sky. A breath of wind fans the trees. The baby sleeps in the shade.

'I've no lover right now,' says Willow. 'I was lovers with Sunny for a while – I'd have liked for us to go on being friends. I'd have liked it if she'd stayed here. But she was more wanting us to be lovers, and I – like it was more important to me we stay friends. I guess she was upset about it all – she's gone back east now.'

And we've come west. Crystal's mother ladled stew onto the plates: 'I put some tomato in, but it's all gone west' – disappeared.

'I think you're real lucky, you two, the way you've stayed friends. I get impatient, I'm more for moving on, if things aren't as I want them I've no patience to work things through. Like with Sunny – I didn't *really* work at it to try and make her see it my way. You two – you've really stuck together.'

'But we weren't ever in a sexual relationship.'

At once, Crystal wishes she hadn't said it – or not like that, not so guilty, defensive – distancing, disavowal – She hurries on: 'Lots of women we used to know – vanished, disappeared. Or got into something completely different. Or we've quarrelled – political feuds . . . We met someone I knew once, down the coast in Sausalito, someone from years back. Used to be a man. Had a sex-change operation. Robin – Robina now. Into mother goddesses and aromatherapy.'

'*We've* diverged, anyway,' says Eileen. 'You're married, I had the baby on my own – '

'Well, we always wanted different things in a way . . . I was never so much of an activist.'

'It's not just difference, it's a moral choice, a *political* choice. You get married – you accept the status quo – and somehow it all goes so nicely with being a psychoanalyst – '

'You used to encourage me – '

'It's led you into conservative value judgments – '

'Oh, but I don't see it like that at all – it's more a questioning – like, how *does* a child without a father, how does it enter patriarchal culture?'

Eileen scowls, her lip sticks out. Willow's dismayed for a moment, but then she sees that the argument is flowing along well-worn grooves. Still, to turn the subject a little she talks about the issue of fatherhood in a more practical way, of how they deal with different kinds of family situations at the summer camps: 'Last summer each girl worked on her family tree, her personal past, we brought it all out into the open – '

It's too hot to be cross, anyway. They are all lolling in the water now, looped in the heavy black tyres. The sun is so hot Crystal thinks it will wipe them out, melt them, nothing left but shadows where they were.

'And you're working together on this book of testimonies, women's accounts of their lives,' says Willow. 'I think that's a *great* idea.'

But they don't agree entirely, even about that. Eileen wants it to be political; Crystal's more interested in 'the varying experience of women'.

'I don't see that as such a split – that's two sides of the same coin really.' For Willow doesn't want to think of them as moving apart, estranged.

They float becalmed until the baby's reedy wail sends Eileen scrambling up the slope to feed her in the shade of the madrone tree. Crystal says she's going back to the cabin to rest for a bit. Willow and Eileen cross the ford in the opposite direction and walk up to the communal buildings for lunch. Willow slaps scrambled eggs on tortillas while Eileen changes the baby.

'Crystal married!'

Eileen shrugs. Some kind of middle-class safety . . . he's

an old friend, an academic, in Australia for six months, Crystal's on her way to join him now, couldn't leave her psychoanalytic training before the summer break –

'So we had this idea of a West Coast holiday, me on maternity leave, her on her way to Sydney – interview you for our project, look up our old friend Karen in LA. She was in our women's group . . . anyway, we didn't find her; another of the Disappeared.'

'You found me.'

'And you're a completely different person, a new woman, with a new life, a new *name* even – your life alone would make a whole book – '

'I sure was different – '

The baby kicks and smiles on her mat.

'She's so *good*,' says Willow. But Eileen sees that the baby doesn't really interest her. Her daughter Cindy a teenager, motherhood's almost a thing of the past for her, of that prison time, the life of unfreedom –

'Did you ever think of being lovers with a woman, Eileen?'

'Not really – not on principle or anything, but I just never – it never got me going somehow. I'll get back with a bloke again quite soon – I'm sure I shall – all this about Rosa and fathers from Crystal, it's so – *stuffy*.'

'Did she want children – thinks she's too old?'

Eileen shakes her head.

'I have problems seeing her as a healer, she's kinda reserved – '

'But that's why she's into psychoanalysis! The analyst never drops the mask. That's part of the game – But you know, since we saw you, what is it, *seven* years! – well, Crystal had some history with a woman you know. All been firmly buttoned up again now, of course. But then there was a lot of that, women dabbling – cracking on how great it was and how you ought to be into women – and now . . . as if it had never happened – I used to feel *really* put down for being straight – '

'But for a lot of women that was an important part of the women's movement, a way of getting in touch with themselves you shouldn't put them down either, as if it's only like authentic if it's forever. I mean, gee, nothing's *forever*.'

Later, Willow drives them down through the hills to the town on the floor of the valley. It's peaceful, has wide streets, wide grass verges, white clapboard houses that are neat and smart; tree shadows draw charcoal lines across the central square where sprinklers hiss and fan the grass.

Friends of Willow are holding a garage sale on their front lawn. Eileen and Crystal sort through the faded tee shirts and second-hand books, and talk to Willow's friends – two tall, rangy women who admire the baby and reminisce about their trip to London. Eileen buys an old leather hat, broad-brimmed, with a plaited cord wound round the crown, a hippie hat. Crystal buys a wooden bracelet, carved into a snake.

'I thought you hated snakes.'

'So nicely carved, though.'

'Reminds you of the python – '

They giggle at the memory.

Willow takes them to a Mexican roadside café, the waitress brings enchiladas smothered in beans, guacomole, sour cream, red sauce and minced meat. Crystal thinks it's sickly, gorges herself on tortilla chips instead.

Willow takes them to a show. A local community group is putting on a children's entertainment.

The school hall fills up. Everyone knows everyone else, at the front children swarm and shrill, their parents move about the rows of chairs further back.

Here it is still 1970. The women wear long, Victorian print skirts, frilled and flounced, full-sleeved blouses and smocks, and their hair is long and flowing loose. The men have long hair too, sometimes tied in a bunch, and they have full beards and those Christ-like faces. Willow says they all came up from San Francisco, and a lot of them grow dope, but you can't build it up into a really big business or

17

the cops come around in their helicopters, and spray the crops, or run guys in –

The lights dim. The curtains creak back, the show begins. Eileen whispers to Crystal, 'It reminds me of those cabarets we used to have at women's liberation conferences – amateur theatricals, women's institute, village halls. That was the tradition, wasn't it, only no one ever said so.'

The older children of the community are putting on the show. The audience recognizes every actor and calls out the names, enjoys the mistakes and hiatuses as much as the intentional effects. When one little girl gets stage fright and rushes off, the audience, caught up in this real-life drama, cheers as she's coaxed back on stage, still a bit tearful. They join in all the songs, and applaud the recitations wildly.

The baby looks and looks about her, does not cry, nor does she fall asleep until they are riding home again in Willow's truck.

Willow's cabin rises straight out of the forest floor. And really it is like sleeping in the open, in the forest itself, for on two sides the walls are simply sliding doors of glass, with no locks, and at each end they are made of faded redwood planks. Willow has laid astro-turf on the floor, and the mattresses on top of that. She turns out the light. The four of them lie in a row on the floor of the forest and stare up at the black sky, which is powdered with stars. They can hear the frogs calling in the creek. In the spaces between their intermittent hoarse hawking, the silence is so profound it seems deeper and more restful than sleep itself.

'*Now* d'you understand why I wanted you to hurry on up here instead of hanging out in LA and San Francisco –'

And Willow tells them about her life on the land, and of how she came to live among women, after she came back to the States – coming out to California to get away from the old life, she still got caught up with another no-good guy –

'I thought I'd help ex-prisoners – thought I'd have a lot to give them, but they were always messing up, doing stupid, crazy things, in the end I thought, like why should I be giving all my energy to these creeps –'

So she joined a women's group in Sacramento – and it went on from that: they'd drive up into the Sierra and there'd be singing and dancing; when she decided to change her name they had a proper naming ceremony – and then they all started to talk about going and finding some women's land –

Going out into the empty hinterland of California – they left the seething cities, the old world behind. . . .

At the Stardust Motel Eileen sits on the wider of the two beds and tosses the sheet of paper back to Crystal.

'It's all right in places – a bit over the top – you'll have to work on it – '

'You think it's pretentious, overwritten – '

'I didn't *say* that. I just said keep it simple – '

'I don't think you're really into this book at all – '

'For God's sake, just because I make a mild criticism – '

The baby suddenly yells.

'Look, when I've fed her let's go out and get something nice to eat ourselves.'

They wander away from their seedy, sleazy neighbourhood and into a phony Japantown. On impulse they walk into a Japanese westernized hotel. There's a tinkling piano at the bar, waitresses in kimonos and obis, pale velvet sofas and curving stairs down which guests float importantly, making a big entrance although there's no audience, no one takes any notice. The waitress brings them Midori cocktails in glasses the size of footballs and there's a tray piled high with free hors d'oeuvres. After a couple of the snowy-green daiquiris and handfuls of sushi balls and rice biscuits they're no longer hungry. Two American businessmen try to chat them up, the baby sleeps unnoticed in her basket.

'They think we're tramps, come on, we're drunk, we'd better go – '

Outside, on the downtown square, between skyscrapers, the real tramps sleep in the rapid, purple dusk, curled foetally. Each is alone. They never carouse in a group like the ones at home.

They're walking up a side street. A car bursts into flames –
'Look, it's burning – '
'Spontaneous combustion – '
'It can't be – '
They walk on. The car burns by itself.

Back at the Stardust Motel they watch TV. A documentary about prostitutes in LA – the city reflects back its own image, closed-circuit reality. Young women, very young, blonde, hispanic, black, their faces flicker on the screen, they have long, luxuriantly curling hair. Their perfect lips shape stories of coercion, lies, addiction, of alienation from the bodies they call their own.

'I wish my insides were disposable, so I could throw them away and put a fresh one in each day.'

Disposable cunts; Eileen's indignant: 'You know, men are *pigs* – really – '

'But .. .' Men, women, that raw edge, we tried to escape it, to create something better . . . as Willow has done; and yet –

Crystal has breakfast at the coffee shop on the corner. Sleepy Eileen and the long business of feeding and changing and dressing the baby, it all makes Crystal impatient, better she waits in peace here. Her irritation evaporates once she's seated by the window and drinking her coffee.

The place is almost empty. A man of about fifty sits at the counter, hunched forward on his elbows as he eats eggs and bacon. The waitress has tied a check bow round her hair, but she must be all of fifty too. Each stares ahead, past the other. In the far corner an old woman with papery thin hands and face devours eggs, hash browns, bacon, whole-wheat toast. The walls are painted yellow. Chrome rims the counter, tables and chairs.

Eileen appears, the baby's curled in its sling. She eases herself onto the bench: 'Stack of hot cakes please, with bacon and maple syrup.'

She's worked out the route to Hollywood, wears a cart-wheel straw hat that shields the baby from the sun.

'We have to get the bus from downtown.'
'I think we should hire a car.'

So many old women are on the streets, dressed despite the hundred-degree heat in finery left over from long-forgotten film premières: brocade dresses sweep the ground, gashed lips mutter behind veils, a fur swings carelessly off a naked shoulder, there are artificial flowers on hats, snub-toed suede shoes, rickety sandals – the parade of ghosts passes by. Hallucinations crowd the air, palpable as smog.

On Hollywood Boulevard the pavement's melting, rock music blares from a tacky record joint, the sidewalk's thronged, here at least it's like a real city. They buy English newspapers at a stand that sells porn.

They stroll along, in search of their turning. Suddenly Eileen pulls Crystal violently aside, out of the path of a painted youth who lurches, dances along the pavement, a python wreathed limply round his neck. It looks pale, faded as an old scarf against the boy's bronzed skin and dusky-rouged cheeks, his crazy eyes outlined in red and gold.

'Oh my *God!*'

At last they come to the turning. The city feeling fizzles out halfway up the block. Grass grows through the concrete, the road winds up the hill towards clumps of trees. On the left the block of 1930s flats must be what they're looking for.

They stop. The flats look seedy. Karen never answered their letters, after all. Apartment B; they ring the bell, hearing distant radio music and voices, high-pitched, not speaking English. A shuffling sound. A Vietnamese opens the door. He shakes his head to their enquiry.

'Lady was here. Lives Venice now.' He disappears down the dark passage, returns with a scrap of paper. The writing might just possibly be Karen's; it's hard to say.

'Venice – where's that . . .?'

'You go – it's too hot for her – I'll go back to the motel – '

'Surely somewhere in this city there must be a pool – '

21

'You'd think there'd be a beach at least . . . I suppose it's miles away – '

'I'm going to hire a car – this is absurd – '

A mother and baby in a sleazy motel at what, in a motel, is the sleaziest time of day: mid-afternoon.

'We don't think enough about you, do we, Baba. Don't take you into account.'

The baby's flushed and damp with heat. But she smiles.

'My darling baby . . . there now . . .'

Crystal drives through back lots, past shacks where creased black women and men sit out on the porch. It's like some Deep South hamlet. Crystal cruises past with the windows wound down. She refuses to lock them. She passes a cop on the corner interviewing two men. When he sees the car he springs out into the road, hand on his gun. But he sees she's white and falls back.

I shan't be able to do this with Andrew. He wouldn't like it – hates squalor and extremes.

My life with women – all that time, those years – was it a zone of freedom I'll never find again?

She drives through what might be a flat African township; roads, telegraph wires and the railroad track converge on a pinpoint in the distance. This is one of the richest cities in the richest country in the world.

Then she is back on the freeway, where the city shimmers, a mere mirage, at the horizon. Later she swoops down again, and the streets are different, yet the same, emptier than ever, the houses inturned, silent and secretive in the flat sunlight. She parks in a side street and walks through to the beach. It's deserted too, just a few kids hanging round doorways, addicts maybe, it's a bit menacing, the atmosphere. She retraces her steps, passes beneath a colonnade, crosses a road and up over a hump-backed bridge. The canals wind round, unmarked. She walks along the mud path beside the treacly water. A flock of geese passes single file ahead of her, beyond them squat palms unfurl by the water. More than ever this could be Africa . . . my mother in Africa . . . the snakes. . . .

Crystal remembers the beach at Pear Tree Bay. With the Robertsons; as they picnic Alan's mother scrambles to her feet, shrieks: 'Look! An adder!'

Zigzag its slithery speed along a rock.

Her mother throws a stone which traps its tail. There's slime, mess. The head and neck still flicker to and fro. A second stone misses, but a third somehow decapitates it.

I didn't want to look, but saw – couldn't help looking again –

I never thought till now – my mother must have been frightened too. Mrs Robertson just screamed.

Eileen says we've sentimentalized the Mother, mother-hood, just produced new stereotypes, or even embraced the old stereotype, when in reality being a mother in itself isn't any one experience, but different for different women – how different for Willow and Eileen, say – and you can't say that motherhood is what it means to be a woman, that it's the core experience, the core identity . . . can you? Eileen wants our book to be about politics, women in action, trades union women, activists, refuge workers, that sort of thing. But perhaps womanhood itself can't operate as an organizing principle at all.

What does Woman want? I wanted to live more intensely, never thought about womanhood, the whole idea was a kind of lie, femininity as masquerade, something you put on for men. I just wanted – Experience, excitement . . . but it came up at every turn: 'because you're a woman – '

Denied there was a problem, excluded great chunks of myself. But now, even if I acknowledge it, it's still a mystery, I'm not sure what it means, like a lost civilization, Freud said, the great hinterland, the lost continent: women . . . To reclaim that lost civilization, or to be part of this world of men; which is it to be?

She wanders past the bungalows, squat dolls' houses, each façade an imitation of some different style, more like a cinema lot than a real city street. She finds – more by chance than anything – the address that's scribbled on the scrap of paper. It's a duck-egg blue house with a pink roof and wrought iron all over the front. The crazy-paving path twists past a gnome, a stone bird bath, a clump of pampas grass. Muslin curtains hang limply at the steel-framed windows.

She walks slowly up the path – reluctantly. Even before she presses the bell she knows there'll be no answer. The ding-dong chime sounds emptily in there. She waits, hesitates (is someone watching from behind the curtains?) – doesn't ring the bell again, but turns away, retraces her steps along the canal paths and returns to the derelict street where she'd parked the car.

Karen wasn't there; we won't find her now – she stays locked in the past. Karen sat on a big red cushion in the cottage where we all went for that awful weekend, and laughing (nearly in tears) cried: 'It's Charles – he makes me feel so imprisoned – it's not exactly him, it's somehow . . . the relationship, locked together, and yet . . . I don't know – I just want to be *free* – to escape – '

Karen imprisoned in the past – I look back to see it all unreel to that pinpoint on the horizon – stretch out my hands, but the empty air slips through my fingers –

Before we created that zone of freedom, that no man's land, were we imprisoned, locked within our feminine subjectivity? A prison of glass – invisible yet so hard to escape – Did each of us sit in the solitary room of her mind, reading of our heroines – the ones who'd escaped – and, raising our eyes to look in the mirror at the scene reflected from beyond the window, catch sight of a woman walking in the garden, in the street, – *out there* – the perfect self, she who has escaped subjectivity, imprisonment, she, the ideal mirrored other –

No, I can't believe we were all the Lady of Shallot. Or perhaps we were – but didn't realize it. For in the beginning at least we all, always, *thought* we were free.

PART TWO: THE SIXTIES

Dali's crucified Christ lunged out in alien hysteria over the shabby comfort of Matron's office. There was nothing in the room to suggest a mother-and-baby home – more like a vicar's study or something. Crystal read a copy of the parish magazine.

The door burst open: 'I'm sorry we've kept you waiting so long – but we're in the middle of a bit of a *do*.'

Matron looked as if she'd just come from the grouse moor, left her fishing tackle in the hall. She sat down and peered at Crystal over her spectacles.

'You must excuse us – we're not ourselves.'

Her hands moved among the papers strewn over her desk and she murmured, 'Now, where did I – '

She stopped, looked at Crystal again, quizzical gaze, above her spectacles, beneath her beetling brows facetious masculinity peered out, unconsciously imprinted from clerical father, donnish uncles; Matron was a tweed-suited, hearty public schoolboy, no truck with femininity for her.

'Perhaps I should explain right away. It's a bit of an upset for us. We've had a death – not *here* exactly, but – one of our girls died yesterday, in hospital. She'd just given birth – well, last Friday, that is.'

'How dreadful. I'm so sorry.'

But Matron seized on the platitude: 'Dreadful? Well – I don't know about that. After all, who are we to question God's ways? One may feel these things are sad, but who is to say it wasn't really for the best? Anyway – we'd better get *you* settled in, hadn't we? No work for you today, we won't start you till tomorrow, but you'll want to sort yourself out, and you may like to look around the town – oh, but you know it already, don't you?'

Crystal smiled and nodded.

'You can come to Chapel with us in the evening, and then have supper if you wish – '

'I have some friends still here, I thought I'd – '

27

'Oh, it's just as you please – entirely up to you, of course.'

The college quads drowned in the honey of this September. So beautiful – yet with its flocks of middle-aged ladies in flowery dresses, its tourists with guidebooks and cameras, its flannelled dons and its students on bikes, the university town basked a little too complacently in admiration. The shops offered home-made scones and pots of jam, pot-pourris and embroidery silks. Life here was an everlasting tea time. A newspaper headline, 'Crisis in Laos', spoke but faintly of a faraway, larger world. Crystal smiled patroniz-ingly on the place. She'd envied Ian for still being here, but now it seemed outgrown and a little provincial, she thought, as she crossed a cobbled back street in the direction of her lover's lodgings.

It wasn't until mid-morning that Matron even mentioned Crystal's programme of work. More guest than student, she found it embarrassing to pass hugely pregnant girls scrubbing the landings or carrying heavy baskets of washing or trays of crockery. Deferential, they stood aside to let her pass.

'Usually we ask our student to supervise the girls doing housework upstairs until elevenses. But I thought as it was your first day you'd be getting straight, and then after coffee you can help Miss Staithes in the kitchen – you like cooking? You do? Good! But anyway, *this* morning – well, I wonder if you would mind doing something rather unpleasant for us this morning. It would be such a help if you would – you will? That's very kind of you. You see – well, Lila left all her things here, naturally, she thought she'd be coming back very soon. And I thought, as you didn't *know* her, it would be less painful for you to have to go through them and sort them out than it would be for any of us. It will all have to *go* somewhere. Ah good – here's coffee now – I hear the chink of cups.'

The door shot open.

'I hope you're not going to drop the tray today, Marilyn.' Matron laughed heartily. Marilyn grinned and blushed, almost holding her breath as she set down her load with its pot of coffee, jug of steaming milk and plate of chocolate biscuits.

'Thank you, Marilyn. Now can you close the door *quietly* this time, please!'

Matron poured.

'Marilyn's a nice girl, a dear girl, really, but you want to be a bit careful with her. She can be very cheeky you know. That's why I say to my students that it's not a good idea to talk too much with the girls. Be polite and friendly, *of course*, but if you encourage anything more than that they won't have much respect for you. It's fatal to bring yourself down to their level. They're only too ready to make a bid for sympathy, you know, and if you give them a chance they'll pour out all their troubles, and that doesn't do much good in my opinion. If they want to talk to me, of course I let them, but I don't encourage it. Healthier to put the past behind them. I don't believe in taking a tin opener to people. After all, if they have a problem to discuss, the right person to talk it over with is our Chaplain.'

'On our Course we learn quite a lot about counselling, the psycho-dynamics of the here and now – '

'Oh I daresay you do – you learn lots of different things, I know. Let's see, we had a student from our own training course last month, she was doing an essay on – let me see, what was it, the witness of prophecy in Elijah I think. She did a wonderful piece of work. Theology's a good basis. If the values are there, don't you agree, the work comes naturally –

'But anyway, let me tell you about Lila. She was a nurse in the hospital here, you see. She showed me her certificates from India – absolutely glowing reports and references she had, they said she was a *brilliant* nurse, but I spoke to the assistant matron, friend of mine, and she said that actually Lila was a great disappointment to them. So often happens with these commonwealth girls; out there they're wonderful, but the standards must be lower or *something*, I don't know what it is, because when they get over here to our hospitals, very often their work is a terrific disappointment.'

Matron drained her coffee cup, wiped her lips and poured them second cups.

'And I think Lila had been leading an unhappy kind of life – she'd moved from place to place over here, and mixed with all sorts of odds and bobs of people. Not a happy life. They said at the hospital, the nurses, she put up very little fight after the baby was born – no will to live . . . almost as though she didn't want to, though it's a terrible thing to say. And then you see' – she lowered her voice slightly – 'the baby is negroid in appearance. Not Indian, quite definitely negro.'

'Does that make a difference?'

'Oh, none at all – I wasn't implying – ' Matron looked over her spectacles and twinkled quizzically at Crystal. 'I'm afraid you suspect us of the most awful motives – but the trouble is we find it very hard to place these babies for adoption. It is an extra responsibility to ask parents to take on, don't you agree, as well as everything else? We have to be very, very careful . . . but you'll be able to talk to our social worker, Miss Jenkins, about all that, she'll take you through the reception into care –

'But anyway, to get back to Lila. She told me – mind you, I don't know how true it is – but she *told* me she came from really quite a wealthy family in – whichever part of India it was. Her father was some kind of businessman – she said they were very high caste. I don't know much about caste, do you? Can businessmen be high caste out there? But anyway, I can quite believe they were *rich*, because she had no *end* of really beautiful clothes, saris and so on –

'Well, I'll take you up to our boxroom shall I, that's where we've stored it all.'

There were piles of what looked like jumble. Crystal opened a suitcase and plunged her hands in among the soft, inert, clinging materials, which gave off a faint scent of joss sticks.

Matron had surely exaggerated the luxury of Lila's wardrobe. Only two of the saris were silk; and there were only six altogether, the others of cheap printed cotton or nylon; there were also under-bodices and heavy underskirts (so that was what you wore underneath). There were half a dozen pairs of scuffed court shoes and thonged sandals. Crystal put them in a separate box. Some of the clothes were soiled, and left a slightly tacky feel on Crystal's hands. There was a sense of untidiness and haste, of unpreparedness. Well, of course –

What was astonishing was the quantity of make-up. Expensive brands, too, but most of the stuff was hardly used. The lipsticks and creams, the eyeliners and different coloured eye shadows had all been tried and discarded. Pale powder and English Rose rouge had been left to spill and moulder in the quilted plastic holdall. The musty, stale smell, feminine yet sexless, depressed Crystal.

She next opened an attaché case full of papers. She sat down on the floor to look through them, but Matron appeared, breathing heavily from climbing the stairs.

'Oh – *would* you mind helping Miss Staithes in the kitchen now? Marilyn's gone into labour and I've got to get her to the hospital. Though whether it'll come to anything this time – she's had two false alarms already. You can finish that tomorrow.'

Miss Staithes was flustered, because she'd lost Marilyn, on whom she depended. Crystal made cauliflower cheese for her, and asked her questions about the hostel. The conversation was a frustrated one, for every question Crystal asked from the point of view of social work and Freudian theory was answered in religious terms. Her only interesting discovery was that Matron had wanted to be a nun.

'She was an aspirant, you know, but she wasn't called.'

'What does that mean, exactly?'

'Why, simply that God decided otherwise.'

'I thought nuns were Roman Catholic.'

'Oh no!' Miss Staithes looked deeply shocked.

'What *really* is the difference between being High Church and being Catholic – apart from the Pope, I mean – '

'Isn't that enough!' Miss Staithes looked most upset. 'I don't want to be under the Pope, I'm sure!'

On Saturday, Matron said, 'You'll be coming to communion with us, tomorrow? We usually go first thing, and then take the girls to church later in the day, to matins usually, sometimes evensong.'

'Well – actually I'm an atheist.'

There was a little silence.

'I see – well . . . thank you for telling us – I don't know how you feel about it, but I think it would be best if you went to church with the girls just the same, don't you? Though it's entirely up to you, of course.'

When the Chaplain dropped in for a cup of coffee, Crystal caught Matron mouthing silently at him: *she's not one of us*.

The Chaplain, a bachelor, reminisced about Kenya, where he'd been a missionary. His faded blue eyes seemed still to be looking out over the blue hills.

'I send the girls to him when they're upset,' said Matron. 'Our little chapel – it's a place where the girls can be peaceful.'

Crystal liked the early evenings, when she helped with the babies, although for the most part she just watched.

'Why do you make them breast-feed, if they're going to have them adopted?'

'Oh, it gives the babies a *much* better start. It does form more of a bond, of course, and then breast-feeding is supposed to be *pleasurable*, you know, for the mother. The uterus *contracts*.'

'It seems unkind if they're not going to keep them. . . .'

Oh, but no girl should be encouraged to keep her child. So hard for a young mother on her own, living in one room perhaps, every girl owed it to her baby to give it a better home than she herself could provide.

'We wouldn't have them back a second time,' said Matron firmly. 'Some homes do – but we feel – well, you can make a mistake once, but a second time . . . There's too much sentimentalism – '

There was Lillian, the thirty-six-year-old secretary, who'd made one fatal slip. Her intense grief at the thought of parting from her baby pleased Matron more than the carefree manner of some of the younger ones. One sixteen-year-old even had a boyfriend in attendance, and might get married after all.

'She doesn't really *feel* it,' said Matron, as she watched the family group from her window. 'Look at her parents, egging her on. Spoilt!'

Lillian on the other hand sobbed and sobbed the day her baby was taken away.

'It's hard for her, very hard.'

Crystal tried to show the girls she was on their side.

'Please call me Crystal,' she said.

Crystal was going through Lila's papers. There was an empty wallet, containing only a few stamps. There were two nursing certificates and a passport. Crystal looked at the photograph. The face that stared out looked pale and heavy. The wavy hair was black and very lustrous. The blackened eyebrows, slanting, kohl-lined eyes and black, shiny, ogee-curved lips were clichés of popular Indian illustrative art. The yellowed, frayed passport and the much-folded and fingered certificates, crumbling at the edges, gave Crystal a sudden sense of the distance to India, of the worry of being a stranger far from home.

There were income tax forms and letters of appointment, and at the bottom of the pile a packet tied with white ribbon. Crystal untied the ribbon and unfolded the first letter, in pleasant, illicit anticipation of being privy to someone's secrets, to private, intimate lives.

His name was Ahmed and he typed badly on what must have been an almost worn-out machine. He had just moved to a good job in Aden. 'Darling,' he wrote, 'it was so lovely to have a lovely f— (!) with you, and now I am thinking of you and how we can meet together again soon. I am here, missing you very much and not looking at other pretty girls. I am hoping we can have good times together again soon. It would be so nice to be lying under the trees with you again having lovely times, kissing and cuddling, and you know what! Instead I shall try to tell you what you ask, all about my life here.' But the letter petered out in a stilted timetable of his week, and promises of another letter very soon.

Following letters tried to excuse their infrequency. References to other girls and to his expanding social life replaced the references to lovemaking. 'I cannot be a good boy forever,' he wrote, 'I hope you are having jolly times, too.'

He moved to Bagdhad. The letters became morose, irritable. They ceased altogether. But then there was one last letter, postmarked a year later than the previous one, and posted in Kenya. It was handwritten – blotchy, ragged writing. He had had many worries over his father's death, business affairs, his mother, his sisters, the shop, the political situation. 'I miss you Lila, I need you here. Why did I miss my chance with you – surely Fate cannot have decreed that it is too late. This life, one long mistake, is all, all for you. I lay it at your feet.'

Most days Crystal saw her lover. Of course it was on his account that she'd chosen this particular residential social work placement – so convenient since he was doing his Ph.D at the university from which they'd both graduated. They laughed at the irony of the situation.

'Don't you think you'd better tell Matron?'

'God, it's an appalling place. What a morality! I'm glad I'm free of all that – I couldn't bear to live by convention. Could you?'

Ian smiled and raised his eyebrows. He was being a bit enigmatic. That girl (smart, dark) she'd seen him with in the High, just a friend, he'd said, from the labs, now don't start being possessive –

They met in his lodgings in the afternoons, and it was exciting to return to the hostel as if nothing had happened, yet savouring the bland, mushroomy smell of sex, and the smell of sweat, like thyme, clinging to her body. Matron smiled briskly, and Crystal felt triumphant – the truth so brazen, yet invisible.

Of course she had no wish to lie. Indeed, she broached the question of sex outside marriage to Matron: surely it wasn't really so wrong? Miss Staithes looked horrified, but Matron listened as if she respected Crystal's point of view. As Ian said, probably more interesting for her to have someone intelligent to talk to, instead of endless evenings with the other old girl.

Crystal remembered, congratulating herself, her visit to the Family Planning, pretending she was married –

'Surely they ought at least to be *told* about birth control?'

Matron listened, expressionless, polite.

Although a nuisance, Crystal found it rather exciting to squash in the dutch cap, slippery with the cream . . . really, why *didn't* the girls use something?

Matron said, 'Anyway – I'm so grateful to you for putting Lila's things to rights. It was quite a do we had, wasn't it? And then Marilyn having twins! I've just written the letter to Lila's people, and then tomorrow I suppose we shall have to put it all in a parcel and send everything off to them.'

'But they'd lost touch – and they won't want all that stuff – old letters – '

'Oh, I think they should have it all. It's only right – and it's not in any case for us to say. It belongs to them, really, after all, and I daresay they'd want to have it. One can never presume to choose for others, can one?'

Matron's harsh Christianity, with its clarity that did not illuminate, directed her thoughts and actions without visible hesitation or doubt. It could never be right to be kind by protecting innocent bystanders from the truth. Matron had to rub everyone's nose in some plain, unvarnished truth that wasn't a truth at all.

'It all belongs to her people now.'

Had Matron seen the letters? Did she know?

What would Lila have wanted? She would not have wanted Crystal to read her love letters, would not have wanted her parents to know of her illegitimate child, would not perhaps have wanted Ahmed to know. But Matron had said they thought she wanted to die, so perhaps she had not cared about what was left for the living.

Crystal decided that she would remove and destroy Ahmed's letters.

The next day was Saturday and a whole day off for her. She and Ian took a punt down the river, and returned home late in the evening.

Matron had not gone to bed.

'Not too late for a cup of tea? Did you have a nice day?'

'My boyfriend was here.'

'How nice – you should have brought him to meet us.'

'We went on the river – '

'Well – I sent the parcel off,' said Matron, 'Lila's things.'

Too late – Crystal had forgotten to remove the letters after all.

'A relief, really,' said Matron, 'but God's ways are best.'

3

The Nervous System

London's a machine furred up with bad weather. No light – you stare from the window at a negative: black sky, white streets, white roofs. Cold cocoons you. You'd like to stay at home, to hibernate. Out in the streets there's clumsiness, things slow to a halt, roads gummed up, railways disrupted, the city's nervous system falters, there's a power cut.

Men and women stagger through the streets in the grip of collective breakdown. Nothing works that you always took for granted. The city's had a stroke.

It's Clinic Day. A quiet morning on the wards, but by one o'clock the patients are beginning to creep into the rows of chairs, gathering like an audience waiting for the show to begin, waiting for Sister to come out from behind the screens and announce the first number.

Behind the screens the itinerant troupers begin to assemble, the latter-day mesmerists, hypnotists and fortune tellers. We call it psychiatry. The consultants leave their overcoats and briefcases with Sister and make for the doctors' dining room.

The Department is just a corridor. Wooden partitions segment it into cells, with Sister's room at the end. From behind her desk she hands out drug slips to the patients, digestive biscuits and tea to the staff. Here the women gather round to hear the departmental gossip.

'You know that boy from Neurology. They couldn't find anything wrong with him, but Dr Darke wasn't satisfied – did a complete re-examination. And you know what? Found a whopping great tumour behind his eye.

'And Mrs Morrison died. Hadn't you heard? Terrible, wasn't it – only thirty, and two small children. Still don't really know what it was. Blood pressure just shot sky-high. Mind you, I knew there was something wrong the minute I set eyes on her.'

The body is treacherous. At any moment something may happen, the system start to go wrong.

'I'm afraid Sister from Lucknow Ward complained about

you, Crystal. Didn't like you coming into the ward in all that black leather.'

'You *do* look rather like something out of prewar Berlin – the boots *and* the coat – looks a bit kinky.'

'Like Christine Keeler.'

'Aren't those heels dangerous in the snow?'

Then Dr Morag MacKenzie, the junior Registrar, changes the subject: 'It took me half an hour to start the car this morning, *half an hour*, can you believe!'

'It's been like this for nearly three months.'

'The worst winter since 1947, that's what they say.'

'Are there more accidents?'

'See all that blood in Outpatients today? Someone's lifeblood I'm afraid.'

Another cup of tea for everyone. They stir and sip.

'So who've we got this afternoon then, Sister?'

'Well, there's Adrian Green – '

'It's definitely MS you know – '

'Dr Anthony says the prognosis isn't good.'

It starts gently, insidiously, double vision, a little weakness of the arms, a dizzy spell. Then you begin to shuffle, to drag a foot, to shake uncontrollably, fall down. Incontinence, the body like a jelly – at last, like that man on the wards; he stares, moves his jaw like a fish, just a hoarse noise comes out. The nurse sits beside him and places the cigarette between his lips. The nervous system goes haywire, in collapse.

Think about it too much, and you'll have all the symptoms. Listen to your body, and you'll disintegrate from sheer fear.

The others, unperturbed, maintain normality. Geraldine Bishop, principal social worker, has had her hair done, as she does each clinic day, swept into a candyfloss beehive.

'You'll be in charge today, Crystal. I'll be with the Professor, it's his special ward round.'

The show begins. Sister calls the patients, one by one.

Crystal interviews in a disused bathroom beyond Sister's lair. She balances on the edge of the bath, and the patients sit in the rickety chair with their backs to the light. Afterwards she ushers them down the fire escape. Better to keep them away from the hall where rows of supine patients now lie wrapped in blankets as they recover from Dr Anthony's electric shocks.

Sister sniffs: 'He's a bit too fond of ECT if you ask me.'

She harks back to the therapeutic community where she worked until last year.

'No ECT or drugs *at all* – and of course we *never* wore uniform.'

'That's what I'm interested in really – psychotherapy.'

But Sister's fishy eyes stare at her coldly.

Mrs Brown leans back in the bathroom chair. She's wan and waif-like, looks about twelve years old. Supposed to be depressed.

'I wonder if you can tell me why – what it is – '

'It's just my nerves. I'm fine, really – '

'Is it your husband – ?'

'He's a good man, really, and so long as I have the tablets, see, I'm okay.'

'Your housing – ?'

'Everything's fine so long as I have me prescription – '

'There must be a reason – there's always a reason for feeling unhappy – '

'How's the little depressive?' Dr Morag MacKenzie smiles. 'What! Lost her prescription *again?*'

'So she says.'

'But it's only two weeks since the last one – are you *sure?*'

'That's what she says.'

(How can you be sure?)

'Well, I'll rewrite it this time, but you'd better keep an eye on her – '

The childish face lights up: 'Oh, *thank you* Miss.'

The next one's a bleached blonde with a greenish-white face. Dr Mackenzie hands the file to Crystal. What's the family background? Some problem with her baby – and a bit paranoid too.

'I don't *know*,' says Dr Mackenzie, squeezing out pinched

39

Edinburgh vowels, 'but there's just a wee bit of a delusionary tinge – could be puerperal psychosis.'

The woman speaks in a monotone: 'Never wanted to be a housewife, you see. Never played with dolls . . . I don't think the baby's mine, really – they keep giving her back to me, though – '

'You don't really feel like a mother – ?'

Every woman wants to be a mother.

'I wonder if you can tell me when you first – '

When life ceased to feel normal. The bathroom, this normal, misused room, is bleak in the glare of the unshaded bulb that hangs from the high ceiling. The bath has a dribble of rust down the inside, the plaster peels off the walls, there's still an old nailbrush, a petrified bit of soap. It's the sort of room that would do as a torture chamber, so ordinary. Interrogation now:

'Just try to tell me – '

'It's just the way I feel.'

The snow comes down again, motes flicker past the dirty window. New snow on old, the thin coating over impacted grey ice; it's treacherous, a different city.

'We'll need to know a bit about your background – '

'If they can just take the baby away – '

Dr Mackenzie prescribes tranquillizers: 'Better contact her local Children's Department. We may have to admit her.'

There's a commotion in the waiting room. A young man with dark curls waltzes through. He sings, talks and laughs, a hurdy-gurdy of joy.

Dr Mackenzie mutters, 'I've arranged an emergency admission. He's high as a kite. St Theresa's – get him an ambulance. And keep him occupied until it comes or he'll frighten Dr Anthony's ECTS.'

He puts his arm round Crystal, can't stop talking he's so excited. She sits him in the bathroom, makes the call from Sister's room next door.

She can hear him singing, and he's turned on the water.

40

She's still hanging onto the phone when he appears, grinning and wet.

'Had a little dip. Hope that's okay.' There's a pool of water seeping out into the corridor.

'It'll be at least an hour,' comes the voice down the phone.

'Hey, mind if I make a call? I've got to ring Peter Sellers – friend of mine. Just a minute, I've got the number here – won't take a second. Don't worry – I've written a song. He's going to love it.'

Crystal hurries back to Dr Mackenzie: 'Morag, please give him a sedative – I can't control him – '

'You'll just have to do your best – look how many I've still got to see – '

He's eating Sister's digestives as he shouts down the phone.

'I'll call you a taxi.'

'Where are we going – ?'

'In a taxi – '

'Oh good – the BBC – '

Crystal pays the driver, tells him where to go.

'I'm singing a happy song – '

Life doesn't warrant this joy. A disease in itself his happiness; they diagnose manic psychosis.

The taxi circles the forecourt at the bottom of the fire escape, and eases out into the grey confusion of streets and traffic. There'll be a row when the ambulance arrives. She acted unprofessionally. And he'll never make it to the hospital. He'll disappear into the winter city, whirligig like a spinning top, can't escape his own momentum.

'What the hell's the mess in this bathroom? And my *biscuits!*'

Sister's furious; and Geraldine Bishop's back from the ward round. The two of them stare at her. Geraldine Bishop puts on her *concerned* look: 'Are you managing okay?'

Hypocrite – it's a reprimand disguised as friendly care. (The work *can* be worrying – the bread and butter part of it *is* sometimes boring, you know, arranging transport, seeing to their social security, that sort of thing – but that *is* social work after all – I know you're more *interested* in psychoanalysis, but – this is part of mental illness too, the practical side, you know. Do *say* if anything's worrying you –

Nothing, I'm fine, it's just my nervous system.)

Geraldine's so womanly. It all comes naturally to her, to organize behind the scenes, to smoothe things over, to calm them down, to manage: flowers for the Professor's wife, a cup of tea for the bereavement case, birthday presents for the secretaries. Soothes the system.

But Crystal's different. Knocks around with Geraldine Bishop's younger brother. An unfortunate coincidence; she met him on New Year's Eve – the night the snow started.

('Of course, you know Simon's homosexual – '

'Of course, you know Geraldine thinks you're frightfully immature – '

'I hope you know what you're doing – you don't want to get *hurt*.'

'She's one to talk – with that husband who beats her up.'

'Isn't it time you *settled down?*'

Simon has no steady job. Just a bohemian, living on the margins, bits of freelance writing here and there. Hangs about Soho cafés. But he sees a psychoanalyst.

'We're all sick, you know. You think you're so sane?')

'He was so manic – I just couldn't keep him quiet here.'

Sister and Geraldine Bishop exchange glances – (emotionally still an adolescent – perhaps we should have a talk Crystal – and she wants to become an *analyst!*)

The Department's emptying now. The Professor leaves, and Dr Anthony. The patients who had shocks have all come to and gone home. Geraldine Bishop lingers; she still has a patient to see. Crystal sits waiting for the end of the afternoon in the dim light of Outpatients. The clinic is nearly over. Only Dr Morag Mackenzie works on.

The telephone rings. Sister darts out of her cubbyhole and rustles down the corridor, swivels her fish-eyes towards Crystal.

'That girl – Mrs Brown – found her unconscious in the street – she overdosed – no wonder she wanted more prescriptions – been admitted to Lucknow. Morag will have to get over there now after Clinic to sort it all out – God knows what time she'll get away. You really could have been a bit more careful, just used your common sense.'

There's another telephone call. This time it's from Casualty. They're sending a patient upstairs.

She appears between two uniformed porters. A fur coat is slung round her shoulders. Her legs are long, thin. She wears lizard shoes.

'No stockings,' mutters Sister, 'that's a bad sign.'

'May I ask what all this is about? Is there any reason *at all* for this fuss? I was merely in search of – '

They brought her in off the street. She was shouting and falling about in the gutter. Nearly ran under a car. Her silk dress is soiled, torn.

'She must be freezing,' says Dr Morag Mackenzie. 'Funny how they don't notice it sometimes!'

'Now – what's the matter, dear – ?'

'Nothing's the *matter*, I assure you, except these men, who've *dragged* me up here – '

'Now let's just have a few details – your address – '

'I usually stay at Brown's Hotel, but for some reason – it was *full*. Can you imagine – I've *always* stayed at Brown's – '

'She's from that hostel – ' hisses Sister.

'My name's Paragreen, Lady Lydia Fox Paragreen. Now please just call me a taxi, darling, and – '

Dr Morag Mackenzie soothes her down. The nervous system slows back to normal. Everything's going to be all right.

'Just a few days in hospital, Lady Lydia – '

But the nervous system goes into overdrive again: 'What the hell are you talking about – I'm buggered if I'm going to any fucking hospital. I'm perfectly well – get me some sandwiches, where the hell is the waiter – '

Up on her high horse again, truculent, refusing to play the game.

43

'The *language*,' gloats Sister, her mouth pursed like a carp's.

Dr Morag Mackenzie's sweet reasonableness is reassuringly genteel. She has the sanest voice in the world: 'You'll be verray much more comfortable, Lady Lydia – '

Subside again – then suddenly something sets her off and once more she's on the gallop, shouting about the buggers trying to keep her here, well you can all fuck off. And she hits out at Dr Mackenzie with a white, scrawny arm.

Geraldine Bishop whispers to Dr Mackenzie, 'All for the best, I really think we'll have to.'

Section her. Slice her up, dissect her, lay bare the nervous system.

Dr Morag Mackenzie nods at Sister. Sister winks and rustles away.

Lady Lydia glares at them all from those turquoise jewels set in her cracked enamelled face. A Bright Young Thing in the twenties: debutante of the year. She knows exactly what she's doing, she's saner than any of us, she just won't play the game. Obstinate. And hungry, hungry.

But when Sister returns with the hypodermic Lady Lydia looks up and knows she's beaten. They all hold her down. She struggles a bit and her dress wrinkles up.

'No knickers,' murmurs Sister as the needle sinks into the wasted thigh.

The ambulance men arrive.

'Have you right in no time.'

'There you go, onto the old stretcher – '

'Easy does it – '

Geraldine Bishop looks at Crystal: concern.

'It's always unpleasant, that sort of thing.'

'It's horrible, I hate doing it,' says Dr Morag Mackenzie.

'She'll be better off in hospital,' says Sister.

Now Dr Mackenzie must dash across to see Mrs Brown in Lucknow; then she and her husband, also a doctor, will be off to a dinner party in Blackheath, despite the snow; the young marrieds. Geraldine Bishop will wait in her softly lit drawing room for her businessman husband, and wonder if he's having an affaire with his secretary that he's always so late. But she won't dare to ask him. Sister's on the shelf, but there's a coffee evening at the Psychotherapy Association; she listens to the speaker, but her eyes swivel right and left to assess the likely men. The consultants, who long since left for Harley Street, are now en route to the warm embrace of normal family life in St John's Wood and Highgate.

The end of the day: Crystal wraps herself in black leather, fur hat and fur muffler. She clambers down the fire escape, spikes across the courtyard on high heels and out into the frozen street.

Does she feel dizzy – a throbbing in the brain – ? It's just my nerves.

The pavements are covered in frozen slush, hard black ice. Cars and lorries squelch and crunch past, sometimes splattering her. The sodium glare illuminates a sky rusted like dried blood. Never dark above the city; it pulsates beneath, its breathing laboured. Somewhere the nervous system palpitates.

She's a young woman, alone in the city, she's looking for those raw nerves, bleeding somewhere, beneath the snow.

4

The Divorce Party

Green leaves were bursting out all over the red-brick city, and the scent of lilacs and wallflowers filled the suburbs. Business was booming, and 'Money Can't Buy You Love' shouted from the airwaves.

Jenny was on her way back to the clinic after lunch when she saw Peter and Di slouching towards her. The combination of their grey hair and their crumpled, studenty clothes made an uneasy, almost sinister impression, as if they were in disguise, gave them a shifty look.

'Hul*lo* Jenny!' Peter massaged her shoulder. 'You're looking well.'

'Have you heard!' shrieked Di. 'We're having a divorce party! You must come!'

'We want to *celebrate* our divorce. It's a *happy* occasion. We thought – we'll invite all our friends round, have a ball – '

Jenny was late and didn't want to chat, but of course before hurrying on she promised that she and Keith would be there.

As she trotted towards the clinic, curved, muscular and healthy, full of vigour and purpose, she reminded Peter of a smart, round-rumped little pony.

Bill Hargreaves, the clinic social worker, flinched when she swung her yellow mane and flashed her large white teeth; her ruddy face and blindly staring blue eyes, all the sexier for being so short-sighted, scared him. He preferred Helen, the clinic doctor.

They'd had lunch a few times, he and Helen, a drink after work, he dared to hope there was a kind of understanding – but she was married, and to one of the city's richest businessmen. Also there was Trisha, his wife, with her postnatal depressions, her miscarriages, her body perpetually bleeding with the stigmata of thwarted fecundity.

The health centre stood in the middle of a windswept prewar estate. The curving roads that led nowhere, the rows of concrete and pebble-dash houses, the rusty prams and swathes of seeding, anaemic grass, spoke of neglect and poverty in the midst of prosperity. Bill called it a subculture, problem families, inadequacy. Tom Horrocks, the NSPCC man, 'the Cruelty' the women called him, railed at laziness, evil, whoredom. Helen sighed. Jenny was brisk and antiseptic.

Even here, though, the pink and white may trees clustered, lilac scented the air, yellow laburnum liripipes drooped. And the clinic was less busy than usual. The clerk said it was the fine weather. The mums had managed to sell their own bodies, or something that had fallen off a lorry, and had taken the kids to Skeggy for the day. Or else they were just lying on the pallid grass, hoping for a Costa Brava tan from the first cold English sunshine. Like white lard, Jenny thought; you told them about proper diets, but they didn't listen, or hadn't the money, or didn't care. It was all chip butties and coke.

'I've just been invited to a divorce party.'

Bill went red. He was Catholic, only semi-lapsed.

'What a strange idea,' said Helen.

'Why don't the two of you come?' said Jenny, both unaware and on target.

That was how she'd walked into Keith's life, unaware, yet with juggernaut resolve. Inconclusively separated from his wife, he'd been living alone in a big, cold flat and waiting for an American mistress with whom he thought he was in love. Almost the first thing Jenny did was clean his cooker. She neither asked him if she might, nor expected thanks. 'I just couldn't bear to see it looking like that.' The American mistress arrived, finally, but found Jenny installed.

The flat was spruced up. Jenny repainted it, and scoured the second-hand shops for comfortable furniture, pretty bits of china, even found a good rug. It would do nicely for the time being. No children yet for Jenny. There was plenty of time.

The university was expanding. An ambitious building programme had just been completed and gleaming glass towers crested the hill. It was much more glamorous than the old poor law hospital where Jenny had trained. In that former world of fellow nurses and hearty medics Keith was a good catch: an older man, but still quite young; an academic and touched with the university's slight aura of bohemianism; separated from his wife, but childless; a writer, a quiet man, but with access to an exciting new circle of friends. Their first meeting had been chance – even in the circumscribed world of the provincial city their two lives had hardly overlapped; but she'd made sure they met again.

True, they were not yet married, his divorce hadn't been sorted out. But on her medical card, on her library card and in the electoral register she appeared as Mrs Pierce.

'Typical Peter,' said Keith when Jenny told him about the divorce party. But then Keith never enthused. Jenny on the other hand felt quite excited.

Before Peter's arrival, university social life had been symmetrical families, a settled routine. There were wives with small children, a few struggled on with their Ph.Ds, there were husbands who chased pretty students on the sly, there were male excursions to country pubs for billiards, darts and local beer, there were suburban dinner parties where the wives wore dolly dresses and pale stockings and gathered at one end of the room.

Then Peter had come, and it was as if a band had struck up. They'd all been caught up in this dance, been swung on the merry-go-round of a Paul Jones. Everyone had changed partners. More like musical chairs for poor Di, though, for she'd been left out, eliminated, ending up without a partner at all.

Some people thought it odd that Peter was keeping on the house, not Di with the children. But then it was Peter who had the job and anyway Di was moving to London.

The house stood in the oldest square in the city, the only eighteenth-century survival. It was cavernous, had original tiled passages and kitchen, and a garden dank and ivied as a Victorian cemetery.

Peter was proud of the period atmosphere he'd created in the large rooms. He'd papered the walls himself with thick, grape-strewn, purplish Morris wallpaper, and had furnished the whole house with Victoriana bought at provincial auctions. There was wax fruit beneath glass domes, a wooden rocking horse, oil paintings of highland cattle. He'd even had a brass bedstead transported from Scotland.

Some of the furniture had been moved out of the double drawing room for the party, but the cumbersome, richly scrolled, red velvet chaise longue lolled in its usual place in the window and the Persian rugs had been rolled up underneath it, to leave the polished floor ready for dancing.

Would Di leave it all with a pang, or would she be glad to see the last of it? No one asked her. Who were her friends? No one knew.

Two strangers flanked Peter and Di as they awaited the first guests; a louche foursome. Peter's new mistress, Venetia, of course was one of them. The man was a seedy-looking journalist from London. He looked like a refugee from a Soho drinking club. He was even wearing dark glasses. 'What does Peter see in Jake?' they all asked among themselves. But he was said to be gathering material for a novel – about *them*, presumably, so they felt quite flattered.

Venetia's hair waved voluptuously over her shoulders, she wore a clinging knit-jersey dress and dark red lipstick, so she, like Jake the writer, looked like someone out of time, a fifties look, rather blowzy, although she could not have been more than twenty-three years old. Peter held her bottom in the cup of his hand and every so often rubbed it up and down.

Keith and Jenny arrived early. In this initial stage of the party there was still a slight stiffness and tension. But Di threw herself into the gaps and silences with childish excitement and much giggling: 'Isn't this a *wonderful* idea – it's all Peter's – I think it's marvellous – '

'Suppressed hysteria,' muttered Keith to Jenny. He hoped her desperation wouldn't overflow and create some outburst. There was nothing he disliked more than scenes.

The men gathered near the French windows, which were opened wide. Crystal, the only woman in the department (and a temporary research post at that), stood with them. There was to be a new Professor. They chewed over the gossip, the intrigue, the politics of it all: who would be on the appointments committee, what the Vice Chancellor had said . . .

Keith stood aloof, talking to Matthew, the department Adonis, whose only two interests in life were drink and films.

The woman stood on the periphery, not yet wound up into life. Jenny – to her relief – saw Miriam. They walked into the garden to look at the flowers.

Keith always said how much he admired Miriam, but Jenny knew she was completely 'safe' – much too strait-laced even to flirt with anyone else's husband, despite the fact that her own husband, Joe, slept around more compulsively than any of the men. With her teaching job and her Labour Party work Miriam was a separate person, not an appendage like so many of the wives. And of course she was the very opposite of the girlfriends who came and went, swept up into the group for the duration of an affair, then disappearing as if they had never been. She was the opposite of Di as well, all control, serious, achieving a dignity Di never dreamt of.

People jammed the rooms. There was a general movement towards the food. Peter had prepared everything. He had made the patés and terrines; he had boned the duck and stuffed it with veal and pistachios, had created the lobster balls in salmon-pink sauce Nantua, the iced Camembert and the Daube Provençal in its pools of red sauce sequined with oil. Di and Venetia had each been allowed to contribute a pudding, however. Venetia's caramelized oranges struck just the right note – showed she took the party seriously, yet without attempting to compete. Di's *Sachertorte* on the other hand was somehow discordant. It had been placed at the back of the laden table, a solid chocolate monument to a

50

family history of which Di had fatally let go, the recipe direct from a German Jewish grandmother who, unlike Di, had known and proudly filled her place in the world. After all the other food it was too rich and sickly, and was destined to be discovered the morning after, despoiled on its plate, smashed and disintegrated, largely uneaten.

Soon sixty or seventy men and women jostled in the kitchen, balanced cardboard plates and forked food into their mouths as they talked. The tide of voices rose, the sky outside deepened to indigo, the air filled with gnats, the Rolling Stones rumbled through the rooms and echoed in the empty square.

The dancing began. Di span round on her own, laughing and waving her arms about. Keith and Peter swopped girls. Keith and Venetia edged elegantly, imperceptibly towards the garden and out into the dusk. Peter gripped Jenny and thrust his groin against hers.

'Don't you think it's time that you and I . . .'

Peter always talked like that. It meant nothing, heavy flirtation was the only way he knew of being friendly to women. Jenny at once became the cheerful nurse with a cold water douche of good humour. Tonight, though, he wouldn't stop: 'Surely you two have an open relationship – '

Then the unexpected little spurt of poison: '*They* are, you know – Venetia's always fancied him – I think we almost owe it to ourselves, don't you?'

Jenny smiled blindly, as if she hadn't heard, but his words, although instantly suppressed, discounted, sent a faint shock wave through her well-controlled system. Was that what had happened to them all? A few words, a glance, even just a thought – until that moment everything would have seemed unchanging, natural, inevitable, but then everything shivered into doubt. You only had to say: this could change; and the surface of life would crack in a thousand places, moved by hidden forces, the existence of which you had never guessed.

Jenny disengaged herself and went for some more wine. Robin Soper stood by the drinks table.

'I must talk to you.'

'Where's Barbara?'

'She's at home with the kids. We couldn't get a sitter. Look, can we go into the garden, it's quiet out there.'

Jenny peered through the dusk, but she couldn't see Keith and Venetia anywhere. Robin led her to a secluded bench. She sipped her wine and stared over the rim of the glass at him, wondering if he would proposition her.

'I must talk to somebody.'

They were the Faculty happy couple, through all the changes they'd stayed together, devoted and content. Barbara loved domesticity, Robin adored the kids, you saw them shopping in the market at weekends, or off in the car for countryside explorations. So a proposition was unlikely and mildly flattering.

But what was this he was telling her now? Insomnia – late at night when Barbara and the children were asleep he rose, left the house, walked the deserted streets. And then one night he'd – it wasn't an impulse, not really, he'd often thought about it.

'It became an obsession – something I just had to do – '

It wasn't a new thing, then, but at first he'd thought that when he got married it'd go away. Instead, it haunted him.

To begin with he'd worn Barbara's clothes, but of course they didn't fit. And he'd tried to forget it afterwards, wipe it out, pretend it hadn't really happened, that it had been a kind of dream. Later he explained it away to himself as due to worry, overwork, he was getting it out of his system. Soon it would go away again, he'd be normal once more.

'I was never normal. Deep down – in my heart of hearts I've always known I'm a woman.'

One day he went to Oxfam and bought himself an outfit. Hid the clothes in the garage. It wasn't that he wanted to be furtive. But how could he ever tell Barbara?

Miffed to discover that he hadn't been interested in her at all, Jenny said sharply, 'You'd better see a psychiatrist.'

'I just can't go on.'

Jenny gripped the edge of the stone seat. The party bayed beyond the French windows. Jenny and Robin sat in silence, both inwardly watching the gaunt figure with flapping skirts that strode along the London Road.

Sometimes he'd thought of carrying straight on out towards the bypass – thumb a lift – just light out and never come back. He did still love Barbara, only –

One night last week, the last time he'd been out, he'd met two coppers up by the roundabout – thought they were going to stop him. Scared him shitless. Frightened to go out again.

'I just have to talk to someone.'

Di and Crystal stood by the French windows and looked out into the garden.

'Look,' said Di, 'over there by the bushes, Jenny doing one of her sympathetic numbers. Why do they all smooch up to her? The bedside manner, I suppose.' She tittered and lurched slightly. 'Must have something we haven't got.'

Crystal moved away, distancing herself from that 'we'. She sat against the edge of the drinks table. Matthew came up to her after a while. She looked up at him, holding her drink against her chest. They talked, desultory chat. Then, abruptly, he said, 'You can't do this, Crystal, you really can't.'

She stared at him: 'Do what? I haven't done anything.'

'You just can't do it to me – I don't want you to.'

'I don't know what you mean. I'm not doing anything.'

She laughed. He turned away. She looked round for someone to talk to. But every circle seemed closed. She made for the bathroom.

Like all the rooms it was high-ceilinged and Victorianized. The mahogany seat had been revarnished, the bath stripped of its hardboard casing to reveal wrought-iron feet, and an old gilt-framed mirror hung on one wall. She looked at herself.

'Christ, I'm nearly *thirty*.'

She turned and looked over her shoulder at her back – and saw it: the stain, an ugly dark red gash across her bottom. Her white dress ruined. She must have sat in a pool of wine when she was leaning against the drinks table, but the horrible thing was it looked like menstrual blood. She pulled at the zip, dragged the dress off and sponged roughly at the stain with cold water and a face flannel. She dabbed and rubbed, and the stain grew paler. That would have to do. She dressed again, but sat for a long time on the edge of the bath, staring at herself in the mirror, ashamed of the stigma of the menstrual stain, not wanting to go back into the party.

Someone banged on the door: 'Are you all right in there?'

It was Jenny. She thought Crystal was looking rather thin and gaunt. That thing with Matthew – over, if it'd ever been on.

'Listen, d'you know what Robin's just told me?'

Miriam circled the room in Jake's arms. Jake held her tighter and tighter. Miriam was smiling. Joe was upstairs with some woman.

Groups were jammed in doorways, people pushed to and fro with drinks held high. The noise was a single, sustained roar. Couples clung and swayed to the music. The rhythm was monotonous and endless. The pleasure cage had caught them, swung them back and forth, this way and that.

Miriam stepped back smartly and slapped Jake's face. The crack of the blow brought startled glances.

'I'm going home. Where's Joe? He'll have to drive me.'

After a hurried search he was located, and appeared, dishevelled, meek. Jake had gone too far. But so had Miriam – cracked a whip across the fun, for a second they all jumped to attention, guilty and dismayed, then annoyed with her for breaking the rules. Of course there were no rules – rulelessness was the rule, and to be cool about things. And you broke out of the new pattern, as out of the old, at your peril. It was uncool to slap a man's face.

'The trouble with Miriam, she's got no sense of humour.'

> I can't get no-oh-oh
> *Satisfaction* –

Jenny grabbed Matthew and they jerked angularly to and fro in the jostling crowd. At last she caught sight of Keith – in conversation with a group of colleagues.

Some students gatecrashed. Peter wanted to send them packing, but everyone else thought that would be uncool. The students joined the scrum on the dance floor. Someone was sick all over the downstairs bathroom.

It was after midnight when Bill and Helen walked through the rooms hand in hand. Jenny waved at them.

'I never thought you'd come.'

'Isn't it a *marvellous* party,' said Bill.

It was the most wonderful evening of his life. At last he'd plucked up courage to invite her out. They'd driven into the country. She felt as he did – she'd said so – almost in so many words. He caught his breath with the happiness, the danger of it. Grabbed her hand and flung his head back as they walked into the mêlée. Oh *God*!

And now here was a chorus of glamorous, benign strangers. This evening was the beginning of a new life.

Helen watched the sweating crowd, toiling at pleasure as if at the sales, struggling to pick up a bargain, to grab something before it was too late. She gazed round at the young, who were not much older than her children; and at the still good-looking of her own age. Some of the behaviour seemed a little sordid.

'Let's go home.'

Hereafter there would be anxiety, guilt, snatched meetings, promises of a radical break, snatched agony of desire, the greater happiness missed perhaps. But for this night at least they'd escaped. They were free.

Suddenly hours had passed. Jenny and Keith swayed in the empty room, too lethargic to leave; only a few couples now. Jake was fumbling with a very young girl on the scrolled, red chaise longue. Robin, white as a sheet, was keeling over as he pinned Crystal to the Morris wallpaper and told her his agonizing secret. Joe had returned to the party, after leaving his wife at home, and was undressing a girl in the garden shed.

At dawn a few persistent revellers lingered. Peter and Venetia had long since gone to bed. Di set off with the last guests to the Blue Lagoon, where you could get pot.

The sun rose. It poured through the French windows. Its rays of light fell on half-empty glasses, spilled food, paper plates and cigarette stubbs on the parquet, on dregs of rice salad and pools of beer.

Robin lay passed out on the chaise longue. The very young girl slept curled up in the chair in which Jake had abandoned her in a fit of temper when she'd refused to go the whole way.

Barbara woke, found Robin's half of the bed empty, telephoned, got Peter out of bed and cursing down the stairs, gripping his towelling robe around his loins, to wake Robin to a new world. Everyone knows now, you'll have to tell Barbara, do something about it.

Upstairs, the children were shouting. Venetia groaned, hungover.

Bill started up in horror in a strange bedroom, sank back as Helen put out a hand: 'It's all right – they're all away, remember – '

He would still have to creep away before the neighbours were about. No one must suspect.

Matthew lay alone. His dreams were even better than the movies.

Miriam had breakfast with the children. Joe returned soon afterwards. He'd driven several of the party home after the Blue Lagoon had closed. Dropped Crystal at the roundabout – said she'd wanted to walk the rest of the way.

Keith and Jenny slept on until noon. When Jenny woke, she lay there making plans, while Keith still dreamed beside her. They would have to move quite soon, she decided, after all. The flat was poky and dark.

If Peter could afford a house like that, why not Keith? An Art Nouveau living room . . . the bedroom dark blue . . . central heating.

Then they could have a party – a really big one, bigger than Peter and Di's: a wedding party.

PART THREE: THE EARLY SEVENTIES

5

The House With No Doors

I first heard about the house in north London from Hugo –
Hugo and Francesca. It was just a house on the margins of
my existence – far away on the horizon. They always
referred to it as 'Formosa Road'.

When Francesca went to live in the house in north London
she cut off her hair. Black and spiky it looked now; no
more curtains, looped behind the ear to show she was
in communication, or drawn across her face to indicate
withdrawal; no more hair like Isadora Duncan's scarves,
ready to tangle in the spokes of her bicycle wheels and
strangle her. They called her Frankie.

Hugo came round to my place a lot to talk about it. His
round blue eyes like marbles got still more round as he told
me about the house.

He went to look for Francesca. He wandered in through
the open front door. The walls inside were bare even of
plaster, never mind paint. It was a big house. He walked
through several rooms. They had taken off all the doors.
After a while he found Francesca seated in a large bathroom.
He sat down on the edge of the bath and started a conversation about their relationship. Only after some minutes –
when she reached for the paper – did he realize she was
sitting on the lavatory, having a crap: 'These long skirts –
kind of hid it, Crystal – sort of teacosy effect.'

For weeks he went round asking people, 'Like – why
d'you think they took the *doors* off? I mean, there are two
hypotheses: it was to stop anyone locking themselves in a
room and committing suicide; or they needed the doors for
firewood.'

Hugo was a sociologist.

Francesca, Frankie now, said it was done in order to
abolish privacy. Privacy and property alike were suspect.
She'd taken some furniture that had belonged to her grandmother, recently deceased, to the commune. They called a
house meeting. The chaise longue in particular was condemned as bourgeois and oppressive, and two of the men

carried it out to the gutter where it perched lopsidedly in the sunshine for a few hours before disappearing overnight.

Hugo sometimes stayed there: 'You can't ever go to bed, in case the wrong person comes up after you.'

Night after night the whole household sat up later and later round the kitchen table. More and more joints, more ciggies and roll-ups were smoked, cans of beer and bottles of wine consumed. In the earlier part of the evening a Diaspora to one of their pubs would have occurred (you were never told where they were, the pubs, just issued with the directive: meet us at the Castle, the Queen, the Bull). At the pub they went in for mixed drinks – whisky-and-blackcurrant, barley wine-and-bitter, gin-and-port, these were all considered more truly proletarian than my prissy vermouth, or Hugo's draggy beer. After closing time they returned to the house, laden with cans.

There were no bedrooms, no one had a room of their own. At one o'clock, two o'clock, the first faint-heart slunk away, made for the most distant and inaccessible room in the house. Downstairs, elaborate but silent manoeuvres creaked into action so that, without anyone saying anything, the mutually attracted might end up on the same mattress. These mattresses on the floor – all over the nation hippies and students and politicos in their pads and squats slung out their bed bases and divan frames and lay on their mattresses on bare, painted boards.

In the house in north London, some fell asleep round the table, some feigned drunkenness, some genuinely passed out, others prowled in search of an empty bed or the right person – it wasn't done to refuse an offer. By three in the morning everyone was settled for the night. A little later the silence was broken by the sound of lovemaking. At least someone had got it on.

Frankie had a phrase for it: the total separation of night and day. Frankie had a new way of talking: 'It's like – you know – I just don't feel like I could – ugh – I don't – dig that shit – but – let's rap about it, Crystal – that would be cool.'

Fragments flew off the word-breakers hammer, hewn off lumps of language.

Frankie's mother phoned me up: 'But is she *happy*, Crystal? That's all I care about – whether she's happy with her life . . . I know I didn't like all that student politics, those demonstrations and sit-ins, whatever they're called, but at least she was at university then, it all had some purpose – I never expected her just to *leave* like that, without taking her exams. I mean, what kind of future – ?'

I tried to explain it all to her.

'Oh! I suppose you're all in favour of this drugs and free love then – not that it's anything new, you know, just good old-fashioned *bohemianism*.'

Frankie's new friends didn't like me much. I was bourgeois – 'bourgey' they called it, they said I was into property because I had a house, a job, and a fiancé.

They started a local branch of the claimants union. Frankie spent a lot of time zapping the ss. They always called the social security the ss in order to remind the world of the repressive nature of the state. The ss bullied single mothers with early morning calls, withdrawal of benefit, intimidated the unemployed, their snoopers were an incipient and sinister secret police – Britain was in the grip of creeping fascism.

The ss was always trying to prove that the women in the house were cohabiting with the men.

'Can't they see – we're not into couples.'

'Everyone should have a guaranteed minimum income.'

The first time I saw all the women together was at a demonstration. The march was singing and shouting along Oxford Street. The women looked like a band of gipsies, with their scarves, trailing skirts, bare shoulders; the whole thing was a carnival.

The women in the house shared all their clothes, and Frankie's expensive boutique numbers were either added to the pool or thrown out as unworthy. On the demonstration Frankie herself was wearing trousers under a second-hand frock cut off just below the waist, to create a ragged peplum effect. She seemed to have grown larger, blossoming, as if

63

the energy formerly stored in her hair had now been released to burst out everywhere else. In the red blouse and with her high cheekbones she could have walked straight out of a 1920s Soviet poster.

At first the women at the house all looked the same to me, but soon I began to see how different each one was – and how beautiful, though you weren't supposed to make sexist judgments of that sort. Luce had a cloud of blonde, frizzy hair like an Art Nouveau angel, etiolated and striking with her greenish-white skin and her moss-green djibbah. Clare looked very English with a pink face and cowslip freckles; Jill had straight black hair and a sallow face with long, cynical lips; Vinny's hair was a bronze hood and her face a rosy nectarine; Alice had a thin, pale face and violet eyes. They – I too – had only just stopped wearing make-up, and the freshness of pure skin and unsmudged eyes was startling. And, in their faded, pooled trousers, their home-dyed tee shirts and their shrunken, slightly matted, yellow, pink or green woollies, they had created a fashion the very indifference of which was stylish in its untidy way.

I never met any of the men from the house, but their reputation glimmered on the horizon like summer lightning before a storm. Three of them got arrested. Frankie said, 'I'm working around the Formosa Road Three Defence Committee.'

But soon afterwards the women expelled the men from the house, having made a political decision to become gay. Even after it had become a Women's House, though, Frankie continued to talk about the total separation of night from day.

'What d'you mean?'

'It's like – ugh – there is this total separation of night from day.'

'D'you mean you're all too uptight to talk about sex?'

Silence. Then she asked me if she could come and stay with me for a bit.

'The house is – like – heavy just now.'

Hugo had not yet quite understood that Frankie was no

longer his chick, so he hung round my place even more. He chatted with me over coffee, because Frankie scarpered over the fence at the back of the garden when he called.

'She says she just isn't into men at the moment.'

'What I can't understand is – how can *six* women all fall in love with one another simultaneously? Like – *two* I could understand – *three*, even – life's rich tapestry, and all that, but – *six* – '

'I think just what it isn't about is being in love.'

'New frontiers of sensuality then – '

'It's the way you turn it into a joke that is just the sort of thing they find a problem with men.'

'Shit!' He rolled another cigarette. People hadn't begun to give up in those days.

Several times the women from the commune ('Don't call it that, that's what the ss and the pigs call it') came round to try to persuade Frankie to go back. They sat in my living room and glared, not at me, just generally.

'Don't heavy me – you're laying trips on me – '

I tried to stick up for her: 'Why don't you ask her what she wants – why she wasn't happy there. Start from where she's at.'

'That's social worker talk.'

'Well, I am a social worker.'

'I'm not *not happy* – what's happiness got to do with it? You sound like my mother.'

I had my own theory of why she wasn't happy, but she wouldn't talk about it, and quite soon she did go back, though she still hung round my place as well. So did the others – they would come surging round unannounced at inconvenient times. My fiancé called them Frankie's Flatmates. He would telephone before coming over: 'I'm not coming if they're there. They're so glum – I don't feel like I can relate to them – '

Men were silly about them, I noticed, they made more fuss than was necessary. They felt threatened for some reason I didn't understand.

I also noticed my place had somehow become a kind of

commune annexe. Soon travelling drop-outs and politicos were unrolling their sleeping bags on my living room floor, and even pitching their tents in my garden. The neighbours turned nasty after a visiting American gay liberationist accidentally set fire to his tent and scorched their pear tree.

Mind you, I did have some good times with the women. There was this other woman, Eileen, who was running a community newspaper and we all helped her with that through the summer. I also helped her with the Women's Issue of *Getting High*. *Getting High* was one of those newspapers of the hippie Underground – its days numbered by then, since rude cartoons with lots of tits, bums and pricks, and overexcited articles about dope and rock had begun to go out of fashion, to be replaced by harder political stuff. It was probably a gesture of desperation to ask us to contribute an Issue on women. Still, we liked the idea, and hurried over to west London in a taxi.

The *Getting High* offices were in the Portobello Road, just where the street market began to peter out. We pushed past rails of cheesecloth blouses and second-hand fur coats, through a grotto-like shop filled with crushed, tie-dyed velvet and the smell of joss sticks, and up some rickety stairs. The *Getting High* editor and his golf ball typesetter (every politico within miles itched to get his hands on that golf ball machine) were alone in a chaotic room. Clouds of marijuana smoke filled the air. The editor was a very tall, very thin old Etonian. He was wearing pink velvet trousers and a green-and-gold brocade jacket with long skirts, probably a genuine eighteenth-century relic from his old man's stately home. His ringlets fell past his shoulders. He wore (of course) National Health wire spectacles. When he saw us his cool was momentarily faintly shaken.

'Www-ow-uh . . . *heavy women!*'

I'd never heard anyone make 'wow' last for three syllables before. I was a heavy woman! Not a weekend hippie any more. At that moment I knew I'd joined the seventies.

* * *

Then the women from Formosa Road got into spray painting.

'We're not reaching enough ordinary women with these magazines – '

'Writing stuff is so bourgey – '

'That's what all the blokes were into – writing all the time – '

Late at night we all piled into an old van and searched Hackney for some empty walls. Two or three at a time got out to spray. The empty, shabby streets were livid at night-time. The sound of a distant car sent us rushing for the van. One time we were actually standing by some corrugated iron fencing, cans in hand, when a patrol car slid by, but by some miracle it didn't stop. So we went on spraying 'Angry Women' and 'If You're not part of the Solution you're part of the Problem' (a quotation from the Black Panthers).

Their most ambitious effort – I wasn't in on that – was a really long slogan above the escarpment of the district railway line: 'Wake up, eat, crap, rush-hour, work, rush-hour, eat, telly, bed. Same old thing, day after day. Get off the treadmill and make the revolution.'

For a long time I thought one of the best graffiti was the one near the top of Gower Street: 'The Tygers of Wrath are Wiser than the Horses of Instruction' (William Blake). Several times the wall was repainted, so as to obliterate it, but someone always sprayed the slogan back on. Then, one time it was whitewashed, and no one painted the words back on – but by that time it was the 1980s and I'd decided I didn't really agree with the slogan after all.

My neighbours started to cut me after the police called round. Some of the women had got done for spray painting in the end. By this time it was the silly season; the magistrate ruled that the women were to go back and clean off the paint they'd sprayed, and the newspapers all loved this story of a 'punishment to fit the crime'. Journalists turned up at my house and wanted to know how I felt about being made to clean the paint off. I got annoyed: 'Whatever made you give them this address?'

''Cos of the Defence Committee – too heavy to say Formosa Road – '

'But I told them none of you lived here – '

'Shit.'

Then they sent Tina and Margaret to stay with me, although the American gay liberationist was still in the back garden. Tina and Margaret came from Australia. They took over my study, pulled the curtains, and lay in the dark all day smoking joints. In the evening they rose, put on their robes, ate some of their vegetable stew, always simmering on top of my stove, and went out to women's meetings, or round to Formosa Road.

One evening I came back with my fiancé to find them all having an argument in my living room – Tina, Margaret and the women from Formosa Road:

'But it's a women's house. We can't have men there.'

'Tina is not a man. Tina is a transsexual. Psychologically and emotionally Tina is a woman. Soon she'll be physically a woman as well – just as soon as we can get enough bread together for the operation.'

Tina sat quietly, said nothing. Margaret was hoarse with arguing.

'I tell you, we're both lesbians. Can't you understand!'

The women from the house just silently looked. My fiancé disappeared upstairs. After a while the Formosa Road women left, still in silence.

I think Tina and Margaret might still to this day have been in the study behind the drawn curtains had Tina not got arrested on a demonstration and deported as a result. The two of them went to Amsterdam from where they sent me a postcard with a picture of tulips, wrote how much they liked Amsterdam, they were spending a lot of time at the Paradiso, 'sisters are less uptight over here.'

I was relieved to see the back of Tina and Margaret, not because I disliked them – I didn't – but because the alien rhythm of other lives was disrupting my ordered existence. I was one of the zombies referred to in the graffiti – I got up and went to work each day, came home at the same time,

68

switched on the telly for the news, had a routine. They made me feel defensive about it.

But with Tina and Margaret gone I could hardly refuse Hedda a room, for she and her baby, Billy George (named after Billy the Kid, and George Jackson, who'd recently been murdered in prison) were homeless, evicted by an unfeeling, Rachmanite landlord. What I got was Hedda, Billy George, a dog called Haile Selassie and Hedda's two boyfriends, Jerry and Jack. Since Frankie and her chums never introduced you to anyone, I did not sort out for quite a while which was Jack and which was Jerry. One was a hippy and had golden hair and beard, like Holman Hunt's painting of Jesus, 'Light of the World' – and from the glum expression on his face you'd have thought he had a crown of thorns too; the other went in for a more macho image, with Dr Martens boots and an army surplus greatcoat. Because of not knowing which was which I tended to try and avoid them; this may have caused an impression of unfriendliness.

Tuesday was Hedda's ss giro day, so every Tuesday night Hedda threw a party. She roasted meat and potatoes, or made a big stew, bought demijohns of wine, stacks of expensive fruit, fresh supplies of dope. People I'd never seen before made merry all over the house. When I found two strangers making love in my bed (fucking, they always called it) I'd had enough.

'You're being uncool, Crystal.'

'Come round to Formosa Road and we'll rap about it.'

It was the first time – strangely enough – that I'd ever actually visited the place. By now they'd done it up a bit, and it wasn't as Hugo had described it – lathe and plaster walls, et cetera. The room we sat in looked like a community nursery: each wall had been painted a different primary colour, the woodwork was shocking pink and lime green, the floor purple and the ceiling bright turquoise. There were sag bags to sit on. We drank instant coffee.

They stared at me.

'It's been very heavy for Hedda.'

'Her landlord slung her out.'

'Only because she didn't pay her rent,' I pointed out.

Now, of course, I was no better than another Rachman. They stared in sullen silence. There was a dreadful atmosphere of reproach.

'I'm not having her – you can have her. You've got room.'

But this was just what they didn't want. The truth was, they were scared of Hedda.

'You're too used to being on your own – a baby needs space – your furniture's oppressive.'

'I've made up my mind.' Now that I'd sussed out the real reason they were heavying me (ie self interest) I stopped listening, stopped feeling guilty, and just watched them instead. At first Frankie and Luce had been inseparable – that was the real reason Frankie had moved in in the first place. Despite her disclaimers – and mine to Hugo – I thought she *was* in love with Luce, she really *was* a lesbian.

But today Luce seemed to be eyeing Clare.

I tried to get Frankie to talk about their relationship. She wouldn't have it, though. Like the rest of them, she had an effective way of turning her moralism on you, so that if you asked an awkward question it simply proved your own false consciousness.

'We don't operate like that – all that bourgey shit about owning people. Look at you – you're so coupley.'

'But you and Luce seemed to be – to have something, well, special together.'

'All friends are special.'

Coupley I might be, but it was virtually a homeless couple now. I spent as much time out of my own house as I could. My fiancé's flat, though, was a pokey little place and he got freaked out if I stayed there too often. ('I need my space.') On the other hand, since he was terrified of coming anywhere near my house by now the whole situation was threatening Our Relationship.

My mother was moving to a smaller flat at the time, and I'd promised to take my friend Alex round there to see if there was some stuff she didn't want but which he might be able to sell. In those days he had a stall in the Portobello

Road and I used to crochet tanktops for him, and shawls from those multi-coloured squares, which had a certain cottagey charm until they began to be mass-produced.

My mother used to go all indulgent with men. She thought Alex was wonderful.

'What about all these cushions, Alex – *she* doesn't need them.'

'I *do*, Mother – '

'No, let him have them. There are lots more. And what about this dress, you never wear it – '

'But that's a genuine 1956 – '

'Oh, I'll have *that*, darling,' Alex nipped in, quick as a shot, 'isn't that *too* camp.'

I was furious – those fifties clothes were just beginning to come back into fashion. But it was only her way of having a little go at me. When Alex went to put the loot in his van, she said, 'What a rather charming young man, dear – such lovely curly hair. Wasted on a man, of course.'

Alex and I drove back to his flat. He gave me advice about my problems: 'You must put your foot down – really. I mean these revolutionaries are all very well – well, what am I saying – *I'm* a revolutionary, we all are. I mean I just regard myself as a complete fucking *anarchist* – but not these *heavy* revolutionaries – I mean we all need our own space, what's right for us. And having them come sicking bloody trannies and babies and *dogs* all over you isn't good for your karma.'

'It certainly isn't.'

'Mind you, drag is *tremendously* revolutionary – but not in that *heavy* way – operations! Ugh! Gives me castration anxiety when you even *mention* it, darling.'

'They weren't as bad as Hedda – '

'They're the conformists, not you – '

'Still . . . privacy *is* a form of bourgeois privilege, I suppose – '

'Stuff *that*, darling. Revolution means freedom, not just another set of fucking rules. You have to find your own space.'

We lay about smoking. He had a large flat in a great big house just behind the Portobello. The walls were painted a kind of dusty chocolate, and the floors were sanded and sealed. You sat on heaps of satin cushions (soon my mother's would join the pile) and houseplants trailed their long locks from ceiling to floor.

Later we went to a party. By this time we were pretty stoned, and carried on smoking in the tube. Alex had some particularly good grass. As we hadn't bothered to buy tickets we didn't take the lift when we reached our destination, but climbed the spiral emergency stairs instead. We came out at the top dizzy and giggling, turned in the wrong direction, and found ourselves in a small room full of uniformed men drinking tea. Luckily we were able to back out again without arousing their suspicion – and we laughed and laughed all the way up the hill.

The party turned out to be for gay men (it was a bit typical of Alex to have forgotten to mention that) so I didn't stay long. The tube journey home again was rather a bring-down, though I still felt a bit giggly. My evening was over without having begun. My fiancé had gone away for the weekend. I dreaded my house, full of noisy strangers. I even considered going to the movies by myself – but suppose someone saw me, that would be too shaming, going to the movies on a Saturday night on my own.

My house was unexpectedly silent and empty; deserted. I sat down with a cup of coffee. At least I could curl up with a book, undisturbed.

About half an hour later I heard an odd noise from upstairs. I went up to investigate.

Billy George was in his basket (Hedda wouldn't have a cot for him, because she said she didn't want her baby to get its first sight of the world through prison bars) and he'd just woken up and started to cry. He bawled louder when I picked him up. It's surprising how quickly a baby's yells can induce a sense of panic, but I managed to warm some milk for him, and that cheered him up.

In fact he went back to sleep quite quickly, but I couldn't

believe they'd left him. I realized it was later than I thought – they must have just nipped out to the pub for a few moments to buy some drinks or something. All the same, it was inexcusable. Mindful of Alex's words, I went round the house from top to bottom and collected all the junk that Hedda had left lying around in every room. I took armful after armful of it and dumped it in her little room, once my study.

I didn't feel like waiting up for Hedda. I'd deliver my final ultimatum in the morning. I went to the drinks cupboard for some whisky – the effects of the grass had quite worn off by now – but they'd polished off all the alcohol, so I just went to bed, took some codeine, and was out like a light.

It was the middle of the night when they woke me. Jack (the army greatcoat one, it had turned out) barged into my room and was looming up in the shadows.

'I'm going to fucking punch your face in for what you've done.'

I switched on the light, but having no clothes on I couldn't really sit up, which put me at a psychological disadvantage. Hedda sidled into the room, and only then did I remember about Billy George.

I didn't scream at her, just coldly, woodenly, told her to get out. I was shaking and frightened, but they were too drunk to notice. Maybe if Jerry hadn't been there Jack *would* have hit me – I don't think so, though, not really. He was too . . . self-conscious, uptight – I can't quite put my finger on it. Jerry was actually worse in a way, because he insisted on us all talking about it for hours and hours – things kept going round and round in circles, and I didn't finally get rid of them until it was getting light.

For the next few days they tried to come round me, Hedda even gave me some money for bills, they replaced the whisky, only then they drank it again. But I stood my ground, in fact I was rather nasty to Hedda, told her she wasn't a revolutionary at all, just a hustler, and not even a very good one at that.

After they'd gone I changed the locks. That made me feel better.

Frankie came round in tears. Hedda had managed to inveigle her way into Formosa Road, and somehow as a result Frankie had got herself chucked out.

'They said I was into couples. I hate Luce, she was horrible.'

'I never could see what you saw in her. I thought she was boring. Beautiful but so egocentric. Very boring, actually.'

'Boring! *Boring? Luce?*'

Frankie stayed with me for a while. But autumn was coming and she decided to go back to university after all. The American gay liberationist struck camp and returned to the United States. Things got a bit heavy – some of the women got done after a big Irish demonstration. I was more friendly with Eileen by then – she got mixed up in that too. Formosa Road was raided by the police.

We've all changed a lot since those days, I suppose. Frankie, for instance: she dropped out of university *again* and decided she wanted to be a nurse. Later on she became a radical midwife. Last time I saw her she'd had a baby herself, but she was still working. She lived with another woman for a long time, but I don't know if that's still on.

Hugo's a professor now; written quite a few books – joined the Labour Party. He doesn't smoke any more. Too worried about coronaries.

Luce met a French film director who was over here to film political demonstrations. Since then she's starred in all his films. They live in Nice and Malibu – except I read in the papers recently that they'd split up.

Clare went orange, stayed with that buddhist community in Poona, then came back and now she's running a vegetarian restaurant in the west country.

Vinny had two little girls, and got involved in the peace movement. I saw her again when I went to Greenham Common on the big mass demonstration. She'd been living there for a bit. It was nice to see her.

Eileen says she sees Jill quite often, because they're both active in their union.

Alice got cancer, and died.

One of the Formosa Road Three got a suspended sentence. He carried on for quite a few years squatting and things like that, but then he decided he was really more interested in culture, and he's quite a successful novelist now.

Of the other two members of the Formosa Road Three, one runs a community bookshop in the north of England, the other's a registered drug addict.

Tina was murdered in Amsterdam. No one knows what happened to Margaret.

Jerry went to the States and lives on a commune in California.

Jack is a left Labour councillor in south London. He got a job with London Transport, on the tube, and has generally gone proletarian, as well as being a heavy family man.

Hedda – more of the same, really.

Billy George is in the A stream of his comprehensive school.

Haile Selassie was killed by a hit-and-run driver.

Alex became Mavis Magdalen, part of a glam drag act on the alternative cabaret scene. He's even been on Channel Four.

My fiancé married someone else.

Eileen – that's another story really.

And me – well, you can never sum yourself up in a sentence, can you.

Anyway, things have happened to all of us which we never expected, but as Jerry and Jack and Hedda would once have said, 'Well – there you go, man – '

Or to quote Mavis Magdalen, 'It's your karma, darling.'

Eileen sat on the stairs to lace up her boots.

'I'm going to be a very cross old lady.'

With the boots she wore a maroon midi-skirt, a red, frilled flannel blouse and a shawl crocheted in cottage squares of purple and brown. Her black curls fell past her shoulders. Over everything she wore a full-skirted, black velvet coat.

'My gran was a very cross old lady. She had a stick she shook at people, and thick, curly white hair. I'm going to be like her when I'm old. Her brother fought with James Connolly.'

'Who's James Connolly?'

'Who's James Connolly! An Irish revolutionary. He was a Marxist.'

'My grandmother lived in India,' said Crystal. She had it all off pat about her family, her childhood. Analysis had helped her acknowledge that past.

'Is that those photographs in your bathroom?'

Her grandfather faced the camera, seated in his white-man's-burden uniform of shorts, long socks and solar topee, surrounded by a throng of bearers in shorts or loincloths, one of whom held the reins of his horse. In the second photograph a group of African servants stood in apparent triumph over a dead elephant. In the third the photographer had frozen tea time at the Club in sepia: groups of men and women sat in wicker chairs round little tables set with English hotel china. But for the palm trees and the black waiters and the dusty bare earth underfoot the scene might have been Bournemouth or Torquay.

Crystal's mother sat slightly apart. Like the other women she wore a pale shift, a rope of beads, and cuban-heeled shoes with a button strap across the instep. Beneath the wide saucer brim of her black straw hat her face was held carefully expressionless for the camera. She stared straight out of the picture with the slightly foolish gaze of the short-sighted, refusing to wear her spectacles for posterity: 'my specs'.

'I think they're quite offensive.'

'It's just a camp joke, really – you know, my grandfather was a big game hunter, backbone of the British Raj, that sort of thing. I loathed it as a child, such a peculiar background, different from everyone else – I've come to terms with it, that's all.'

'But imperialism isn't a joke – or a psychological problem.'

The meeting had already begun. The hall was dark, although spotlights flared across the dust, but while most of the room was in shadow, the dais was sharply illuminated. Dressed in scarlet a woman with a halo of red hair sat flanked by two others at a small round table, up there on their own. All the other women sat on the floor, looking towards these three, or clustered on the wooden stairs that led up to a gallery.

A woman in a ragged tee-shirt was jabbing the air with her finger and shouting, '. . . grassing to the pigs – '

Women clapped sporadically as she was still talking. The woman in red raised her hand for the right of reply.

'We were *concerned*. Don't you see. We found all this communist literature at the Centre. Surely – don't we want the Centre to be for *all* women? How can Communism help women? We surely don't want the Russians dictating in our own Women's Centre! I was only trying to protect – '

'But what did she *do?*' muttered Crystal.

'Went to the Special Branch – told them she'd found these pamphlets – it was only some stuff that idiotic group of Maoists had left . . . Some women are feeling *really* threatened – you know Formosa Road's been raided by the Special Branch . . . look, there *are* the women from Formosa Road – let's go and sit with them – '

They edged across with difficulty, stepping over other women. When they reached the group Eileen started a whispered conversation with them. Then she stood up and spoke: 'I don't think that I actually *do* want the Women's Centre, or the Women's Movement for that matter, to be for 'all women' – in the sense that I don't see what most of us have in common with Tory women, with right-wing

77

women. We can't just fight for all women. We live in a class society, don't we? Women's struggle has to be a class struggle too – '

Alice went in behind her, in support, talking about their women's claimants' group, and how the police hated the claimants: 'They think we're all anarchists.'

More women joined in, arguing. Others milled to and fro at the back and up and down the stairs; shuffling feet and murmured conversations made it difficult to hear the main debate. A baby began to yell from somewhere in the middle of the throng. Smoke drifted above their heads. Crystal looked about her. How strange it all was. Not what you'd think of as a *political* meeting. More like a gathering, a happening, spontaneous, anything could erupt. There was this current of restless energy, a hot lava spring, seething, muttering. Yet it was somehow thwarted, negative, not like the marches and demonstrations. The Formosa Road women were grumbling among themselves.

Frankie said, 'I'm dying for a drink – the pubs'll shut soon, it's Sunday.'

There was uncertainty and restiveness in the hall. No one knew what to do, how to proceed. The meeting was degenerating into separate conversations, the women on the platform almost forgotten. But then a hoarse voice came from the gallery:

'All of us 'ere, we may not agree with Maoists at Women's Centre, and we may 'ave different views about Tory women, or whatever. But what I think is so disgusting is to think that any woman could actually report us to police – in any circumstances whatsoever. *That's* what we're on about. Yer don't 'ave ter be a politico to get arrested, yer know. Sum of us, we're single mothers, we're on social security, we're pestered by bloody police and snoopers the whole bloody time. And you bloody dare to go to the bloody coppers in order to protect us from ourselves. We're not 'aving that – no way whatsoever!'

There was clapping, shouts of approval, cheers.

'Right on!'

'That's settled it,' muttered Eileen. 'They've had it now.'

And in fact the red-haired woman gathered herself and her two friends together and stood up with a gesture as if to ward off attack: 'Very well – we'll leave. If that's how you feel – we're not wanted, okay. We've obviously been very, very naïve – '

They hurried from the hall, heads down.

The pub across the road was jammed. The women, who'd seemed picturesque in the dim hall, looked mad and witch-like in the sallow light of the shabby pub, less respectable even than the regulars, shifty, shabby men from the desolate estate at the back of the mainline terminal.

Eileen eased through and ordered beers, then found a secluded corner where there actually were some empty seats. Women pushed to and fro, many paused to speak to Eileen. They banged and surged round the bar as if they didn't care, demanding space, freaking out the men.

The trouble started when one of the regulars made a remark. Insult or sexual appreciation, it went down badly. One woman squared up to a knot of men.

'She's tiny – what are they so fussed about – '

Glass shattered, caused a sudden, split-second hush, then uproar.

'Oh my *God* – Grace threw a glass at the mirror – '

'*Out*! All of you – OUT!'

'Come on – better go – he'll call the pigs any minute – '

The men jeered, the women jostled towards the door. There was heaving and shoving. Both men and women were shouting, exchanging insults. One man raised his fist.

Then, knots of women stood on the wet pavement outside, some were shouting, cursing, seething with thwarted anger, but most were laughing and chatting, didn't care. The incident petered out.

'We're going over to the Gate – wanna come?'

Frankie was at the driving wheel. Six of them crammed into the car.

79

The room was of course familiar. Crystal had never been there before, didn't know who it belonged to, but she'd seen the painted floorboards, the cushions, the picturesque tat. . . .

Frankie rolled a joint. Eileen opened a double litre of red wine. Two women began to kiss. Crystal looked away, embarrassed.

She'd promised Jon she wouldn't be late. She was meant to go round to his place, but now she'd been borne away over here, and it was almost too late to telephone. He resented her meetings. Last week he'd even referred to them all, her new friends, as 'those bloody lesbians'. Of course he'd retracted immediately, but she was still shocked – and even ashamed of this sulky, spiteful stranger. She'd always liked effete men, once she'd have said they weren't so 'conventional' – maybe she'd meant male chauvinist, without realizing it of course. And then, like social workers do, he was always talking about feelings, emotional nuance. So she'd assumed he was sensitive, aware, unprejudiced.

Now he did nothing but nag – yet he wanted to know all about it, the meetings, the friendships. Didn't want her to be part of it, and yet didn't want to be left out.

She wanted to keep this new, different world quite separate: separate worlds, separate selves.

Eileen plunged into the currents of talk and laughter and defiance. She had a boyfriend too – black hair, thin and wild, not English. Ben they called him, but that wasn't his real name, Frankie had said. Eileen had met him at LSE – all those student sit-ins, he'd been in the thick of all that, of course. . . .

The coaches stood in a line, three of them, alongside St Pancras Station. Crystal had her weekend things in a paper bag, and she queued up with Eileen, waiting to get on and claim their seats. Women swarmed round the doors. Surely there weren't enough places for so many. There was panic about women left behind, children missing, tickets lost and places double booked, but Eileen and Crystal sat snugly in

80

the middle, and after much waiting and running up and down and shouting from coach to coach by the women in charge, everyone was seated, the drivers sprang up to the wheel, the engines revved up and the coaches roared away under the railway arches.

Lights smeared across the tarry darkness as they droned northwards. Women at the back were singing and drinking. It was like being in a coachload of football fans. After two hours or so there were shouts to stop and some women struggled down the gangway and peed in the lay-by, their white bottoms like balloons in the glare of the headlights, not even bothering to get out of sight. Northwards again; Crystal's sandwiches had gone squidgy, but Eileen and she ate them hungrily and would have liked more. The rocking motion lulled Crystal into a daydream, she was only jerked out of it when the bus swung off the motorway and into the services area car park. They joined lorry drivers in a queue, someone got into an argument, there was nearly trouble, like in the pub the week before.

They'd been scheduled to arrive in Manchester by ten, but it was past eleven when they drew up in front of some university building. Women milled about on the steps. You plunged through a golden disc of light into the hall to join more women crushed round a table.

'We have to register – '

'Where are we staying – ?'

'Will the coach take us – ?'

'I forgot my sleeping bag – '

Even this wasn't the end of the journey.

'They've fixed up for us to stay in some hostel,' said Eileen. 'Wish I'd gone with the Formosa Road lot, they're staying over the other side of Moss Side – '

Moss Side was just a name on election night: 'I've never even been to Manchester before.'

The coach swung them through quiet streets off the city centre until they drew up outside a neo-gothic portal.

'Here you are, girls.'

It looked closed up and unfriendly.

'I'll fetch you from outside the Union building at four sharp on Sunday. Now don't forget, girls, I'm not waiting for anyone.'

One of the women had a baby bundled up in a crochet blanket.

'They said no children here, so I bloody well hope she doesn't yell.'

'Just keep in the background,' said Eileen, 'I'll do a spiel.'

They all trooped upstairs – bare, stone steps, varnished pine walls, ecclesiastical. The woman with the baby tripped on its trailing blanket. There were suppressed explosions of giggles, but the child never cried, only laughed along with the rest of them.

The dormitories were partitioned with pine panels, each cubicle contained a high iron bedstead and a rickety chair.

'Jesus, you know what this is, some kind of Salvation Army place.'

'It's a women's dosshouse.'

More giggles. They set one another off. They couldn't stop laughing.

'Not so inappropriate really.'

Crystal lay on her back in her narrow institutional bed. Jon seemed to have ceased to exist . . . where was he, she didn't know, she'd even forgotten what he said he was doing this weekend . . . Only trouble was, she hated the thought of being an unattached woman . . . To be with these women in groups was fun, exciting, but on your own . . . And most of them had shadowy blokes in the background – when you came down to it. You never met them, but they were there, hovering about in the wings somewhere, for when the women went home after their meetings, left this brightly lit stage and stepped back into humdrum anonymity. . . .

One by one they emerged, tousled and unrefreshed after being stowed away for the night on their high shelves. The harsh sheets had felt like tablecloths, and Crystal had kept waking herself up because every time she'd turned over her foot had caught in a rent.

'Where do we wash?'

'Woman last night said it's in the basement.'

Downstairs Crystal looked round her. The place was full of ghosts, madwomen in white nightgowns, wandering, muttering, grunting in the washroom. Water ran away along open drains beneath the thick white sinks, and cockroaches slid to and fro. Not even a mirror. And these women –

'Christ this is awful – '

'Poor things – '

'Don't think they'll be coming to the Conference – '

The lost souls stared ahead, their white faces framed in limp, uncoloured strings of hair; others glanced sideways, menaced, paranoid.

'Let's get out of here.'

They stopped at a caff for breakfast. There was a smell of steam and washing-up water and stale fat. Again, the men looked up from their tabloids and tankards of tea, and glowered at the loud group of women. Crystal did not even know the names of her companions, but she felt as though she'd been travelling with them forever, this trip had gone on for days.

An initial briefing: more than two thousand women in an auditorium – Crystal couldn't decide which workshop to go to, so she followed Eileen. They sat in a circle in a classroom, the furniture had been pushed back against the walls. More women crammed in as those who'd arrived early sat in silence to read the stencilled sheets passed round by the six women leading the workshop.

This workshop is organized by the *Termagant* collective. We produce *Termagant* six times a year; our aim – to bring together women's liberation and revolutionary politics. In our discussions and in some of the articles we've published, we have identified women's role in the *reproduction of the relations of production* as a key feature of late imperialist capitalism. . . .

83

'Language is heavy,' muttered Eileen.

One of the *Termagant* women began to speak.

'That's Eddie Macfarlane,' whispered Eileen, 'she's in the Communist Party.'

Eddie Macfarlane had a rich, beautiful voice and she emanated warmth, the words she used weren't difficult, she talked about their struggle to find words to articulate oppression –

'When you get down to the nitty-gritty, women have been silenced, we've been *speechless*, literally – '

The woman next to her spoke in a posher accent, some-how more disdainfully: 'We're trying to work out how women's personal sense of oppression in the home relates to the workings of capitalism – '

Crystal's attention wandered from the words, instead she watched the severe, pale woman with her much more didactic manner. After she'd finished speaking there was a silence, perhaps the listening women were intimidated, but after a while a woman at the back began to talk about teaching and her sense that in her infant classroom she repeated the functions she performed for her family at home: 'I'm always *servicing* someone – children – my husband – the parents of the children I teach – my own children – '

'Yes! That's it! Exactly! It's all *work* – '

'I think the trouble is housework – '

That set everyone off. And slowly something began to make sense for Crystal. Until now she'd felt she'd been thrown into the middle of things, in at the deep end, Eileen and the others took so much for granted while she was still stuck before the start, hadn't read a word of Marx, knew nothing about politics –

Now, suddenly, she spoke: 'I'm a social worker – in fact I'm on the point of beginning my training as a psychoanalyst, at least that was my plan until a few months ago. But lately . . . somehow it's all become more and more oppressive. Yet I've never been able to explain to myself why or how, exactly. Although I have seen more and more clearly how the whole psychoanalytic world is *so* anti-women, so reactionary. It's not Freud's work *so* much, it's more –

'Anyway, now it seems to me that what we're talking about is what happens in my job too – like you said about teaching. Only with me, it's more that I'm helping other women to be better servicers, to perform their female role more effectively. It's all backed up by this vulgarized Freud stuff . . . and then the women I see, the *State* labels them as inadequate – so I come along, and I'm supposed to tell them how to do it better, help them reproduce the same old situations, only more effectively, to be more *efficient* at being feminine – budget, be more house-proud. Of course, I'm an *absolute* slut myself, but – anyway, it's only now that I *really* see just what's wrong with it – '

It was wonderful – they laughed, she was amusing them, they agreed, she wasn't alone any more.

'We're *all* sluts,' said another woman.

'We shouldn't even use the word – '

Afterwards Eileen said, 'You were good, spieling away like that – '

The tall, severe *Termagant* woman came up to Crystal.

'We're starting a study group – in London – to talk about psychoanalysis. A Freud-reading group, really. I wondered if you'd be interested in participating – '

Crystal laughed: 'But I've just put all that behind me!'

'But we think it's so important to understand Freud if we're to understand the way in which femininity is constructed – '

'But don't we understand that quite well? I should've thought what we needed was to break free of it, not just dwell on it more and more – '

The other woman shook her head: 'It's absolutely essential to understand how gender is constructed at the level of unconscious, because sexuality and gender are at the root – '

This woman had light, prominent grey eyes. There was an insistence, a stubbornness about her which Crystal felt immediately.

'I'm not sure it's compatible with Marxism,' said Crystal.

'And it's as if you're saying it's an oppression within, but it's outside, it's out there, that's what we have to change – that's why we're socialists, isn't it? I mean I'm a socialist, I thought *Termagant* is a Marxist-feminist paper, isn't it – ?'

'Oh yes.' The woman smiled, and raised her eyebrows just slightly, so ironically. 'But the oppression is outside *and* inside, don't you agree?'

'Yes, but – '

'I'll give you the address in any case – '

'I'm sorry – I don't know your name.'

'Celia Howard.'

But Crystal, although she took the piece of paper, turned away, her resolve strengthened; definite.

Goodbye to that stale old romance with her analyst, Dr Haversham. All that money – all those hours; and just to dig further and further into yourself, entrenched so that you'd never get away. Yes, goodbye to Dr Haversham, high priest of the past, and goodbye too to Jon. No longer romantic, those stale old relationships – lover, therapist, the same old routines for years – four years at least with both of them –

> Thy lovers were all untrue –
> 'Tis well an old world is out
> And time to begin a new –

Eileen said, 'They might ask us to join their collective.'

'Who?'

'*Termagant*, of course. Partly because you spoke good – '

'Really?'

'They're rather fine,' said Eileen.

So these women, strangers, intimidating, bold – they accepted her, liked her, had taken her to their hearts.

After lunch some of the Formosa Road women wandered away; Eileen and Crystal followed them, loitering along a run-down main road with shuttered shops and derelict houses in the weak November sunshine.

'Where are we going?'

As the light faded they sat in another empty, dusty room, passed a limp joint from hand to hand. There were a couple of men there – lank and lean, strange beings after all those boisterous, round-limbed women.

Frankie and Luce came laughing in; more escapees from the Conference.

'All that heavy rapping – we went window-shopping in the centre of town – '

'*Window shopping* – nudge nudge, wink wink – *know what I mean!*'

'Get anything nice?'

'This was a real bargain, don't you think?' Luce displayed a thick cotton smock, richly patterned in green and blue and edged with crust cream lace.

'*Really* nice.' They nodded with the mellow certainty of the stoned.

Shadows fell across the room. The lethargy congealed. To lift your arm took too much energy – it was a bring-down, Crystal felt depressed, smoking gave her a headache –

'Let's split, we're missing things – ' said Eileen.

They walked back along the road in the blue of dusk.

'Bit uncool – kiting cheques, shoplifting – '

Crystal hadn't realized, didn't want to admit her naïvety, appear uncool.

'Good fun and all that, I suppose,' said Eileen, 'not *serious*, though – no good politicos getting into that kind of stuff – they all think it *is* political of course – ripping off capitalism . . . just adventurism, actually – '

Crystal heard herself say, 'Yes – it's objectively reactionary.'

Was the Social in the evening objectively reactionary too? To begin with there was a sort of entertainment, a cabaret it was called, women wearing a lot of clown's make-up and ranting and shouting a bit; afterwards women stripped off, danced with bare breasts through the dust and strobe lights to the hard percussion of the Women's Band.

In this throng, you didn't need a man after all – what

was sexual love, anyway: just couples, possessiveness . . . whereas here you felt free, untrammelled –

'I'm not going back to that hostel,' said Eileen. 'Let's go back with Formosa Road, shall we, they're crashing out together in this place – '

They drove in someone's van through a concrete landscape of high-rise towers and corridors in the sky.

'You know, they smashed up the old working-class districts and built this prison. Yeah – there's only one way in and one way out, they got you, when the revolution comes they'll pen everyone up – herded in with no escape – '

'Yeah, but that's always a two-edged thing, they can never sew it all up – a People's Army – well, think of Bogside – '

'Bogside today, Moss Side tomorrow – '

They started to sing *Bandiera Rossa*, and then Irish songs.

They reached a quiet suburb beyond Moss Side, and a corner house with a turret over the front door. Dead tired they trooped upstairs and into a small kitchen. A man with ruddy cheeks and black curls offered them tea.

'So you've been at the Women's Liberation Conference. Uh-huh. Uh-huh. Elvira – that's my, er – well, we live together – she's been there too. She'll be back shortly – we're SRG comrades. Socialist Revolutionary Group. SRG supports women's liberation – from a revolutionary perspective, naturally – We're part of the Fourth International –

'For myself, I regard myself as a complete – how shall I put it – as someone who has undergone a process of complete sexual change and – liberation is too pretentious a word, but – well, anyway, as a result of my experience of revolutionary struggle I've recognized my own homosexuality. Actually I regard myself as a complete transsexual. Elvira totally approves. She's into relationships with women, anyway. We regard monogamy as utterly reactionary, completely counter-revolutionary – '

The women, white-faced with fatigue, sat watching him, drinking the tea.

'The problem is, we are all so totally chained by capitalism – Reich's notion of character armour has a place, I feel –

mind you, his theory of orgone energy diverged from the objectively revolutionary, however, he was a committed comrade at one time and –

'I think I'll have to go to bed – '

'I first became aware of all this at a Tendency meeting – do you know we'd just been discussing the role of avant-garde art and – I suddenly realized: almost all great innovative artists in the twentieth century have been homosexual. Well, you're familiar perhaps with Trotsky's views on the avant-garde, he was absolutely in favour of – '

They split one by one, trying to trickle off without being rude or at least without his noticing.

'He'll be talking to the wall soon.'

'He always was.'

There was a lot of giggling.

'When he said – '

'SRG wankers – '

Bodies rolled into sleeping bags were laid in a tidy row. There was a warm, rank smell of feet, pungent yet endearing. Someone snored.

'Goodnight,' whispered Eileen and, with odd formality, 'sleep well.'

When Crystal heard voices she knew she'd been asleep. The room was now fetidly hot, the snoring oppressive. She lay, watching the line of light beneath the door, and listened to the voices washing up and down along the corridor, breaking over her consciousness, unwilled, unstoppable.

'So all you can do is take – take – take – '

'But look, you said – '

'Don't tell me what I said – '

'You said unselfishness was a bourgeois emotion. Self sacrifice, all that crap, you said – '

'On both sides – on BOTH SIDES – '

'And what does *that* mean? Who said there was anything one-sided about this particular bourgeois hell?'

'All I know is, I've had enough, more than enough – '

* * *

89

In the morning a different man was making tea in the kitchen. Like the man from the previous evening, he played host. Perhaps they'd imagined the other one.

Eileen and Crystal pulled on their clothes and left the other women sleeping. Keen to get back to the Conference in time for the morning plenary, they waited for a bus in the red-brick suburb, no idea where they were.

Eileen said, 'You know, we ought to start an action group on all this housework and social reproduction stuff – could organize things round social security, role of the state, all sorts of things, take it wider than just claimants, that's a narrow focus, other working-class people don't relate too good to that – it's central, actually: the State. And did you know – I'm going to join a *Capital* reading group. Why don't you join too – you should. We haven't enough *theory*.'

'One of the *Termagant* women asked me to join a Freud reading group – '

'Oh . . . interesting – will you?'

'I'm through with all that – Marx would be better.'

'Do both – you could suss them out anyway – '

'Anyway, Eileen, you don't need a *Capital* reading group, you know lots about Marx – '

'Naah – I'm just spieling away most of the time – '

And soon they were back in their coach and the coaches were going like bulls through narrow streets and out towards the motorway. Under grey clouds a dreary landscape spread away, but Crystal hugged her euphoria, slipped an arm through Eileen's.

'I'm glad you made me go. It was great.'

'It was okay.' Eileen shifted away from the physical contact. She was already onto the next thing in her mind: 'Shall you come to the *Termagant* meeting?'

'Oh *yes*.'

'Be good fun. And we'll work on this social security stuff. You'll help, won't you – be good, you know about that.'

'You think this is all good fun, don't you, not dreary duty – ' That was the difference – politics would give life and importance to that which had been do-gooding, tedious routine.

'All what?'

'Politics, grass roots stuff, activism – you know – '

Eileen laughed: 'The people are making the revolution.'

Dark Glasses

The man, when Crystal answered the door, said he was from the college, Eileen's work. It was Eileen staying with her now.

(Can I crash at your place for a while? It's getting a bit heavy over here . . .)

And Eileen came out onto the upstairs landing just wearing her knickers, she'd been having a rest, some women were coming round, and Crystal was cooking a meat loaf, chatting to Alex in the kitchen, he'd dropped by as well. And before they knew where they were the house was swarming with men –

It's a raid. They wouldn't let her see the warrant. Two suavely suited men went through all her papers. Eileen screamed at them to wait until she was dressed. You could see these men thought they were flash, the Special Branch. But they were coarse, vulgar, it was all in character when they leafed through Crystal's love letters, with sniggers and smiles. She was pleased; she could despise them.

They turned the place upside down, slit open the life-sized papier maché sheep that Eileen had brought home from a window display for a joke, pop art she said. The faithless cat wound herself round the Inspector's legs ('she's a friendly little cat'), they took Crystal's papers, her address book, shopping lists, stuff about France – a summer holiday –

Then it was over. They stood by the door. They were going. Waiting for the last man to come up out of the garden.

'Nice place you've got here,' the young one said.

Crystal looked away. Insolence – trying to trap you into being friendly. At least they hadn't torn up the carpet. She'd heard how they took up the floorboards at Formosa Road, used sniffer dogs –

Now they were going. It was over.

Then the Inspector pounced.

'You're coming with us.'

Eileen.

'Where are you taking her?' said Alex.

No answer. As they drove off Eileen looked out of the window of their car, her face a white smudge.

That was finally the end, with both Jon and her analyst. Jon wanted her to wash her hands of it.

'Why did she come and stay with you then – bit fishy, wasn't it?'

It was something to do with Ben. He worked with a group – they called it The Politics of Repression Group – involved with the claimants' union, doing Irish stuff –

Now the cops were trying to say they were terrorists because someone had thrown a bomb at a cabinet minister –

'You're a bloody voyeur – it gives you a vicarious thrill,' said Jon.

The analyst talked of a rebellion against authority, as if what kind of authority it was was unimportant.

'There seems to be a lot of infantile excitement – things exploding – '

He thought explosions were a substitute for orgasm.

Eileen would always go further than everyone else, of course. On demonstrations – that time she'd kicked a policeman in the balls and got away with it, run away. She'd shout and yell, taunt them, try to stop other people being arrested, run after them, pull them away. And always laugh afterwards, reliving the escapades with that strange mixture of anger, indignation and glee that set her apart from all the other women. The *Termagant* women were a bit scared of her, you could see.

Yet where did it come from? She told how she'd been a terribly naughty child, always into scrapes, running wild in the country, a complete tomboy, would never wear a dress. But her parents – a cook and a valet before the war, upper servants, visiting former employers afterwards, after the war was over and there were no servants any more – Eileen would tell how she remembered the houses of the rich, the excitement of it all, the soft rugs, Lady Rose. 'My mum and dad weren't working-class Tories, though – '

But Eileen ran away as a child, put lighted matches in a drawer – 'I thought it was exciting – '

It all changed, though, when she passed the eleven-plus and went to the girls' grammar school. It was such a long journey, they had to cross from the island by boat, and then there was a train –

They were worried about her at school, at first, said she never spoke, never spoke at all, she was so shy, so terribly shy – 'they talked of sending me to a speech therapist – '

It was because she'd changed class. Gone middle class. And then she was the only one who went to the university. So far away – in London – she was all by herself. Until she met Ben.

The first time Crystal ever saw her was at a meeting about radical social work at the college where Eileen worked. It was before Crystal had met the women at Formosa Road, and when she saw Eileen with them, later on, she recognized her as the woman from that meeting. She'd dominated the meeting – a hundred people or so – and Crystal had thought she was a crazy woman, with her wild black hair and her raucous voice and her violent, almost hysterical gestures. That was how it had seemed to Crystal then. It had all seemed exaggerated. So small, like a rag doll, but she'd waved her fists in the air.

She no longer saw Eileen like that at all. But Eileen hadn't changed, so it must have been she, Crystal, whose perceptions had altered.

I wanted to live more intensely, it's true.

Now nothing mattered but to get her out of prison.

Even on weekdays the small, octagonal waiting room was crowded and smoke-filled. Furtive the visitors, as if ashamed to be there – the men waited, awkward, standing hands in pockets, grinding out a fag on the floor, while the children wriggled and whined, and everyone coughed.

'Visitor for Kelly.'

'I have some books.'
'Hand them in at the office.'

Eileen walked demurely beside the screw, who was one of the nicer ones. Quiet, she didn't try to make conversation. Some of them were too friendly on the surface, called you dear, treated you like a mentally defective child, most were pretty hard and rough, a few downright twisted. Only the black ones were ever at all decent.

Eileen hated the ugliness, the cruel surfaces – ice-blue stone, glassy lino in shades of shit, walls that looked as if they'd been painted with margarine.

A few prisoners waited with a screw by the pseudo-medieval door that led into the courtyard. The wind froze them after the stifling heat of the cells. The remand visits took place in a kind of hut. Each woman sat behind her own little table. They waited. At last they heard footsteps and a murmur of voices as the party straggled across the courtyard. The door opened. For a second Eileen saw no one, just a group of strangers, then Crystal stepped forward.

She looked haggard today. 'Ben couldn't come,' she muttered.

'Give me a hug – I'm so cold.'

There were eight visits in progress and only the two screws, one at each end of the room, so it was easy not to be overheard. Crystal's large, pale eyes stared into Eileen's face – Crystal always looked so worried.

'Cigarette?' Crystal produced the new packet – it had to be unopened – peeled off the layers of wrapping and pulled at the first cigarette, then as she held out the match she placed her hand over Eileen's and Eileen felt a little pellet of paper being pushed into her palm.

'They raided his flat – lucky he wasn't there – '

'Things got too hot, I suppose – '

'There was a query about his visa anyway.'

'What sort of query?'

'He said you wouldn't be surprised . . . He said don't be upset, he'll be in touch – '

Crystal's solemnity was tinged with self-importance to be acting as romantic go-between.

'It'll make things look worse for me – '

'No it won't. Why should it?'

'Sh – sh – ' For Crystal's voice had risen with alarm. 'They can drag in any old thing they want on a conspiracy charge – '

Conspiracy to cause explosions.

But Crystal dismissed conspiracy with a wave of the hand. 'They've got *nothing* on you. I must say Formosa Road aren't much help. All this Defence Group stuff, they just want to make political statements. But I say, you and Vinny gotta get off.'

'Innocent or guilty?'

'Oh, come *on* – '

'Everyone in here is innocent,' said Eileen. 'You know, like *out there* everyone's riddled with guilt and uncertainty – not in here. The repressive state's a very freeing thing, my dear. Frees the prisoner from all her hang-ups. They don't need all these social workers, father confessors, drugs and all that stuff, all the crap they dish you out, 'cos once you're banged up in here you're bound to be innocent – they're heaping so much shit on you, you could never in a million years deserve it – '

'I brought the books you wanted.'

'Someone sent in *The Well of Loneliness* – but they wouldn't let me have it, Vinny and I are going to complain – '

'*The Well of Loneliness?*'

'Lesbianism – not that you'd need a book to find out about that in here – '

'Yet they let you have all that Marx and stuff – it's the Lenin I've brought in today, oh and Gramsci, *Prison Notebooks*.'

'Thanks – listen – ' Eileen leaned closer across the table, 'two things – did you get hold of the solicitors?'

'Yes – and it's Eddie, she's coming tomorrow – she's a clerk at Cohen's now.'

'Oh great. The other thing: I share a cell with a nice American woman. Cathie. She's all alone here, doesn't get any visitors at all. Got caught passing through with pounds of grass, she's pleading guilty, she's sure to be sent down. If you could somehow fix to visit her – '

'How can I?'

'Oh, just write a letter saying does she remember you from when you met in the States or something and you've heard she's in trouble and can you visit her – you know.'

'But I've never been to the States.'

'Oh *Crystal*.'

Already the visit had to end. Fifteen minutes was nothing. They hugged. Crystal smelled faintly of mothballs, the old-fashioned smell of second-hand fur coats.

'Come again soon – '

Crystal waved, then disappeared out of the door. Eileen waited with the other remands and the screws to be taken back to the wing.

The youngest girl began to cry.

'Don't be silly, dear. Now be a good girl – '

Hustle, hustle them back across the yard to make way for a fresh contingent. Round the corner, up the stone stairs, along the corridors in the twenty-four-hour glare that dried out your eye sockets, gave you a headache –

Back on the wing; doors slammed, locks ground.

Eileen had a visit every day except Sundays, when there were no visits for remands. Cathie enjoyed the short period of solitude. She sat cross-legged on her bunk and tried to write a letter to her daughter. She tried to imagine her, to visualize her, but the focus was all blurred; a muddled yet sharp emotion – anxiety, guilt, frustration jammed together – tensed her up so that it was impossible to get words down on paper.

The dash to Heathrow – she'd just thrown everything and Cindy into a taxi. Then, as she'd hauled the trolley across the check-in hall with Cindy tugging on her hand and crying, jostling against other passengers, the beefy man in the blue suit had stepped forward, Cindy had yelled harder – they'd just yanked the kid away –

The key ground in the lock. Eileen had been gone it seemed like only five minutes.

'Hi! How'd it go?'

'Okay.' Eileen climbed to the upper bunk, lay down with her hands behind her head and looked at the ceiling. Somewhere along the corridor a woman began to scream. Eileen half sat up and took the little ball of paper from her pocket. It was softened and dirty, but when she smoothed it out she could just read his jagged writing: 'You'll understand the news. It's better this way. Love, and Power to the People.' She rubbed it between the palms of her hands, then tore it into three smaller pieces, rolled them into pellets, made saliva gather in her mouth, and managed to swallow them one by one.

She lay back, waiting for the drug to work. He'd never told her *all* he was into – so many of the women in this place got dragged into trouble on the coat-tails of their boyfriends – prostitutes, receivers of stolen goods, it was all the same. Even the few who'd murdered – even *her*, the famous one – it was mostly all to do with their men . . . but surely not she, Eileen, as well.

The rapid walk, almost a run, the sharp jerk of his head to shake aside the tangled dark hair, his machine-gun speech, his weird silences – he seemed far away, the drug wasn't working (but then everything *out there* seemed distant). The three little pellets she'd swallowed (almost, she thought, ex-Catholic as she was, like the communion wafer) had failed to perform a miracle, the word wasn't made flesh, he wasn't close to her. She remembered the moment when she'd lost her faith: she'd been explaining to a student friend, in her first year at university it was, the meaning of transubstantiation, and suddenly she thought, I don't believe a word of this; it all fell away at once in one great wedge.

So Ben fell away. She was on her own. Better forget him.

A bang on the door; a screw thrust some paper bags into the cell. 'Your meal that was sent in.'

The screws hated that – her and Vinny knowing their rights, getting food sent in, newspapers, books –

'Oh goodee!' Cathie grabbed the bags and took out the little packages wrapped in silver foil.

'Crystal does the best meals.'

Eileen climbed down and sat beside Cathie, felt down the bags for the half bottle of wine, hoping it would be the kind with a plastic cap, but it was a conventional cork. A woman with whom she'd shared a cell for a few days before Cathie's arrival had taught her how to press on the cork until it slipped down into the bottle. It wasn't so much brute strength, just a special knack –

'Here – ' She took a swig and held it out to Cathie. But Cathie was more interested in the food. 'Houmus – and a terrific salad.'

'I'm not really hungry.' Eileen picked out the lumps of kebab.

In this dark suburb Dr Crippen had lived. The houses were big and bleak, their heavy façades were overloaded with plasterwork and half-hidden behind Victorian shrubs. Fleshy shrubs they were, as overdressed as the Victorians themselves, with a surfeit of thick dark leaves and poisonous-looking berries, but never any flowers, or only whitish, sickly ones, like children kept in a cupboard. Victorian families once filled each house to bursting, the petty bourgeoisie; the mistress of the house, a grim Victorian wife with lantern jaw, pacing the rooms in creaking stays and dusty skirts, imprisoned in those high cold rooms and bullying the skivvy below-stairs.

Now lonely individuals lurked in rooming houses, the mentally disturbed, the unemployed –

Crystal shrank into her fur coat against the east wind. I wanted to live more intensely . . . but it's still the same, I'm still a social worker, Eileen's now, running errands for her instead of for those isolated individuals – shall I ever break free, shall I always somehow be passive, bent to the will of others, looking into the mirror to live other people's lives –

Yet this was different. She had, after all, moved through the glass into a different world. For, like the Victorian world that haunted this suburb, there was another invisible world beneath the surface of the ordinary, the everyday, the palpably visible. Suddenly you put your hand on the glass and it began to dissolve – so that you moved through into the other world of which they talked in the new movement of women: the world of repression. The women she met now all spoke of society as a prison for women, a world of iron necessity, a world of rooms with no doors and streets with no exits, one-way streets. You could call it the underworld. It had started for her in the Blue Lagoon where they'd all smoked ganja, and then in the gay pubs and clubs where Alex used to take her. Now she'd just gone further into the invisible world – the world beneath the façade of normality. Because of her poverty-stricken, genteel childhood she'd always known the façade was only that – behind it lurked danger, excitement, the raw truth, madness, violence: experience.

But she hadn't quite bargained for this forbidden world. Outside the law – men and women passed by in the street, brushed against you, unaware, believing they were free. They didn't even notice the electric fence, invisible, but if you fell against it or strayed into the space it enclosed you had crossed forever into the underworld, the hinterland, the seamy side where, as in the Victorian below-stairs, there was no escape, no allowances were made, life would be bone-crushing, drag you down.

Fear: is *she* afraid?

The east wind blew dust off the street into Crystal's face as she folded her coat tighter round her and held its collar pinched about her face. Strip off the veil of illusion; see things as they are.

'You know it's my trial next week,' said Cathie. 'I guess I can take five years. I'm just counting on that, praying I won't get more.'

'You are pleading guilty?'

'What else can I do? Eileen – it's just hopeless – they found all the dope in the hotel room – can you *imagine* – all that dope, enough to keep you in smokes for *years* – well, I wouldn't feel right anyway, pleading anything else. It was all my fault. I let Al talk me into it and now, well I guess I'll just have to pay my debt to society. I've prayed about it and I'm sure that's right.'

'With remission and the time you've done on remand you'll be out the year after next – '

The locks ground. The parcel of dinner for Eileen was pushed through. As usual Eileen ate the meat, Cathie ate the rest.

'You're putting on weight, Cathie.'

'Oh I *know*! I eat all their stodge, and now your meals as well. And I don't get *any* exercise. But you know I really don't care. Al was always on at me to be thin. 'Why can't you look like Twiggy,' he used to say. Day in, day out: 'Don't eat so much, I want my wife to be real thin, like Twiggy.' Guess that's how I got so into drugs in the first place, popping pills the whole time to keep my weight down.'

That summer when things began to go crazy – they had this walk-up above a laundromat; just a room, really, with kitchen and shower in cupboards, and the hot steamy smell from the laundry stifling you. Over on Avenue A. The streets were full of girls like Twiggy, and Al kept bringing home more dope. Evenings there was always a party some-place, in rooms whose windows opened onto streets filled with excitement and noise – and always the old rock music. Took the baby to the parties, she musta got stoned too, breathing in the smoke as she lay on some cushions in a corner.

She went to work in the mornings, she was still stoned. Lump of dope in her purse, a big thick square, sometimes as dark as liquorice, sometimes green as henna, she felt great, laughing and giggling with the clients, humming as she pranced with the dryer, quick out the back room where they did bleach jobs for a coupla drags – it stank of perming liquid out there, a metallic, *mean* smell, but it covered the smell of the dope.

Left the baby with her friend, on account of Al had no job and they had to find the money somehow for the rent, food, diapers, dope. And you couldn't leave the baby with Al. With Al it was terrific if they were both stoned. She just fell down, down, the pit of her stomach, the floor fell away – and there was nothing, nothingness –

Yet all the time she knew he was getting it on with other chicks.

Cathie struggling through the heat with the baby on one arm and the bag of groceries on the other . . . floaty, light-headed, I've eaten nothing today, really, coffees and one biscuit, that's all, the baby's yelling, we'll soon be home, sugar, don't pull, don't scream –

Al's bad-tempered too, worried about the draft. I said, why don't you go back to school, wouldn't that be one way of –

That was the first time he hit me. I was in shock. I never would of *dreamed* he'd act that way – but the baby started to yell, and I tried to quiet her, pretend it hadn't happened.

Anyway, I guess I got stoned, and then I didn't think about it. The pills, more than anything, they were terrific, 'cause that way you didn't eat and then you were thin, so thin. Got my figure back real quick that way, after the baby.

Cindy, her name's Cindy. Al thought she was so cute at first, but soon he kinda lost interest, and anyway he was hardly ever there. . . .

These days Al only came by when he needed some bread, or to shack up for a few days, like he was lying low or something. He still kept her in supplies, but now . . . he was starting to encourage her to get stuff for her friends –

'C'mon, it's real cheap – good stuff, you're doing them a favour baby – '

She didn't know who she was with any more. Sometimes she thought she was still with Al – other times she thought she was with Pete – or Andy – or Vince. But she was always with Cindy.

They set off in the old, sagging Buick. She's driving. Cindy's in back. As they gather speed northwards in the morning traffic, against the stream, there's a glitter off the industrial wasteland across the Hudson river on the New Jersey side. Vehicles slide over the Williamsburg bridge like an army of ants. Northwards: Manhattan left far behind in its shimmering dreams. Now they drive through flat suburbs. The sun shines. Vince smoking at her side, his friend, what's his name, snores in the back alongside Cindy.

Need more gas. Vince has no money – wants her to make a break for it without paying, Bonnie and Clyde stuff. She pays herself from her old, fat purse which is giving at the seams. He nags at her about it, resentment begins to rise, she grips the wheel, keeps her mouth shut, the way she's learned. The sun sweats down on them. So hot inside the automobile. Anger bubbles like water in the engine. Steam smoking up; she pulls into the side.

Don't stop here – the middle of nowhere. I'm hungry – someplace we can get something to eat –

Can't you see the engine's overheated –

Bicker, bicker, the words flicker in the cruel heat. Give us a drag – thaaat's better. They drive on. Cindy wakes up. Starts to shout, soon she's yelling for her dinner too. Vince's friend is slumped sideways, grunts and frowns in his dreams. Cindy pokes his face, trying to stick her finger up his nostril. Cathie draws into the forecourt of a drive-in hamburger joint. Eat something here, I'll feed the kid. The man in the back groans, slowly moves, sinks back into sleep. Leave him.

Cindy grabs her glasses, dashed to the ground they break. *Shit!* WhaddamIgonnadonow? She sips black coffee. Smokes. Cindy drains her bottle, throws French fries on the floor. Vince thrusts the hamburger into his mouth. Mayonnaise like pus oozes out, a shred of lettuce hangs down, clings to his beard.

How much further –

My shades'll do. She hitches her shawl around her, scrabbles in her deep basket, fishes them out. The bridge is broken, just mended with tape, they sit askew on her nose . . . better than nothing. They are prescription lenses.

Hit the road again. Late afternoon sun slants down. Traffic begins to gather, soon they find themselves in a line that stretches ahead as far as the eye can see. She squints through her lenses. Gradually there gathers a sense of like they're part of something that's happening, though it's all a bit blurred. Men and women walk along the line of vehicles, they're selling cool drinks, dope cookies, hash brownies, food. . . .

There's music booming from distant amplifiers, and there's a guitarist ahead of them on the road.

After they've inched forward for more than an hour Vince says he guesses this is it. They're here. This *is* Woodstock.

Hours pass. Light ebbs from the sky. Cathie frowns through her glasses, can hardly see at all – I guess we'll sleep where we are, draw into the side . . . only someone calls through the window, offers to share a tent. Long skirts brushing through long grass. Fires have been lit. Long hair falls forward beneath the broad brims of their hats.

Time melts down to sensation, to the weight of the sleeping child on the shoulder, heavier, heavier, to the taste of stale smoke in the throat, to sweat in the armpits and a shiver of cold as the shawl clutched around feels thin . . . they roll out their sleeping bags as dawn turns white. . . .

Then it's sunlight across fields and woodland and a distant sound of music and cheering in the open air, and crowds, crowds everywhere. She peers through her glasses, holds them to her nose, hitches up her skirt, lifts the baby, Cindy grabs her hair. . . .

She wanders through the crowds, stoned for days. The tent, Vince, the strangers, the man in the back seat, the Buick – all left behind, she and Cindy float on this sea of faces, voices, the waves of sound bang down, recede, flood forward once more – the tide going out or coming in. . . .

The waves, indifferent, close over drowned faces, roar forward once more. . . .

'So you were *at* Woodstock.' Vinny was impressed.

'Only it wasn't Woodstock – there were so many people, they relocated it. I went back afterwards – the next year – with a friend, and I didn't recognize the place, and I thought, well, was I *that* stoned, that I don't recognize it at *all*, and then I guess I realized it had been someplace else – And then, you know, when I went to see the movie, you'll never believe this, but the same thing happened – like my glasses broke, and I was sitting there in the movie house peering through my *sunglasses* all over again, and they were still held together with this bit of tape – so like my whole memory of Woodstock is through dark glasses – '

There'd been an influx of new remands before Christmas, so Vinny was sharing a cell with Cathie and Eileen. The night before Cathie's trial they got quite drunk, Vinny and Eileen had each had a half bottle of wine sent in, and Crystal had made a trifle with Advocat instead of custard.

'Crystal's awfully bourgey, isn't she?' said Vinny. 'Still, she does do good meals.'

'What d'you mean, bourgey?'

'Oh, you know – she's such a fine lady – '

'No she's not, you only think that – she's worked *really* hard on our bail, they're going to judge in chambers now, we should be out after Christmas – '

'Oh, don't be too hopeful – '

Cathie finished sorting through her property. She gave Eileen her purple velvet jacket ('I've grown too fat for it anyway') and Vinny an embroidered scarf.

'I guess I might as well drink to tomorrow. To the start of a new life.'

'We'll miss you Cathie,' said Vinny.

'Well – I guess – in a weird kind of way I really don't regret being here – Like, I *do*, of course, but outside of this place, I'd never have met you – '

'We're part of a tradition,' said Eileen, 'the suffragettes

were here. When we come out we'll start a campaign for prison reform, like they did.'

'Committee of One Hundred women too,' said Vinny, 'in the sixties.'

'We're political prisoners, like them.'

'I've learned a lot from you two,' said Cathie, 'like I never thought about *women* before, working together I mean, for a better deal, a better world – when I get out I'm gonna try and do some work around women, get something together.'

'Isn't it *wonderful*,' cried Eileen, 'that we're sitting here in a prison in the heartland of imperialism and things can still change – there's the contradiction, the might of the State spawns its own undoing – '

'Some women just get smashed,' said Vinny.

'Let's drink to you,' said Cathie. 'Success in your trial.'

Lights dazzled Crystal as she ran down the steps to tell Alex and Hugo the news – they were waiting in the café. The cameras slewed after her.

'It's not me you want,' she screamed, running faster and slipping on the wet stones, 'they'll be coming out in a minute.'

Dusk in the courtroom – they read out the verdicts: Not Guilty for Eileen and Vinny. Some of the men went down.

'There'll be a press conference later,' she shouted in the direction of the blurred crowd of journalists.

Eileen's minder, that's what she'd become. But it was over now. They could step back from the edge.

Eileen doesn't realize yet, but nothing will be the same again. After the euphoria there'll be a letdown. But it's more than that. We'll always know it's there now, the other world, the world beyond the electric fence, the world outside the ghetto of middle-class safety.

Now I understand what Eileen meant when she talked of revolution – that middle-class redoubt extinguished, overwhelmed as the hidden world rolled forward, lapped wider and wider. That's what a revolution would really be like.

All that oppression, repression, seething, bubbling up out into the open, out in the streets instead of hidden away in prisons and mines and sweatshops. Injustice rising up in a tidal wave, crashing down, it'd break all the windows of our middle-class world –

Crystal took the letter with her to the *Termagant* meeting, to show it to Eileen and Eddie.

'Look – from Cathie,' she said. 'Read it – she's gone out to the West Coast and she's living in a women's commune there . . . she says . . . "We're looking for some wimmin's land, up here in Oregon, we might move further south, down into California. I had a tough time, when I first got home, out of prison . . ." There's a lot about that, it was very difficult with Cindy – I'm not surprised – but that seems to be all right now, and listen, she says, "When I first came to the community we had a naming ceremony. We all gathered in the wilderness – out in the hills – when there was a full moon, and one of the wimmin had created a special dance – so we danced and smoked and I was renamed, to symbolize my new life, so I'm no longer Cathie Robbins, I've become – "

'And then it's signed "Willow Tempest".'

Karen's car bumped up a lane and came to rest on some lumpy grass. It was dusk. After the hot autumn day a chill crept up from the valley. The empty black windows of the cottage stared down the hill.

'In a way I'm glad the others aren't coming till tomorrow.'

Crystal and Eileen followed Karen into the dark downstairs room. There was a smell of damp, and the charred remains of a fire in the grate.

'What a mess – let's clear up first and then eat.'

Later they sat round the fire and ate sausages and fried bread with baked beans. They were drinking red wine.

'I'm *so* looking forward to this weekend,' said Karen. 'Now we'll get to know the others better.'

'I hope we have some good political discussion – I have a feeling we will,' said Eileen.

Karen said, 'Charles kicked up terribly you know, about letting us have the cottage – '

Crystal didn't much like Charles, but she just smiled and looked sympathetic.

Karen was seated on a red velvet cushion, her blue skirt spread out over the shabby old rug on the floor.

'I mean – why should he *mind*? It's not as though he'll have to look after Venice, my mother's having her. He can get on with his work, do what he wants . . . actually I think he's got another woman – well, he can see her for all I care – '

'You think he's having an *affair*?'

'I don't *care* if he's having an affair – what I mind is his making such a fuss if I want to come down here with my women's group.'

'They hate it – us getting together,' said Crystal.

'Just tell him to get stuffed, that's my advice.' Eileen was always impatient when women complained about men. What did they expect? Jam on it? And anyway, why put up with that shit? Get rid of him if he's such a pain. But then Eileen was one of those woman who, without seeming to have much time for men, always *had* one. Perhaps Eileen's men, like Eileen, were above all interested in politics. They found a mate, a comrade, and then got on with life. Her latest was Gareth, who led the *Capital* reading group.

Karen laughed: 'But he makes me feel so . . . *trapped* – it's as if – we're *locked* together in this relationship – I really didn't feel I had the right to come down here with all of you – I really felt guilty – '

'Can't you talk to him about it?'

'Oh, it always ends with a row and he somehow gets me into a corner, he stomps about on the moral high ground while I'm grovelling in the mud of self-abasement – '

'Forget it and let's just enjoy ourselves,' said Eileen.

'Is enjoyment the aim?' Crystal raised her eyebrows, yet felt her irony was misplaced, half-mockery to cover her actual tension, a formless melancholy. It was all very well for Eileen, but actually life without a lover, without a man, was strange, it made one anxious, vulnerable.

They drank another bottle of wine, and played Janis Joplin and 'The Harder They Come', dancing in a circle of three, swaying in their long skirts, then faster, round and round, their hair flying out – as Eileen said, like whirling dervishes.

Termagant had filled the summer. The collective had sat round a table and puzzled over layout and paste-up. Eileen said they made her feel scruffy, they were all so glamorous. They were older than the women at Formosa Road.

In the morning the Communist Party women were the first to arrive. They tumbled out of Eddie's car, and Crystal stopped feeling sleepy under the impact of the loud voices and the energy of women who'd got up at half past six to be here by ten.

Before she'd met Eddie and the others, Crystal had always imagined Communists as old and grey. That's how she'd imagined Eddie – Edwina Macfarlane, it sounded like an elderly woman's name. But all these women were young – and Eddie was the star. Janet was quiet and rather strained,

Maggie was rosy and plump, a community artist, and Helen was the same age as Crystal. She always seemed calm and sensible.

Eddie and Helen came from what they called Party families. They meant their parents had been in the Party too.

The second group arrived in Juliet's little post office van. They were the 'non-aligned' women – the ones who weren't in the CP or a Trotskyist group. They struggled out, cramped and hobbling, but vivid as ever: Anita in red, Sally bubbly and laughing, Wanda with newly hennaed hair, and Juliet who always wore black. Celia got out last. She had wrapped herself in a grey cloak.

Celia began. No chink in her armour of course, as always the stiff smile on her face, the self control. Her clipped, swallowed voice described with neither irony nor apology her upper-class childhood. No one, she implied, could compete with the awfulness of that, the unloved child between nanny and governess, mother a far-off Cheshire Cat smile in a distant tree. The hell of boarding school – Eileen thought she made it sound worse than prison.

All told with such deadpan precision – but behind her words was a silent challenge: trump me if you dare. For Celia had not only had the most nightmarish childhood, she had also, it seemed, had every experience to which any of the listening women might lay claim. She'd been married, got a Ph.D, been a community worker, written for left-wing journals. She'd been in analysis (with a famous analyst of course), she'd been to China, she'd even been in the Communist Party for a bit.

Still kept the stiff upper lip, though, the steely good manners that sawed off your legs as you stood there. And Celia's voice was a monotone, stray shards of individuality broke off, splintered in front of them, but what could you do with them, you couldn't pick them up, they'd cut your fingers, you couldn't see your reflection in them, they simply lay there waiting to jab at you if you got too close.

There was a strangeness, an otherness about this story; you couldn't identify. When one woman talked for so long it was difficult to concentrate. Her life might be a mirror held up to yours, but you wanted in the end to turn away from it, get back to yourself, her words were a trigger for self-absorption rather than empathy.

Celia talked on. Outside the trees flamed, autumn put a torch to the Gloucestershire hills.

All our childhoods, and now here we are, all here together: Movement Women, assured, confident, perhaps gifted. That was what Crystal had noticed first of all about the huge meetings, the conferences, the marches – how *striking* most of them were. Unusual.

Yet they were here, sitting round in a circle, revealing themselves in order to affirm their sameness, mutual identification was the purpose. The difficulty was, that to forge a group identity you perhaps had to be more different to begin with. And aren't we all alike, really, privileged, educated, demanding something from life?

But they all, of course, denied any such sameness. The sameness they sought was not at all of class or educational origins, the sameness they wanted was of women oppressed and in struggle, forging a common identity to brandish against the world.

At the same time, each of them wanted so much to be unique. Perhaps that was the reason for the emphasis on childhood. Your childhood *was* unique. Only as you grew older did you become more like the others.

It hadn't been as easy as they'd expected to work together all year. You couldn't explore your differences because the constant imperative of sisterhood stifled dissent. They didn't even know what their disagreements really were.

Eileen cut through it all: 'Why don't we just get on with it, just do it?' she would mutter to Crystal, or rage on the journey home after a particularly turgid session. 'All this psychic agonizing over every bloody article. No one says what they mean. Why can't we just have cards on the table?'

But as Helen, the older CP woman had once said, 'The

trouble is, we find it so hard to criticize without being destructive.'

Under the original clothes and the beautiful hair and the pure unmade-up faces they were all riddled with insecurity, competitiveness, guilt.

Time unwound, spun out with words. Karen refilled the electric kettle. The coffee jar was passed around, milk in the bottle, a sticky spoon. Sugar spilled on the rug.

Sally talked of coming out, of discovering her lesbian sexuality. It sounded tremendously affirmative, the way Sally talked about it . . . yet intimidating.

Perhaps one should love women. Perhaps that was the solution. Perhaps if you went that far . . . Politics collapsed into pleasure in the vast erotic embrace of the feminine. 'It's about prioritizing women,' said Sally. 'It's not about being like a man, it's about getting in touch with womanliness.'

Sometimes Crystal thought that Sally was looking at her as if – but the whole thing embarrassed her, she couldn't get into it, wouldn't it all be too . . . soft and sugary . . .?

The group swallowed up Sally's love for women in its deep silence. Her companions saw in the mirror she held up so strange a reflection of their own lives with men. Could it be that bad? No, surely – their minds shied away.

Sally had been to China too – she and Celia had done the trip together. The Chinese condemned homosexuality of course – that was a problem. And they'd found the unmarried status of Sally and some of the other people on the tour most puzzling. Everyone in China was married. They didn't understand how any woman or man could or would remain single. Yet they were more independent than we Westerners, they didn't depend for their whole emotional sustenance on the one relationship, didn't live for romantic love. A man and wife might easily be separated for ten or eleven months of the year because of their political or other work. Why should they mind? Wherever they went they had friends. Their friends were in the Party, in the struggle, making the Revolution.

The women in the circle nodded, looked serious. That was their ideal too: the support of a network of sisters, comrades, and independence from those shadowy partners, those Others absent from this gathering, the men and the children. They'd hardly even met one another's lovers, husbands, kids. Yet, resolutely excluded, these maintained a subversive existence in the group, like ghosts at the feast.

The morning had begun vivaciously. But already by noon there was both a dullness and an edge. Celia had talked for so long, and so had Sally. The others were longing for their turns.

Juliet was talking now. Juliet was like a diamond, so beautiful, hard, how you could envy that beauty. But that in itself, of course, was a secret never to be admitted: that you could envy another woman's beauty, or even admit that some were more beautiful than others. Juliet, anyway, would have hated any mention of her looks. There was something dour, angry and arid about Juliet, some bitter contempt for herself, for her men – and for them, her sisters.

She poured her bleak and humourless rage on the communist women. The others listened, stunned, as she denounced the Parliamentary Road to Socialism, the betrayal of Trotsky, the Purges, the bureaucracy, Lenin's sexual conservatism – a thunderstorm of rage broke around them. Janet was almost in tears.

But they sank even deeper into their silence. No one stopped her. Perhaps the non-aligned women were secretly pleased. For the Party was another of the silences in the group – and the women who weren't 'in' didn't analyse their distrust – they just *knew*, the way everyone knows, that the Communist Party was wrong, bad, it pulled the strings behind the scenes, it had its 'line' to be pushed at all costs. They carried the beliefs they'd absorbed all their lives, unthinkingly, along with the rest of their cultural baggage on their hectic journey leftwards.

But perhaps they also hated the Party because in a peculiar way it was real, it was *theirs*, they were responsible for it, landed – since they called themselves leftists, socialists, Marxists – with its betrayals and failures. They felt contaminated by it. It was like a horrible, shaming, elderly parent, old-fashioned and shabby, yet smugly self-satisfied, and unaware of the seedy figure it cut.

When Juliet paused, Eddie was red in the face, but it was Eileen who came to the Party's defence.

'If you'd been in the situation I was in,' she cried, 'you wouldn't sneer at organization, building unity – a lot of the stuff we're into, it isolates us, we're cut off, it doesn't seem relevant to the working class, we have to make it relevant, build bridges, we need support, we can't do it all on our own. The idea of the Party – to unify struggles, to create something that draws in all the different interests – I can't see what's wrong with that.'

Another silence.

After a long pause Juliet continued; now she was talking about her visit to Berlin with her lover. They'd met people 'close to' Baader-Meinhof, the terrorist group. So what did everyone think about armed struggle?

Again the uncomfortable silence. After some time it was Helen who spoke: 'Well . . . I don't think you can talk of armed struggle like that, as if it were just a choice – or – or an act of faith. I mean, it might be something you were driven to, something the movement was driven to – like liberation struggles; it's only when all other avenues have failed that you are driven into armed struggle, it would always be a response to the violence of the state, not this kind of . . . exemplary violence – with no movement behind it.'

Eileen and Eddie nodded in agreement.

'We must go for a walk,' cried Karen after lunch, 'it's so stuffy in here. There's a phone box down the road – we can ring Jenny.'

Crystal walked with Eddie across a field of stubble.

'Pity Jenny's ill – she wanted so much to come.'

114

'She's *wrecked*.' Eddie's deep look and her deep, rich voice implied intimacy, some secret, shared understanding.

'How's the weekend going?'

Eddie put her hand on Crystal's arm: 'The trouble with *Termagant* is women are *disabled* from speaking. The atmosphere is terroristic – it's *horrendous* – '

Eddie always spoke not for herself alone but for other women, for all women, assuming a shared experience, managed to call into existence a vision of women in struggle against a composite foe: the state, trade unions, men – women were totally embattled, yet managed to survive in some wonderful, specifically female way.

Eddie and Crystal walked across the field of stubble towards the forest fire of beech trees against the blue sky. Eddie was talking about the big trial of mass picketers taking place in the west country. She was attending the trial as lawyer's clerk.

'They're going to go down, and nobody's doing owt about it. It's terrible.'

'Not even the Party?' One or two of the men on trial were Communists.

Eddie shrugged: 'Not much – legally, yes, but . . . it's *beyond* the Party, all these trials. It's a whole new ball game. And when you get down to the nitty-gritty, the Party's good at doing what it's always done – but the new politics – it's a non-starter.'

The new politics – women, anarchists, black activists, Ireland; Crystal sighed. 'In a way it's a pity to be shut up indoors when the weather's so glorious.'

Eddie suddenly put her hand on Crystal's arm again: 'Are you all right?'

'No – not really.'

'What's up?'

'Sometimes I think I don't really like women at all, you know.'

She was close to tears – no idea why. She waited for Eddie's disapproval. Instead Eddie laughed.

'I don't blame you with some of this lot. I could have murdered Juliet. Bloody hell!'

'Celia is such a know-all too – always has to be in the right. But I suppose I'm just too judgmental – too critical.'

'You're too hard on yourself.'

'No.' There was still the lump of self-pity in her throat. 'It's other people I'm hard on. You've no idea how easy I am on myself.'

'Oh come on – you're no way so self-righteous as Juliet.'

Soon they were both laughing. There was relief in this secret treachery, this bitching.

It was Eddie's turn; she talked about the Party. She spoke of all the Party women, oppressed by the Party, oppressed by its structures, oppressed by Party families, oppressed by Party Men.

All the women could respond to that. When it came to Eddie, no one despised her for being in the Party, she was somehow exempt from their distrust. They felt she was heroic to try to bend the structures of her sinister, dingy organization. Her struggle inside the prison of the Party became the struggle of all of them to free themselves, to insist on recognition, to take on the world, to free the voice of womanhood. They identified with Eddie. She was their heroine – or rather, the heroine in each of them identified with her.

But Crystal wondered, 'Why be in a political party if you hate it so much? Why don't you leave – you say it's so terrible?'

'It's horrendous, but – *but* – there's the Reactionaries, the leadership, the bureaucrats – and then there's *us* – '

'Us?'

'The Revolutionaries!' Triumphantly. 'The Party *can* change – become a democratic organization – if there's enough of us to make it, that is – '

Her voice wrapped you in black velvet, she had a wonderful voice – Yet there was something angular and beaky about Eddie. Somewhere she too was insecure.

Crystal wanted to hear more about the Party. However imperfect the actual Party, if you were a Marxist you ought to be in a Marxist Party. That was how the debate went in their *Capital* reading group.

To Crystal the attraction, secretly, was more of taking the leap – to fling yourself into the wholly unacceptable, the forbidden, to claim that sinister heritage – Communism – as your own.

Eileen had no time for such romanticism. She just thought it would help you organize. And wanted to be finally shot of the anarchists.

It was Crystal's turn to speak. And she did what she'd known she'd do – she produced the amusing performance, she made them laugh by making a joke of her childhood, middle-classness, genteel poverty, guying it all to mask the embarrassment and pain of those memories.

Shadows filled the room. The splendour of the day had gone. They had missed it.

'Let's get dinner,' said Helen.

Maybe the mistake was the wine. They started to drink while the food was cooking. Karen lit a fire and they sat cross-legged on the floor to eat.

Maybe the mistake was the dope. Juliet made coffee, and it was Karen who rolled the first joint.

Anita, silent until now, began to talk. Words gushed out.

It was not that she was or ever had been mad. You had no idea how wild it was, the life they lived as children, after her mother had committed suicide, her father was a painter, half the time they never went to school, mother taught them at home.

University was her first taste of normal life, so called. It was bleak. The days passed, the land was flat, bleakly bare all round, the campus a new one, concrete, winds whipped across you as you sped through the central square. Her long hair blew against her face; she couldn't see.

He was called Colin. They made love. There was something – it was frightening, she didn't want that kind of dependence. She slept with other men. He was jealous, wrapped her hair around her throat, threatened, made scenes. Then left her.

You could start to feel so strange after a while. The horizon circled you endlessly all round. The trouble was she didn't get enough sleep. She stopped going to classes, it was hard to concentrate. . . .

Anita's was the familiar story: the woman dashing herself at the bars of her prison, the iron system, the iron machine –

'I stared out of my window and through the glass the air shimmered as if it were a very hot day. Yet it was freezing – '

The view trembled, dissolved. Lights flashed across the sky, a great rent in the sky, light poured through.

Karen rolled a second joint. Eileen drained her glass and poured another one immediately. Helen coughed and tried to find a more comfortable position on the sofa.

They dragged her to the ambulance after she'd tried to throw herself out of the window, and then she was in this long room filled with crazy people –

'I was the only person left alive – '

Eddie began to sob. Her sobs shook the room. Helen put her arm round Eddie's shoulders.

Anita's voice rose. She was speaking faster and faster, almost incoherent, denouncing the psychiatrists, the analyst who'd treated her –

'But Anita,' said Crystal, 'don't you think – I mean couldn't therapy at least have helped you understand – '

Anita sprang up with a loud scream, flung open the front door and rushed into the darkness as a sweep of cold air blew towards them. They could hear her screaming down the meadow. Sally followed her outside.

Eddie sobbed. They all stared at her. Then Celia's voice broke through the paralysis, cool, almost cold, she got Eddie to calm down.

The women murmured, cooed, fidgeted, made sympathetic, awkward noises.

118

Eileen drank off her wine, stood up, stumbled, made blindly for the stairs and climbed out of sight, bent like an old man.

Celia shut the front door. Karen threw more logs on the fire. Helen whispered to Crystal, 'I think this is decadent. We shouldn't have been smoking and drinking like this. We should have taken it more seriously.'

'It's your turn, Karen,' said Crystal. 'We haven't that much time, we ought to go on.'

Karen's story was another familiar one. There was the thralldom not so much to sexual love as to men. Charles. None of them had admitted to sexual inadequacy, or a lack of desire; no, it was rather the collapse of identity when you became emotionally involved with a man. But was that really the heart of it?

You were meant to go further than that, the sharing of your experience with other women was meant to reveal a similarity in the pattern, to lead you to understand that it was not your own inadequacy, but also not even the man in question – nor indeed 'Men', but a system of which both men and the state were a part. Really it was the whole world (call it 'ideology', 'capitalism', 'patriarchy', what you will) that slotted you into place like a cog in the giant machine.

No, actually you were not a cog, you were fodder – the machine swallowed you. And yet bits lay about discarded, bleeding on the floor. And that was *their* task, the task of these women: to reclaim the bits that the machine had spewed out. We are the refuse of the political world. Their task was to sweep up the discarded shavings and slivers of experience and identity from the floor and reclaim them. All the bits of yourself that the great machine would not use were actually the most valuable bits of yourself, your strength, your anger, your autonomy.

The tedium of the process was that the meanings it was supposed to reveal were known in advance (it's not me, it's ideology, patriarchy, capitalism, the state). Yet beneath those correct feminist meanings something still more disturbing was revealed; even the affirmative answers, even the women's politics masked a deeper level of cracks and incoherences, of hostility and ambivalence. Things were still being left out, discarded. Scraps still lay bleeding on the floor.

Crystal cut through it all: 'If it's all so awful, why don't you just ditch him?'

'You're so strong, Crystal. You ended your relationship – I'm not like that, I need relationships – '

And now *they* were quarrelling. But as Crystal felt the warm, self-indulgence of the tears that oozed slowly down her cheeks, she found comfort in them. Self-pity was a balm, a security blanket.

Sally brought Anita back into the warm, fuggy room. Anita kissed them all and hugged Eddie for a long time. They could all go to bed, relieved.

The Communist woman slept in one room with Crystal and Eileen, who was lying there, snoring, her body slumped across the sleeping bags. She didn't wake when Helen and Crystal shoved her over, unzipped one of the bags and wrapped it round her.

'She's pretty much passed out.'

'Probably the most dignified thing to do.' said Helen.

The other women slept in the second bedroom, Karen's room. Except for Celia. She found an eiderdown and rolled herself into it on the large sofa in the sitting room. That way she had a room to herself and the warmth of the embers of the fire.

In the morning Eddie came down before the others were up, sat on the floor by the sofa and leaned her head against the eiderdown where it covered Celia's legs. They talked about other things, of the trial of the pickets, of an article on ideology that Celia was writing, and of whether they should start to get breakfast. But silently they ached with fear of madness, of loss of control, longed to be mothered, thrilled to the possibility of intimacy, didn't know whether they loved or hated each other.

After breakfast the group somehow had to get back onto an even keel. The personal testimonies were over. All the women had spoken in turn. Now they had to talk about political strategies, plan the next issue of *Termagant*. It was to be on the relationship of feminism and socialism.

There was an atmosphere of dissent.

'Do we have to take on *everything*?' sighed Karen. She pictured them surging along with a crowd, a huge demonstration of all the oppressed: Irish, miners, anarchists, one million unemployed, blacks, gays, the whole of the Third World – they were part of a vast throng; yet different.

Eileen said she was going to join the Communist Party. There was another silence. Then they went on talking about *Termagant*.

They were edgy, bickering, hungover. And rapidly they made themselves queasy with too much instant coffee and cigarettes.

They were agreed on an article about socialist communes in the nineteenth century, and one about a women's strike at a Midlands hosiery factory. Juliet had written a poem about a German woman terrorist who'd been shot by the police, but all the others objected to its inclusion. Sally wanted an article from a woman in the Socialist Revolutionary Group, but Eddie and Janet disagreed.

'I'm going to make spaghetti for lunch – a very special Italian sauce,' said Celia.

Eileen and Crystal washed salad at the sink.

'What's in your sauce?'

'Oh – tomatoes, onions . . .'

Eileen had a splitting headache: 'They said *nothing* when I said I was going to join the Party. They didn't even acknowledge it.'

'I know – outrageous.'

'Shall you join too?'

'I expect so.'

They carried the salad and the plates into the living room. When they returned Celia was standing in the middle of the kitchen, holding the huge saucepan with strings of spaghetti hanging over its side. There was a mound of steaming spaghetti on the floor in a pool of water that was creeping over the tiles.

'What happened?'

'I spilt it.' Celia was calm.

'The spaghetti's okay – look, some went in the colander and we can get most of it off the floor – let's clear up, put it down for a minute – '

'I say – are *you* all right?'

'Some went on my foot.'

They all sat round in the sitting room and spooned up Celia's spaghetti Napolitano.

'Are you sure your foot's all right?'

Helen made Celia take off her shoe and sock. They gazed at the reddened, angry, blistering skin.

'You've scalded it.'

Helen bathed it in cold water. She said butter was no good.

Celia seemed oblivious, uninterested in her foot. They made her rest it up on the sofa. When she spoke it wasn't about her foot at all.

'I have more to say – you've all spoken, you all had longer than me. I have things I still want to say.'

She talked about her time in the Party. It was an attack, directed against Eddie.

'The trouble with you, Eddie, is that you're not working class – that's the trouble with the Party, actually, so many of its members come from Party families, and no one from a Party family is ever working class, not really – they're cut off from their class origins.'

Hers was not an angry denunciation like Juliet's had been, it was measured, abstract, interminable. It was worse than Juliet, since Celia had actually been in the Party and knew more about it.

The women were impatient, they wanted to interrupt, to

stop her, but they couldn't, they didn't know why she was speaking, what it meant.

She talked on and on in her cold, clipped way. They should have started back for London an hour ago, but Celia kept them there, imposed her will on them all. Even when she at last stopped talking, they couldn't break the silence, couldn't voice their anger, she hadn't released her hold.

It was her foot. She silenced them with her foot. It made them feel somehow guilty, as if it had been their fault, as if they owed her an apology.

It was getting dark.

'We *must* go,' said Karen finally. Charles would be fuming –

They scattered to separate vehicles, there was now no time to bring the weekend to a proper close, to heal the wounds, whatever they were.

In spite of Celia's attack, it was Eddie who helped Celia down the path towards her car: 'It'll be too uncomfortable for you in Juliet's van.'

Car doors banged. They called goodbye through the sharp autumnal air. Mist came up from the valley.

Karen locked the front door. The cottage was in darkness, its windows black, facing down the hill in the dusk.

In the car on the journey going home they said little about the weekend, about the other women. They reminisced about childhood, talked about the little girls they once had been.

PART FOUR: AFTER THE WAR

In the summer we moved to London. It was hot. There were crowds in the streets.

We lived in an hotel. There was a park across the road – couples writhed on the grass, and children called across the open spaces. In the shadow of the chestnut trees footsteps slurred along the gravel and old men and ladies sat on benches. Sometimes a band played.

'The War's over.' It was night-time, but there were still crowds in the park, densely banked, swarming bees. A great murmur went up when a burst of white showered over the black; emerald and magenta stars hung in the firmament, then silently dissolved; next, blue and gold stuttered across and melted into the sky. Afterwards we drifted with the crowd in the darkness. How soft it was. Someone spoke to my mother. She pulled at my hand: 'It's late – better get back.'

Why was it sad – with her?

In the gilded lounge an American soldier offered me chewing gum. I knew to refuse.

'Such an ugly accent,' said my mother, 'never know if they're *educated*.'

My mother said she must speak to the manageress: 'Could you possibly serve breakfast earlier, just a little, ten minutes, so the child gets to school in time?'

Her quick, high-pitched voice splintered against indifference.

'The War – no one cares, no service. We can't possibly afford it here, anyway – '

We moved, to Fitzroy Mansions. You came through an archway of blackened brick into an enclosed well of somnolence. In the unlit hall, which smelled like a bomb shelter, you cranked the cage-like lift to the third floor. We had one room in a warren of a flat. At its centre: the communal room – this was furnished with easy chairs, but no one ever sat in them, a large table was its centrepiece, but no one ate at it. Only Mrs Smith, the landlady sat there.

Mrs Smith had a pale, suety face, and her dark hair, parted in the middle, was drawn back. She wore a dress of faded black silk. She waited, as if for a séance to begin, her hands folded together like a packet of sausages on the chenille table cloth. Her smile was as unchanging as the smile of some painted Italian saint, varnished into fixity in the oleaginous light. And even if she herself were to disappear, her smile, like the Cheshire Cat's, would float forever, disembodied, in the stuffy depths of the flat.

Our room was second on the left. The other guests were shadowy. What went on in those other rooms? You heard voices, music, sometimes. Once a woman sobbed.

Every evening we ate at a wobbly little table by the window. My mother washed the plates in the wash basin.

'Let's get the beastly Put-U-Up thing down.'

My godmother came to see us often, now we were all in London. She and my mother sat on the Put-U-Up. They kept their voices low, but I could hear, although I went on reading.

'For God's sake, Daphne, don't be so tragic.'

Aunt Miranda wore her hair in a page-boy, rolled luxuriously under at the ends. The shining wave of it lay on her shoulders. She wore high-heeled shoes and nylons. She crossed her legs, and sometimes scratched absent-mindedly at her thigh with scarlet nails, a rasping noise against the filament. She reached for her cigarettes and they lit up together, held their Craven A at an angle, started to murmur again.

When she turned round I saw that her dress did up with tiny buttons like a row of peas down her back, each secured into a loop made of the dress material.

'Isn't it difficult to get undressed?'

She laughed. 'I call it my tease.'

After she'd gone a hint of scent lingered – an artificial smell, more like gin than flowers.

'We used to have such *fun* before the War, your Aunt Miranda and I.'

Once, Aunt Miranda took me to see my father at his club. We rode in a taxi.

'So how do you like your new school, Crystal?'

'It's all right.'

'Don't let them make you work too hard – men don't like blue-stockings.'

'There's a Maharajah's daughter at my school, and lots of Jewish girls.'

'Ah – the chosen race,' said my father.

There was only one room in my father's club where ladies were allowed. Carpeted in beige, it had peach lights reflected in chiselled mirrors, and a receding vista of beige velvet sofas.

My father lit Aunt Miranda's cigarette, and her fingers lightly settled on his knuckles. I ate the cocktail cherry from my father's glass.

'She won't forgive you,' said Aunt Miranda. 'Once she's got an idea in her head – you know how obstinate she is – '

'And Jack's cutting up rough I hear.'

They drew close together. Her shining hair fell forward; he, poised, dark, above.

'And what'll you do, now it's all over?'

'Oh – carry on as usual, I suppose,' he said.

'But we're forgetting Crystal – she's got so much to tell you.' She turned towards me and her hand drew me into the magic circle.

My mother asked me if I'd enjoyed myself.

'What's happened to Uncle Jack, Mummy? The War's over now, but he hasn't come back.'

'You'll understand when you're older.'

The hot days continued. We went on outings. Waiting for the bus, we peered down the vista of the empty, endless street.

'Is anything coming?'

'No.'

We lay on the grass at Kew Gardens. Above our heads the trees sighed and frothed against the blue. I lay on my back and stared until it all went colourless in the glare. I'm here forever and ever; this is eternity.

'Let's move to somewhere shadier.'

We wandered across the empty lawns and came to a wilder part with high clumps of rhododendrons and secluded glades. It was very still. We unwrapped our sandwiches.

There was a man there. He wore a dark, heavy suit, shabby, and too hot for the hot day. He was doing something.

'Come along – I think we'd better go.'

The midday glare drugged the deserted gardens. We hurried through the silence.

'Look back to see if he's after us.'

He'd vanished – an apparition, a ghost at midday.

For once we sat in the communal room. The fellow guest leaned forward, smiled. He was portly, with white hair through which a pink pate shone, and he had a pink face with bulging, horn-rimmed glasses. My mother called him the White Frog. 'He wants to tell me about some way of improving my eyesight; wouldn't it be wonderful if I didn't have to wear my specs any more?'

But one visit to his room made her agitated: 'It was all nonsense – something about exercising your eyes. He made me take off my specs. Said I shouldn't wear them – rot I call it, the man's a fool.'

More outings: the Zoo, Madame Tussaud's, the Tower of London, Hampton Court – in a way they were always the same. There was the long journey ('Is anything coming?'); the queues, the crowds, a hot mass of people all wanting to look – at where they cut off Anne Boleyn's head, at the haunted corridor where they seized Catherine Howard, at saints being flayed alive, at the electric chair with its leather straps and a thing like a bell.

Death everywhere.

'My friend Hannah says they tortured Jews in the War.'

Aunt Miranda laughed when she heard about the White Frog.

'You ought to get out of this dismal hole, Daphne – let's get a place – buy something – we girls must stick together.'

'How can we – they've requisitioned everything. Either that or squatters.'

The summer was over. We moved again. It was a house like a lift shaft; dark. Aunt Miranda had the rooms upstairs. She worked at the Ministry now.

'You see to the rations, Daphne, I'll just give you my book.'

My mother always had something nice when I came home for tea: 'They had these lettuces at the market – "three for a tanner," he was shouting, poor chap. I 'spect you'd like a lettuce sandwich – and they had chocolate biscuits, lucky I had some points left.'

Aunt Miranda came home from work, drank a cup of tea standing up, and ran upstairs to change for the evening.

'You're not going out with that American again – '

Miranda laughed. Her roll of hair was caught up in a coarse net snood.

On Sundays she was still in her kimono at lunch time, went without make-up, her hair tied in a scarf while it set. She and my mother sat at the kitchen table and drank tea; low voices again.

'What's custardy, Mummy?'

'Run along upstairs and play, darling – '

Custardy thickly clogged up the machinery of life, dropped sweetly, cloyingly into the cogs, stifled everything in a thick, yellow curtain.

'Can't afford to have the Man in to see to the basement until the custardy's sorted out.'

'No men *at all*, darling – I was good for six months. Lucky you, it was Henry who went off – oh don't look like that – '

'He might counterpetition – '

'Against you! But you're so pure, Daphne!'

'It's all very well to laugh – but I don't know what I shall do – slaving away all day – no money for nice things – '

'Well, at least *I'm* not making a martyr of myself.'

'I don't want to discuss it *any more*.'

They always made it up later. Aunt Miranda came swinging down the stairs carrying a bottle: 'What about a gin-and-orange, darling.' Or my mother called up through the bannisters: 'I'm having a sherry.' They drew cigarettes from the cartons and sat close together, leaning forward over the table, absorbed.

Once Aunt Miranda said, 'I know, let's all go to a show.'

That was a wizard day. The play made us all laugh, and afterwards we had high tea at Lyons Corner House in the Strand. Three women played a string band; the waitresses flashed about the room.

'Wasn't it a *scream* when – ' My mother was pink from laughing.

We did not go on many outings now. My mother had a job she did at home. 'My Appeals'. Every Tuesday she said, 'It's my day for seeing Canon Higgins, up in Westminster, I'll leave your tea.'

'I don't like being here on my own.'

'I have to make a few pennies somehow – that's why I'm sending you to a good school, so's you'll never be in my frightful position – '

Sometimes Aunt Miranda got off work early, sat at the kitchen table while I had my tea, and told me stories about the War.

'Did you like it in the Wrens, Aunt Miranda?'

She laughed, but instead of answering the question, she said, 'Your mother's had a hard time you know. You must be kind to her, Crystal.'

When my mother came home from Canon Higgins, her attaché case was filled with little black-and-white printed brochures, secured in batches with rubber bands, and hundreds of envelopes to be addressed. She poured herself a cup of tea and sat down at the kitchen table, opened her copy of *The Lady*, turned to its small ads columns and scoured them for likely addresses.

'You are a game old thing, Daphne – fancy thinking of that – *The Lady*. God, what a dreary magazine!'

'We can't leave the basement much longer.'

I came home to find the hall floor taken up. I walked along the cross beam like a tightrope above the intestinal horrors of bare wires and spiders.

'Mr Lugg's men have found dry rot.'

The two women sat at the kitchen table.

'Perhaps Tony might come up trumps.'

'*Tony*! I won't hear of that! You said yourself, the man's probably a gangster.'

'That was a joke, for God's sake. Have you no sense of humour?'

'Not another word! The idea!'

'Daphne, do be sensible – '

'If the worst comes to the worst I'll just have to get a cleaning job, go out charring.'

'Tony's terribly well off. He's rolling in lolly – and he's going home soon – '

'I do dislike the way you talk sometimes, Miranda.'

'Make hay while the sun shines – '

'He's not *married* – ?'

'Oh God, Daphne, do grow up.'

Lugg's men excavated the basement. The house smelled of damp earth; there was dust everywhere. Winter had come. Some days there was no water; sometimes there was no light. Power cuts; it was always cold, cold.

'I don't know what Lugg's up to – the man's a fool – or dishonest. Both I daresay. Well, I'm going to speak to him. Cups of tea all day. Miranda's too familiar with them – '

Lugg, an urban Caliban, had taken up residence in the interstices of our deconstructed floors. A malicious spirit of anarchy, he and his men slowly took the house to pieces. Soon we would be bombed out – living on a bomb site.

Aunt Miranda went out more and more. Some evenings Tony in his funny American khaki or an American suit that was even funnier (no waistcoat) came to collect her. And one Saturday afternoon a car purred to a halt outside our door. My mother hovered behind the net curtain.

'He's got a Bentley, then.'

I wouldn't look: 'Let's play cards. I'm tired of reading.'

Once, Uncle Jack came to visit. My mother put out the silver teapot and the good cups. Aunt Miranda looked pale and wore her black suit. Afterwards she and my mother sat in the kitchen. The door was shut. I could hear Aunt Miranda crying. The voices murmured, murmured.

Every Saturday the Bentley crept up to the front door. It was pale grey. A small, grey-haired man wearing a Homburg hat got out when Aunt Miranda appeared on the step.

'But he's old!'

In the spring Aunt Miranda had a new dress. It was navy blue and white. Her little straw hat was covered in clusters of white lilac and had a veil across her eyes.

'You really must smarten yourself up Daphne – do something with your hair – '

'What *can* I do? If you had falling hair – '

'It's not as bad as that – anyway, you could have a hair piece – '

'On this National Health rubbish? Fine fright I'd look.'

'It's only worry – '

'If you *want* to know I have tried – all sorts of things. Don't think I haven't. I even put mange lotion on it, you know, for dogs – absolutely hopeless.'

'Oh Daphne!' Miranda shrieked with laughter, just like she used to. 'Mange lotion – you think of everything!'

'Well – ' My mother pursed her lips, like a little girl.

'Come on, I'll take you shopping, for Crystal's school play – '

We went on the Piccadilly Line. Then the shop opened out before us. We tiptoed through hushed, carpeted salons. The assistants wore black and called my mother Madam. There was a dress on a stand. It was black, splashed with red flowers, and it was crowned with a straw hat garlanded with corn and daisies and set at an angle.

'Get that one, Mummy – '

'Oh – I think – navy, or grey – I've only enough coupons for one, quite apart from the expense, it has to do for everything – '

When we went to have lunch in the restaurant her face was pink.

'Are you sure you can afford it, Miranda? I know you had a rise, but the cost of living's so frightful – '

She went to the ladies room and Aunt Miranda winked at me.

'Don't tell your mother, but you know my Mr Thing – well, never mind – '

At the end of the meal they lit their cigarettes. Aunt Miranda stirred her coffee.

'You know, Daphne, it's time I settled down – got my decree nisi now – and Arthur's very keen – '

'Oh do be careful dear. Are you *sure* – ?'

'I'm not getting any younger. And the War's over now.'

We visited her once in her new house. It was rather like the places we used to go to, the hotel, my father's club, the shop with the dress – softly lit, with carpets and silence. Aunt Miranda looked different. She had a dress with a tight waist and a long, full skirt, and her hair was tidied into a ballerina chignon.

Uncle Arthur was out, 'in the City,' she said. She showed us round the house and all over the garden, it took ages, it was all so big, and then we had tea in the drawing room. Afterwards Aunt Miranda and my mother lit up their cigarettes.

'Just like old times, Daphne. How I miss it all – what *fun* we used to have.'

'You're lucky, really. He seems awfully kind.'

There were little silences. Aunt Miranda started to talk about a foreign holiday, and something about the black market.

My mother's high, quick voice: 'Oh Miranda!' Shocked.

But they didn't quarrel now. Aunt Miranda talked about Spanish servants. Soon my mother said we must go.

It was a long journey home on the 28 bus. My mother muttered, agitated, 'The man's nothing but a spiv. How could she! So common.'

'I liked the house, Mummy. Wasn't it lovely? And so warm.'

'Leaving me in the lurch – having to take in lodgers – '

'Why do we have to, Mummy?'

'You'll understand when you're older.'

We didn't go there again.

Sullen summer – so cold you didn't want to go out, to move
even, just sink into the lap of the chintzy, overstuffed
furniture that crammed Mrs Hancock's cottage. The teacosy
cottage sat in a fold of the heavy green countryside. Mrs
Hancock was in the same mould, ample and squat, her
features coarsely embroidered onto her quilted red face.
Her voice was hoarse and her lips left carmine stains on
cups and cigarette stubs.

'Nose in a book again – well, Phyllis said you were brainy
– but perhaps you'd like to give me a hand with the washing
up – '

The task completed, Crystal returned to her sofa and *War
and Peace*.

A car drew up outside. It was *him*. She ran upstairs to her
bedroom and shut the door. The room was a mess. She'd
pulled the bedclothes up anyhow. Mrs Hancock had been a
nurse once, she'd shown her the proper hospital way to
make a bed, but it was too much fuss. She hated dragging
the heavy covers straight. And anyway, who cared, you
only untidied it again.

She stooped towards the mirror and picked up her lipstick,
looked at her face from different angles. The short haircut –
she wasn't sure if she liked it now; it seemed to make her
nose longer, her face more crooked. You've got a face like
a foot, Jenny at school had said.

The rustling of her cotton skirt and petticoat made her
feel self-conscious, for they all looked up as she came down
the stairs.

'*There* you are, we wondered where you'd got to –
daydreaming again – what a funny girl.'

Captain Sheridan smiled at her. Rodney. His hair was
brushed back from a widow's peak, his moustache was just
a slight line along his lip. He wore a tweed jacket of russet
brown.

'Here's a silly magazine for you.' Her father flung her the
latest *Woman and Beauty*.

'Those books are so expensive, aren't they,' said Phyllis, 'and really there's nothing in them. It's all advertisements.'

Valerie Sheridan looked even more elegant than the fashion photographs. She was not really beautiful, for she had one of those Pekinese faces, but her eyes were smudged with green and she'd painted her bulging lower lip scarlet. Daddy said she had sex appeal.

Julia Hancock sat on the arm of the sofa and swung her leg, admiring her green lizard-skin shoes.

'I bought this suit, and, darling, the *next week* the New Look came in. So I got this skirt to go with the jacket – '

'Julia's always been clever with clothes.'

'An actress has to be.'

But Julia looked all too actressy next to Valerie. Her name wasn't Hancock either, she'd had two husbands and this Jim wasn't really a husband, although Mrs Hancock kept saying, 'They're going to get married.'

Julia was in Agatha Christie's *Ten Little Niggers* in Wimbledon or somewhere. They gossiped about Bertie Baker, who was a friend of Mrs Hancock.

'Have you seen his show, Crystal?'

'I'm not too keen on that sort of thing, actually.'

She flipped over the pages of *Woman and Beauty*, and wished Captain Sheridan – Rodney – would say something. He went and stood by the window, looking out at the garden. Her father read the *Daily Telegraph*.

'We must go, darling, Nanny will be getting restive.'

Julia and Valerie kissed as though parting indefinitely.

'See you this evening.'

Crystal sat on her bed and wrote a letter:

> Dear Mummy, I'm having an interesting time down here, although the weather has been very cold and amazingly unseasonable. We have not been out much, but Mrs Hancock has had some friends round, she seems to know quite a few people round here. Her daughter is staying too. The most charming people are the Sheridans, he was in the army during the War, and

now they live in Chelsea, but they have a country cottage near here. Would you mind if I called you Daphne in future, Mummy? Julia calls Mrs Hancock Mabel (!) and it seems more modern now I'm fourteen. Tomorrow we're going to Petworth Castle, and then to see where the rhododendrons bloom.

With lots and lots of love from
Crystal.

The restaurant was crimson, with candles and Regency stripes.

'Place looks like a brothel.'

'Oh *Henry*!' But Phyllis seemed delighted. 'Isn't he a naughty man!'

Crystal had a glass of sherry; the others drank gin. The head waiter had seated them at a long table, and Rodney was on the same side as Crystal, which was a disappointment, because she couldn't really see him. Valerie wore black. Crystal was almost as much in love with her as with Rodney. They studied the printed menu cards.

'I'll have a mixed grill please,' said Crystal.

'You'd better watch your weight – that's a man's dinner.'

'Oh, I've seen her put away a mixed grill before now.'

Valerie chose fish.

'You should have fish Crystal, for your brains – ' Mrs Hancock again.

Phyllis laughed: 'She hardly needs more *brains*!'

'You won't want to stay on at school, will you, not after you're fifteen? You'll want to be out in the world, you'll see.'

'I couldn't *wait* to leave,' said Julia, 'all those old cows telling me what to do.'

'Telling you what *not* to do, sweetie.'

Everyone laughed long and heartily.

'Oh – I don't know,' said Valerie, 'I rather wish I'd stayed – *done* something.' She toyed with the pleasant dream as she crushed the crumbs of her bread roll together.

Crystal was relieved when the talk refocused away onto

the government and the price of everything. Jim and Rodney were deep in some discussion – cars, business, *flying?* Crystal strained to hear. Julia and Valerie giggled together, and then Valerie was telling Mrs Hancock about Jeremy, her little boy. Crystal was left at the end of the table with her father and Phyllis.

Over the puddings and cheese and biscuits, talk became general again.

'Don't you fancy anything from the sweet trolley, Crystal? What, cheese and biscuits, like your father? My goodness me, you are grown-up! And black coffee too. Not even any sugar – that'll keep you awake, won't it?'

'I don't mind. I'll read.'

There was talk of air disasters and of war. They grumbled about public events as though these were personal affronts, yet at the same time directly due to the malevolence of the government, a Personal Government like a Personal God, calculating the results of Its (His) every act on You.

'It's a sin to be middle class, these days.'

'Middle class! My dear, we're the Nouveau Poor.'

In bed she continued with *War and Peace*, Prince Andrew Bolkonsky had been wounded now, but she could still hear the murmur of voices through the floorboards. (We're just going to have a nightcap – don't you think it's time you were in bed?) Later the stairs creaked. Then there were muffled sounds and movements from the room next to her own as Mrs Hancock prepared for bed, sounds of the routine preservation of an ageing body. In the morning Mrs Hancock would appear without her teeth, her sagging face gleaming with grease, her body pulled together with a dressing gown cord.

She was too tired to concentrate on *War and Peace*, so she turned the pages of her magazine again. Perhaps Valerie had been a model – a mannequin for Jacques Fath or Christian Dior or Balmain. Crystal was dying to go to a real fashion show. She imagined its perpetual motion, the haughty, swaying women with heads like snakes and eyes like jewels as they tracked to and fro – hems swoop and dip, they strut like cranes, their sightless eyes on some distant horizon.

'Going out' with her father and Phyllis meant sitting in the back of the car and watching the chilly landscape slip by. With her mother it would have meant a complicated journey by train and bus, a walk up long lanes and drives and a whole afternoon spent exploring the stately home or art gallery. 'We don't want to miss anything, do we?'

Today, they barely even got out of the car at Petworth, and drove swiftly on to a roadhouse hotel, where they ordered drinks and sandwiches in a fumed oak lounge. It was always the same round of drinks: a pint of bitter for her father, gin-and-tonic for Mrs Hancock and gin-and-It for Phyllis. Crystal had tomato juice with Worcester sauce. The amount they drank never seemed to affect their mood. Phyllis and Mrs Hancock always talked nonstop; her father, as usual, unfurled the paper.

They drove on again. Crystal sat cocooned in the back of the car. The cocoon span out of some source of desire that secreted an endless filament. Yet this thread of fantasy was monotonous, repetitive. Just as Crystal wore down her favourite records by playing the same phrases until either the grooves had gone or she was sick of it, so now she ran the same frames of a kind of film over and over in her head. The same movements, the same phrases, the same scenes lulled her, drugged her, and, like a drug, removed her to all intents and purposes from the scene.

They were driving now through indeterminate terrain, neither forest nor open land. On one side ragged lines of silver birch and pine wavered against the cold sky; on the other, dark, glossy bushes, banked up like thunderclouds, rolled past, mile after mile, heavy and threatening. This was where the rhododendrons bloomed.

'But look, Mabel, they're all over.'

Only a few rusty-brown flowerheads remained.

* * *

The telephone rang quite late, after dinner.

'That'll be Julia – when she's down here she's always itching to get back to the bright lights, but once she's back in London, every five minutes she's onto her old mum.'

But when she returned the creases of her face had settled into masklike fixity.

'It's little Jeremy – he's dead – what a terrible thing.'

The poison seeped slowly into their after-dinner torpor.

'The darling little boy – Valerie will be heartbroken – in terrible pain – rushed to hospital – peritonitis.' Her lips settled round the word: 'a peritonitis, that's what they said.'

Her avidity to know, to delve into death, was a sickness itself. She dwelt on the details, then sank back as the fear of death acted like hemlock. They all three fidgeted in the comfy armchairs, writhing in the discomfort of moral indigestion, trying to swallow the leaden lump of news, disturbed against their will, hoping to regurgitate the thing, wanting, in the end, not to know, their evening paralysis gradually, thank God, returning.

'Well, there's nothing much we can do.' Her father retired again behind the paper.

Yet Phyllis and Mrs Hancock continued to pick over the details, hunting for new bits, chomping at the tainted meat.

'Mind you, she did leave him a lot with that nanny – '

'That's hardly – '

'*Terrible* – '

'D'you think the hospital – '

'Ambulance probably took hours to come – this National Health has a lot to answer for, if you ask me – '

Something had gone wrong with the projector in Crystal's head. A glimpse of the dead child kept interrupting the familiar frames of looks, embraces, declarations. Then it adjusted itself, and now the images ran on unimpeded. She held him in her arms and stroked the sleek, dark birdswing of his hair, yearning over him in aching, erotic sorrow.

Later in the week they passed near Captain Sheridan's cottage while they were out for a drive. There, at a turning in the lane, stood the couple. Mrs Hancock wound down the window and talked to them briefly. They did not notice Crystal in the back.

'I want to have a talk with you,' said Mrs Hancock when Crystal went to thank her for her holiday. She was smiling: 'I'm going to be quite frank with you, young lady.'
It was all about housework.
'You never once offered.'
Crystal listened in silence.
'. . . wonder how you've been brought up . . . a little pleasantness and willingness . . . your mother . . . not firm enough . . . only children spoilt . . .'
You could tell she was enjoying herself – the gleam of self-importance was there again, the dwelling on other people's calamities. But it all seemed to Crystal to be about someone else, about something that had happened somewhere else. The film wound forward in her head again.

There were still weeks of summer holiday left. One after- noon she and her mother went for a walk into Chelsea, right along the King's Road. When they reached Markham Square, Crystal said, 'This is where the Sheridans live, you know – those friends of Mrs Hancock's I told you about.'
'Wouldn't it be simply *lovely* to live in a house like that – just think – '
The square was empty, secluded. Which house was it, which door was theirs, the red, the blue, the black?
'Do you want to walk round?'
'No, don't let's, Mummy – let's get on.'

Crystal went to her mother's bureau to look for some writing paper. Behind the flap lay little sets of inner drawers and compartments; in them her mother kept hidden odd-shaped stones, exotic stamps torn off envelopes, dried flowers, 'sayings' cut out of newspapers, pins, brooches, old buttons – oddments, pretty or curious, which irritated Crystal, she did not know why. Then there were letters, typed business

143

ones, flimsy ones from friends abroad, and stiff blue ones from friends in outlying corners of the British Isles.

Crystal recognized one from her father. The typeface of his rusty old portable was familiar from the days when he'd written to her from abroad. She drew the letter from its envelope.

'. . . never lifted a finger – atrocious manners – Mabel will never have her here again – ungrateful – ' Crystal read it through to the end – 'I don't know what she learns at that expensive establishment you insist on sending her to, but it certainly isn't charm or good manners.'

Crystal replaced the letter in its envelope, the envelope in its compartment, closed the flap of the bureau and went upstairs. She sat by her bedroom window and stared down at the yard, and the flats opposite, which closed in on her like a well. The projector in her head had broken down. The film had stopped.

The crammer was in a street that looked like one long, stucco palace, north of the park. Once the Bayswater bourgeoisie had lived sumptuously here; then it had declined and become rooming houses, bed sitters for the garish women who lingered along the Bayswater Road; now the area was smartening up again, becoming chic and even official, with legations and a secretarial school.

Inside there was dark lino, partitioned rooms and the smell of paraffin. Crystal ran up the stairs to the windowless box in which her tutor sat all day. Anna the deb, and Gillian, whose parents lived in the Argentine, were already seated on bentwood chairs, huddled towards Adam as if he were the fire. Anna wore black stockings. Gillian's feet in ankle boots with fur were twisted together as she talked.

'Ah . . . there you are. We're discussing why one likes ruins.'

Adam's voice always sounded the same tone of irony, about to expire it lingered, insinuating immense sophistication, a weary, smiling satiation with the world. A lock of straight, greasy hair fell over his forehead, muddy-coloured, like his eyes. He wore a corduroy jacket the same greyish brown, and a spotted bow tie.

'Before the eighteenth century no one was interested in ruins . . .'

The poster on Adam's wall was a genuine Spanish one, a poster for a bullfight. It was Ken Tynan, he told them, who had made bullfighting fashionable with the British intelligentsia.

'But isn't it terribly cruel?'

'The Spanish aren't afraid of cruelty.'

Adam had been at Oxford with Ken Tynan. Now Ken Tynan was a famous theatre critic. Adam was writing a play.

Adam teased them about Oxford: 'Why *there*, after all? All you'll learn is how to pour sherry and make decent coffee. You'd probably get a better education at London or

Manchester. Oh – I know it's no use arguing – there are six men to every woman.'

At lunch time the three of them sat in a coffee bar opposite the entrance to the park.

'I know the cappuccinos cost a shilling, but the clientele's so intriguing.'

Gillian, whose brother was up at Oxford already, said there were masses of nurses, physiotherapists, au pairs, so the ratio wasn't as good as all that.

'And then there are trogs, you know, men who do nothing but work.'

'And queers I suppose.'

'Oh, hundreds of *them*.'

'I wonder if Adam's queer?'

'But he's married.'

'My dear, lots of them are.'

But by now anywhere other than Oxford was unthinkable. The very word acted as a magic mirror, which showed Crystal herself as she wanted to be. Or a window – a window opened onto a new life, of escape, of adulthood.

But Adam's smiling irony hinted at something they didn't see. The three virgins, so eager, so blooming, looked forward. He looked back. The room was a staging post in which by chance they'd met as they travelled in opposite directions. The circumstances of the meeting compromised them all, the crammer was a behind-the-scenes establishment, a kind of house of assignation of the educational world. Was not Adam prostituting himself a little – even if he argued that he was gaining valuable experience for his first, picaresque novel of contemporary British life. Were they not paying for a coating of fluency and confidence, which went to make up the ability that should have come naturally, to cope with Oxford entrance interviews. They were cheating in a way. And he was somehow pretending too.

It was their last day, and towards the end of the afternoon Adam read them part of the final section of *Ulysses*. But before he reached the very end he stopped and laughed:

'Well, even *I* can't read you this bit. You're too young for it. Wait until you're a little older – until you go to Oxford.'

This was the end then? Should they shake hands?

'Come back and see me. Come and tell me how you get on.'

The view of spires across the fields from the train, the warm, sombre college where the passages smelt of polish, and the wait outside an oak door, none of it frightened her now. Crystal felt sure Adam would see her through.

Her mother looked up when she walked into the kitchen. 'I didn't hear you come in. How did it go?'

'It was all right.' Crystal refused her the pride, the shared excitement, the bit of rubbed-off glamour. She went to her room and wrote in her diary: 'I think it went okay. The don, Mrs Rose, who interviewed me, asked easy questions, and what I wanted to do when I'd got my degree. Some of the other candidates wore awful hats, as if they were going to church. Soon I won't have to live at home any more, cross fingers anyway.'

Then – nothing; Anna had gone to Paris, Gillian rejoined her family in Buenos Aires, some of Crystal's school friends were abroad too. She rose at noon and lay on the sofa reading a biography of Byron.

'You'll have to get some sort of a job, you know, whatever happens.'

'But I want to go abroad. Why can't I be an au pair?'

There was just one party; sweaty dancing in a darkened room in Fulham. The pale, dark boy had looked at her, wordlessly held her to him. He wore a black polo neck. His name was Mark.

'What do you do?'

'I'm at Oxford,' he murmured, 'don't talk.'

They were anonymous in the dark. Later they embraced on a sofa.

'I'd like to find you in a bed,' he murmured. His voice sounded like Adam's.

She was silent with disbelief. Afterwards, after she'd given him her number, she felt scared, she'd made a promise, too late to go back. Had he thought she was tarty?

For days he didn't phone.

Then, one afternoon, it was him. Was she free – now? There was a film –

It was a wet Sunday afternoon. In a way she didn't want to go. It would have been easier to stay curled up on the sofa, lost in her book. She'd almost forgotten what he looked like until he stepped forward from the entrance to the tube station. A lock of dark hair fell over one eye. He was a bit Byronic, really. In the cinema they sat stiffly, not touching, quarantined in rows of empty seats. She felt cold, but sat there, trusting in the memory of the melting embraces in the dark.

Afterwards he said, as if it were all agreed: 'We can go to my father's consulting rooms. I've got a key.'

They walked along Oxford Street. It was still raining, and they huddled into the hoods of their duffle coats.

Adam's coaching in conversation didn't work for this situation.

'What did you think of the film? D'you like Italian neo-realism?'

Should one like it or not? But then she remembered that you were supposed to ask *them*, be a 'good listener'.

They walked a long way up Harley Street in the rain. At last he said, 'Here we are.' On the steps he turned and looked at her. It was a blank, impersonal smile. Too late to go back now.

Inside it was warm. The entrance hall was panelled in oak, and Victorian oil paintings hung on the walls. They mounted the stairs to the first floor. The whole house was empty, deadly quiet.

'My father's a psychoanalyst.'

There was a divan upholstered in crimson velvet and covered with a rug; Turkey carpets deadened all sound; the lighting was soft and tasteful; an intimate yet impersonal atmosphere. He lit the gas fire, lifted her coat from her shoulders, drew her down by the hissing jets.

A memory: her father takes her to see a doctor. The two men stand over her. There is a couch. The doctor pushes her down and injects her bottom: 'This is for diphtheria.'

At first he kissed her with a closed mouth, which was strange, yet exciting because it was unexpected. He kissed her neck, stroked her breasts under her black sweater, then pushed it up. In silence. She watched all this from a distance, as a twin self was passively sucked down a long tunnel beyond the point of no return.

He stroked her legs, twisted his fingers under her suspenders, pushed his hand in under her knickers. They stumbled awkwardly, half-undressed, towards the couch. He smiled at her again, the same blind smile, a smile that wiped away her personality and left her naked, while it masked, protected him.

He put grease of some kind on his prick. She hoped it was birth control.

When he came at her, still silent, there was none of the pain she'd expected, although the whole thing was clumsy and slightly brutal, more like wrestling than romantic passion. But at its heart – nothing; she would have welcomed pain and blood, they would have been better than this – emptiness. Everything was still just as mysterious. She still had not really crossed the threshhold, was still looking into the mirror, through the window, hoping for the future to arrive. Yet this was the future.

Mark smiled in a different way afterwards. But it was no easier to talk than before.

In her diary, after her mother had gone to bed, she wrote: 'He took me, there, on the couch. I felt the ghost of his father was watching. It was an experience like silent music. Afterwards I felt a great sense of freedom.'

He did not kiss her when they met by the gate. The park was colourless with cold, the dead time of year, and across its expanses a few figures were bowled along the paths by a numbing wind. He stopped and turned towards her. She stepped forward for his embrace, released from shyness by her good news, about to say: I've got a place at Oxford. He however spoke first:

'Why did you tell your mother?'

She shook her head.

He was quite calm, he spoke quietly, led her to a bench. They sat, still turned towards each other.

Her silence locked her in again; to him it must seem like an admission of guilt.

'She rang my father, threatened to take some sort of legal action.'

A futile smile of embarrassment atrophying on her face, Crystal looked away, into the distance, down the vista of bare trees.

'Of course he doesn't take that sort of thing too seriously – just told me to avoid girls who tell their mothers.'

They sat side by side, in silence. Later they started to walk again, their movements stiff, their talk gruff and jerky – as if they'd suddenly aged. He took her to a coffee bar, bought her a cappuccino. They smoked. Later they walked back along the High Street, and he said goodbye to her at the tube station.

The house was dark and cold. Crystal sat in her bedroom without turning on the lights. When she heard her mother's key in the lock she went on sitting there. Later she went down to the kitchen where her mother had made tea. They exchanged bright 'hellos'.

'There's macaroni cheese for supper.'

The stove was warm, the kettle hummed, the radio burbled in the background.

'What did you do with yourself today?'

'Nothing much – oh, the letter came. The post was late. I've got into Oxford.'

'Oh Crystal! That's wonderful! Why didn't you say right away! You are a funny little thing! Aren't you going to show me?'

'It's there on the dresser.'

Her mother's hand trembled, tears blurred behind her spectacles.

'Oh *Crystal*. It's what I always hoped for.' Her face looked naked. If only she'd wear make-up. She said, 'You will be careful, won't you?'

'I don't know what you mean.'

Miss Vanbrugh from school came to tea. She was very sweet, boyishly shy at forty-five.

'You know Crystal, it's jolly good you've got this chance – it's a *marvellous* place – had the best time of my life there – and your mother's worked so hard for you, too, now don't do anything to spoil it, will you – it would be such an awful pity if it all went wrong – '

'Why should it, Miss Vanbrugh?'

Afterwards her mother said, 'Miss Vanbrugh was only trying to be helpful, there was no need to be so rude.'

'Was I?'

'You'd do well to listen to what she says – no matter what they say, there's nothing safe, not French letters or anything.'

French letters! How horribly vulgar – where could her mother have heard such a phrase?

She dropped in on Adam to tell him her news.

'Yes . . . your mother phoned me as a matter of fact.'

He made her a cup of instant coffee. It was nice to be back in his little cupboard. She found him easier to talk to than other people.

Afterwards, though, she couldn't remember what they'd talked about, only the moment when he'd somehow managed to drop – so naturally – into the conversation the words: 'Perhaps your trouble is you like men too much.'

She looked at him. On his face she caught the unmistakeable, instantly recognizable, blank, impersonal smile.

'Your mother seemed a bit worried about you.'

Silence – but her tongue-tied prison had become a refuge

151

now. She simply smiled woodenly and waited until he spoke again, about something else.

As soon as she could she got away and made for the coffee bar she'd frequented with Anna and Gillian. She stared out of the window at the park, letting her cappuccino get cold. Perhaps your trouble is you like men too much. Did he mean she was tarty?

Such a short time – a few weeks – since she'd sat at this window with Anna and Gillian. Well, that was being grown-up, wasn't it; being on your own.

She waited until she felt sure her mother must be asleep, then took the three volumes of her diary from their hiding place in her wardrobe, trod carefully down the stairs to avoid the creaking boards, and turned on the light in the kitchen. Her mother had banked up the stove for the night, but it was beginning to burn through. There was a special iron implement with a ridged end to lift off the round lid. Crystal had to push the books down with it, breaking their stiff cardboard spines and covers, jabbing and pushing at them with the blunt end. At first they wouldn't burn, but at last they began to smoulder, and then, finally, they caught fire.

PART FIVE: THE LATE SEVENTIES

The city was a honeycomb. The hum of the late-afternoon crowds rose from the squares locked into the labyrinth, the susurration of footsteps, voices, indoor sounds.

The hotels were full. They climbed a flight of stone stairs. The courtyard smelled of cats. They knocked on the double doors, pushed them open, and stood in a long, dark *salone*.

The proprietor wore a greasy woollen vest, open at the neck, shiny trousers, scuffed slippers.

'*Momento.*'

They waited. Curtains, heavy and dusty as those in one of the churches, shielded the room from the light that glittered off the lagoon. A long marble table down the length of the room displayed baskets of wax fruits under glass domes, polished stones, little boxes, chipped ornaments, a pile of faded visiting cards: an inedible buffet of bric-a-brac. Heavy furniture stood round the walls. These were covered in brocade and hung with darkly varnished paintings, classical scenes, landscapes, oleographs of Christ and the Sacred Heart with its endless ambivalence of bleeding wounds shot round with rays of gold. An old photograph of a naval officer stared out, heavy lidded. Lighter squares on the walls showed the places where portraits of – perhaps – Mussolini had once had pride of place.

The proprietor returned, with him a second, a double almost. They both had black tongues of hair drawn across the forehead; flat faces with an unhealthy red breaking out over nose and cheeks; wore unkempt deshabille.

'*Viene.*'

One stood aside, the other led them into a maze of partitioned rooms and narrow corridors. They were shown a room crowded with high brass bed, yellow-varnished cupboard, old-fashioned wash basin, and a large red chair. Above the bed Christ died in agony.

'Well – '

'It's incredibly cheap,' said Eileen.

Crystal took the plunge: '*Va bene. Grazie.*'

The bathroom was at the far end of the flat, next to the proprietors' rooms. You could see into their big living room, which was much lighter and brighter than the rest of the flat. Always a woman sat by the window, with her back to the room. She had black hair piled on her head, and wore a red-and-yellow dress. She talked without pause to one of the men. He stood behind her chair and bent slightly forward, occasionally interjecting a murmured word.

She was always there by the window, looking out onto the square. When they left in the morning, in the late afternoon when they came in to change, even late at night they heard the torrent of Italian as she screeched on.

'You'd think they'd put a blanket over her cage sometimes, wouldn't you?'

Every morning they had coffee in the square. Then they wound through the maze until they'd found – the church with the Carpaccios, the late baroque façade. Each day they walked into the hinterland. Crowds jostled in the passages near the main Piazza, but a ten-minute walk brought them to dusty, empty closes and deserted backstreet canals. At the back of the city, behind the shimmering façade, they looked out at the industrial coastline across the estuary. They walked on, on, until a turning brought them up short on yet another quayside looking out over the blue void of the lagoon, or until a dead end brought them to some remote corner lost in the silence of self-absorption.

They laid their fruit and cheese in its paper on a stone ledge, and sat with the view. Crystal read her book, or an Italian newspaper, Eileen opened her sketch book.

'Like a couple of Victorian spinsters,' she said, pleased with the comparison.

'Oh, don't say that!'

Eileen looked at her: 'You're hardly the one to mind about that now.'

'I don't mind. It's just – '

Towards late afternoon was the hour for their daily visit to the post office. The suspense was brief, but painful, as the uniformed man behind the counter flipped through the *poste restante* pigeon holes.

'Anything?'

'*Niente.*'

Each afternoon they went to the same elegant café to recover, sat in the wicker chairs to sip the first apéritif of the day. Eileen smoked. Crystal read *The Times*. Never mind – perhaps tomorrow.

Two women alone; they dined every evening in a different little restaurant, then wandered through the square, sat in another café, listened to the mandolin music and the sentimental tenor who serenaded the gondolas at night.

Eileen laughed: 'How corny!'

Yet the soft-centred, easy chords throbbed with erotic longing. Everything was different now. She felt so vulnerable, hated not having a man at her side, yet to feel that made her feel so guilty . . . Why didn't they pick up a couple of blokes, there'd been those men at the Lido. But it was unthinkable, a betrayal of the new life, the new longing –

They pushed through the listless crowds again and back to the airless room at ten thirty. They crept through the flat, which smelled dank and sour like the canalside churches. The woman at the window chattered on. They saw no other guests – only empty rooms.

Primly propped side by side in the high *letto maritale* they read their books. Then: 'Well – shall we turn out the light?'

Crystal lay flat on her back. A ray of light fell through the gap in the curtain and onto the wall. Even a sheet felt too hot. Eileen always fell asleep at once. Crystal held rigidly to the edge of the bed so as not to slip towards the centre where their bodies might embarrassingly, ambiguously touch. As a clock struck midnight over the city she allowed herself a movement, cautiously easing herself into a foetal position. Later she stealthily propped herself onto one elbow, and reached for the water and the sleeping pills. One o'clock struck – she lay thinking, thinking. Two o'clock – and she still lay pinned, electrified, longing, afraid.

In the light of day everything seemed hopeful, even normal again. They sat over their coffee and planned their expeditions, their wanderings: which day to go to Padua, which to Ravenna, whether to go to the Lido again. It was only as they walked on through the pall of heat that it began to be like walking through a dream, that she began to feel not quite real.

One evening there was a Communist Party music festival in an unfamiliar square. There, it was noisy, full of life, she felt more normal. It was late when they left.

A few yards from the noise, red flags and flares and they pattered down lonely alleys. They turned left. The sound of dripping water punctuated the silence. They hurried, hesitated at every turning, hurried on again.

'Aren't we going round in circles?'

'It's all right, for Christ's sake!'

'We've been down here before.'

'Why didn't you bring the map?'

He was there. He stood in a turning. Crystal stopped still. He loomed before them, barring the way. His prick gleamed. He grinned – motionless – silent.

'Go back – *go back*.'

They fled along the passage.

'He's after us.'

They clattered shrieking down some shallow steps and reached a wider street that was suddenly populated. Strolling couples looked up, startled by the noise.

'Quick – quick – he's still there – '

They lurched, seasick, from crowded streets to deserted passages, from canalsides to closed-in squares, disorientated. Many wrong turnings, and they came out at last not into the Piazza but to an empty *campo* far beyond that. They sped across its shadowy spaces to emerge on the deserted quayside. Here at last it was open, but they still half ran until they reach the main square. Even here the crowds had thinned out and the orchestras were packing up. They turned into the alleyway that led back to the flat.

'Oh *God* – it's *him* – '

'It can't be – '

They took another route, glancing behind them every few yards. One last look as they reached the stone stairs and the flat; the little square was empty.

'Why did we get so hysterical?'

'It's this city, this place.'

Crystal could not sleep. The clocks struck midnight – then one. It wasn't the city, the city only made her more aware that there was no longer solid ground beneath her feet. . . .

Someone in the flat was moving things about. She listened. Footsteps passed the door; then returned, and there was a dragging sound, a sweeping, terribly heavy noise of an inert weight being pushed, pulled along. So close; just outside the door. It moved away. There were more noises – from the *salone*, perhaps. It sounded as if they were packing to leave. The double doors banged distantly.

She lay rigid. It seemed as if she was there forever. Then she felt less frightened and crept out of bed to lock the bedroom door. But it was locked already. Had Eileen locked it? Unlike her . . . In the end she slept.

They swam at the Lido next day. In the afternoon there was at last a letter for Eileen at the *poste restante*.

'I'm to meet him in Trieste on Thursday – it's a day earlier than we'd planned – '

'I don't mind going home a day early – I'll change my couchette – '

Dying to get back. I'm longing for you. . . .

'No letter for you?'

Crystal shook her head.

It must have rained in the night, for on Thursday they had to pick their way through puddles to the station. They drank a last coffee together.

'I've enjoyed our time here.'

'You know – the parrot lady wasn't there this morning.'

'What?'

'You know – the woman in the flat. She wasn't there today – or yesterday.'

'Are you sure?'

'I'm sure she wasn't there. We always heard her talking.'

But Eileen wasn't really listening. She was thinking about this last, half-reluctant meeting with Ben.

'I wonder how he'll be . . . the same, unfortunately, I suppose,' Eileen mused.

'Does Gareth mind?'

'Oh *no*!'

Eileen would cope. They hugged. Crystal did not wait to see the train draw slowly, irrevocably away from the station. That always made her too sad.

She turned left out of the station and back towards the centre of the city. Now she was alone. She walked from street to street, drawn ever closer back to the knot of passages near the Piazza.

So they'd put a blanket over the parrot lady's cage . . . forever . . . She roamed on, wandered through the alleys and crossed the canals, until, tired and giddy, she looked up, hoping for a café, and saw that she was back in the little square. The smelly stone stairs waited to lead her up to the double doors.

She would climb the steps. One of them would open the double doors – waiting for her –

'*Viene.*'

The double doors banged echoingly. . . .

The Last Time

The sky is a brass gong. Banked-up fumes turn it bronze, lock in the heat forever, the ozone layer is destroyed. It will never be cool again, the heat endures from day to day until the earth begins to crack, the city falls apart, Europe a desert.

Drought jolts the foundations, houses crack, structural faults, subsidence. The reservoirs are sinking. The grass turns white. Trees wither in the dust.

The affair has been over two years. It was like nothing else. Now London is empty, made strange in the deadly heat it's suddenly a southern city that cracks open in front of me.

At eleven at night the temperature's still in the eighties. All over the city curtains idle at windows, windows gape open all night, unprotected, who cares any more – only to get cool. The city draws breath from all those open mouths, a vast collective sigh for air.

I lie naked, alone. The one limp sheet burns like a poisoned shroud.

What is it? Why can't I get over it?

I thought of murder, planned it all, how I'd go to her new woman's house – leave her or I'll kill you. My hands were round her throat, I bashed her skull against the wall. Did she feel it, the violence of my jealousy across the intervening miles? Did she ever shiver for no reason, did she ever think: a goose walking over my grave? Did she ever feel faint, did her head ache? Or did my hatred fall harmlessly somewhere in the miles between?

I dreamed every night. I dreamed I was drowning in the lagoon at Venice. Woke sobbing.

Eileen said, You can't go on like this, you must get out of it, move on. But night after night, the same movie in my head, the machine's stuck, plays the same scenes over and over, but always they're a little different, always there's a detail you hadn't noticed, another sign of betrayal, another wound, but always unexpected.

She ditched me. Overnight – total withdrawal: well, you wouldn't live with me, would you, you didn't really love me, why did you go to Venice with Eileen?

And now she's written. Tomorrow I'll see her again. After all this time.

Her letters were always ambiguous, you had to read between the lines. And this isn't even a letter, just a card posted in the north. The picture's a place in France, the *Pays des Landes*. An arrow-straight road cleaves the pine forest at dawn – what is she saying to me – *Pays des Landes* – the land of the land, the wild zone, the land of the women.

We spoke on the phone. It was calm and matter of fact, as if we were just old acquaintances. She has a meeting in the morning. She'll come to my place at two.

I lie on my bed. It's too hot to sleep. I'm waiting, not thinking. The machine in my head has stopped. I just float in a void, I'm waiting.

Was she ever there? Love like drowning – desire pulls you into the depths, what pulls you down is what your life depends on.

At first it was the novelty, the thrill of the forbidden – except of course that all my friends were doing it, I couldn't be left out. They talked of the thralldom of loving men – identity collapsed, there was jealousy and pain. But this would be different: women loving women. And then there she was, giving me the eye across a room.

I was a weekend lesbian. And anyway her too tense adoration turned me off, I distrusted it.

I don't know if I want to be loved. What is *love*, anyway?

You just want my body.

I don't mean that.

But that was it, wasn't it? I wouldn't live with *her*, but I couldn't live without *it* – and yet it was more than – It was a cycle of eroticism that had to be played through to the end, every time. It started with excitement, opened up into the deeply emotional, took us on into a nameless, anonymous place of total surrender, annihilation, kamikaze – going over the edge – and then I'm the servant, the worshipper who dominates, who demands, who forces out those cries, those startling sobs of pleasure.

I heard the pigeons' throaty cooing in the roof. Thought it was some woman, coming forever, over and over again, monotonous, always the same, you never get tired of it. But that was somewhere else, long ago.

Only afterwards we can laugh, we enter the social again, saunter out to the shops as innocent as friends. Yet slowly her anger grew. I would not bend to her will, I was only hooked on that cycle of emotions, the record played over and over again, only now I'm frightened of it, frightened of her, distraught because she isn't faithful. And suddenly, one day, months later: you're too intense, she said. We've changed places.

In the afternoon the rooms are shadowy. Beyond the French windows the garden lies in a white heat. She's late – Crystal knows where her meeting is, even the woman whose flat it's in – she rings the familiar number. No answer –

Crystal wanders through the empty rooms, haunts the cool depths of the house. Indoors and out there; a knife of shadow slices them apart.

Crystal steps into the empty street. A song echoes from an open window. The tube's cool and shadowy again. A rushing wind brings the train. She sits in an empty carriage, doesn't see the station names that come up beyond the window. Yet at the appointed stop she leaves the train, walks along the dark platform, rides towards the surface of the city again, the white light hits her. People mill along the pavement.

The mansion block stretches away from the corner. She walks in at the first entrance. But the number, she can't remember the number. No names in the hallway, nothing by the doors. It would take so long – she can't walk up and down each flight of stairs, hoping to recognize the door.

She paces the pavement, getting jostled and pushed. She'll wait, watch. She stands by a plane tree.

Even if you knew the number of the flat, how could you

just walk in there and ring the bell? What would they think, it'd look so odd. And who says she's there anyway? She might have left, probably back at the house by now, ringing your doorbell and getting no answer.

Crystal runs along the street, hails a taxi, dives in. She cowers against the window, glad he drives so fast, shaking her from side to side, jerking, jolted, like a puppet, some sort of punishment for this crazy flight across the city. Faster, faster – but still it may be too late.

She pitches forward into the hall. The phone's ringing.

'I'm with Deb now – still at her flat – meeting's over, leaving now, be with you soon – '

She was there all the time.

Crystal lies on the sofa and watches TV. White figures spring across green turf, staccato ball, burst of applause, Connors to serve.

Sweat under the arms – she goes upstairs and sprays herself with scent, but keeps on the old jeans, doesn't want to look dolled up. Lies down on the sofa again, as if relaxed, but poised to spring into life at the sound of the bell.

Shelley smiles down at her: 'Hello.'

'You're so late.'

'You're in a muddle – I said I'd come at four.' She doesn't come in. 'Where shall we go?'

Why go anywhere? Why not stay here? Then it's not going to happen.

'Let's go to the park.'

'It'll be so crowded.'

'Doesn't matter.' Shelley always liked crowds – fair-grounds, Wimbledon.

And now they're sitting on the grass by the Serpentine. Shelley bends towards her. She smiles and smiles.

'You really turn me on.'

But Crystal rolls over and looks away, watching the families that stroll along, so brightly dressed, so many nationalities. Then why don't we make love? But she's locked in silence, she's mesmerized, as she always was, passive, wooden, just waiting for Shelley to bring her to life.

'We could go to a film.'

A film! There's so little time. And she wants to see a film.

We talk about our work, our lives, our politics. But there's always this gap – she thinks I'm middle class, élitist, I think she's anti-men. Now I wish we were back in the park, I'm filled with desolation, time passes so quickly. I'm nostalgic for the park, now that we're sitting in a café with bentwood chairs and palms, a café American-style. I watch her wolf a hamburger as I sip my coffee. I've lost nearly a stone.

I watch her. Did I love her? She looks boyish, flat-faced, boring really, breezy.

The strong silent type. She's so like a man – and yet she isn't a man. Is that what turned me on? That magic combination of masculine and feminine – was that her power? Am I outside it now? Have I escaped it?

Does love transform the ordinary, like they say? What is love anyway, just an idea. Those evenings in the dark room, when I drew the photographic paper through its bath of chemicals, then watched it floating in the water in the sink: at first there's nothing, then imperceptibly the image begins to faint in onto the page, it steals on so gently at first, then slowly, slowly deepens and strengthens until it's finally indelibly *there*. The dark room of love in the mind – at first when she looked at me it meant really nothing. Only gradually the image of her stole across the blank sheet, so gradually at first, until it took possession of me, and now she's all over me, stamped all over my body, never to be got rid of again.

I'm lost without you –

We walk into the cool auditorium, smiling and calm. It's surprisingly full, but perhaps that's because it *is* cool.

As soon as we're seated, in the centre, in the middle of a row, she takes my hand. That's nice, it's friendly. Maybe we can be friends now, not lovers. Maybe that's how it has to be.

The lights dim. We sit demurely, our noses lifted towards the screen. Her hand feels smooth and safe. Isn't it strange how I always feel safe with her, and yet she's so dangerous. She eats an ice cream in the interval. Then the main film begins.

And then it starts to happen. I used to have a fantasy of making love in a cinema. In my fantasy a stranger would sit beside me, and take my hand. In silence he would kiss me, pushing me backwards so that I was half lying across the seats. He would touch my nipples, pull at the zip of my jeans, guide my hand towards his, I'd feel the cock harden, he'd force me down between the rows of seats. . . .

In the fantasy, though, the cinema was dark and empty. The pleasure heightened by the danger of a public place was still covered by darkness, paradoxically private.

But now the cinema doesn't feel dark at all. It isn't so bad when she just kisses me and – but surely she won't do more than that. But she is. I try to withdraw at first, but she won't stop. She *is* trying to unzip my jeans, her hand's under my tee shirt, she pulls my hand towards her crotch.

This is awful, I don't feel aroused, I don't want to go on. This is no furtive pleasure, no secret between us that seals us off from the rows of twilit faces that stare ahead at the screen, it's a public event, I know our neighbours can see what's going on, I'm numb with embarrassment, but I don't dare to reject her, all I want is for it to end, I caress her mechanically, frantically, trying to get it over with as quickly as possible. It's going on forever. She even groans.

When the lights go up we move towards the exit with the crowd. I stare at my feet, there are arcs of sweat under my arms, my hair's all tousled, I just want to get away. Shelley still smiles. We walk towards the car, not holding hands, sedate.

The car is parked in a side street. It's like a stove inside, Shelley grabs me again. Can't we at least talk about this? Why don't I say something, protest? But I let it go on, and it's not as bad as in the cinema, but it's not a joke either, although she's laughing, and it's a travesty, a caricature of the past, and I stay wooden, apart from it all, I don't come, but I lie to her about it, pretend I did. The windows have steamed up. Shelley laughs: 'You knew all along – you meant this to happen – wearing those old jeans with a great gaping hole in the crotch – you've seduced me again – '

She's driving me home. A crack is opening up inside me, some new void. I feel so vulnerable. I seize on the word, as if it were an anchor, something apart from myself. I feel so vulnerable: as if to name the feeling will exorcise it.

Shelley parks the car round the corner from the house.

'Won't you come in?'

She shakes her head: 'I'm driving home through the night.'

To the north – the *Pays des Landes*. Will you live there forever – oh come back to me –

Shall I see you again. . . .?

I get out of the car without protest, it's all so casual, I walk away round the corner and let myself into the house. The others are at home, I can hear them talking in the kitchen, but I slip upstairs and into my room. The window is open. I lie down on my bed in the dark. It's hot, so hot.

There's a big rally about abortion legislation at Westminster Hall. The speeches grew tedious, so Crystal and two of the Formosa Road women escape across the square and sit outside a pub drinking beer. Women are spilling out all over the pavements, milling around at the mouths of all the streets that lead off from the square, they drink sitting on steps and on the curb, it's like cup final night, but for women. Crystal, slightly drunk, feels at one with all these women – their shared purpose, she feels at this moment, is the bedrock of her life. This women's movement makes her safe, supports her, keeps her afloat, buoys her up.

There's a crowd in the pub, they shout and laugh as you struggle through for drinks. There's a crowd outside, there's chatter and gossip.

'Hey – you know what – ' shouts Frankie above the din, 'Deb's having an affair with this woman from up north, big thing apparently, she was down a week or two ago, Shelley she's called, Deb's thinking of moving up there – '

'I saw Deb with someone this evening – ' says Vinny.

'Must be her – '

'You all right Crystal?'

'Just a bit hot – going outside for a minute – '

She runs, flings herself onto a bus, any bus, anything to get away from the horror of meeting *them*, gets off again at Charing Cross Road and walks, walks forever, slowly edging towards home and the empty streets further north.

The others are there, round the kitchen table as usual, and she chats to them for a while – nothing's changed. Then she's alone in her room, she's restless, she prowls up and down, turns on the radio, turns it off again.

It wasn't rape of course, you could never say that.

You were dying for it, love – that hole in your jeans –

Consent was hardly the word for all those other times, all those con-sensual acts. But I didn't want it like that in the cinema, I was just too afraid to say no –

I'm lost without you –

I'm mad about you –

You're all I ever wanted –

Crystal turns the phrases over in her mind, like stones, like foreign objects. Archeological remains from some distant past, broken shards of pots, lost bits from buried treasure, they are evidence that she was once alive, all that is left of the cycle of desire.

It was rape in the cinema, an act cynical and empty, you wanted to prove you still could, that I couldn't say no. And I was falling apart with hope against hope that you were going to come back to me –

Oh this emptiness –

Why wouldn't I live with you then, if I'm so lost without you?

Crystal stands by her window and the hot, heavy night air nudges her, nuzzles her in unwanted intimacy; she stares down at the garden, where white flowers glimmer in clumps and a hush of expectancy presages – nothing. And the void opens again.

I thought I wanted love. Was I really searching out your cruelty, seeking the thrill of psychic pain?

I'm mad about you.

You're all I ever wanted.

I'm lost without you.

Sometimes it seemed like it was the future already. '*Now* is past.' She felt giddy as the doors slid shut while the hollow voice of the intercom still echoed through the passageways.

The train gathered speed into the tunnel and the roar drowned the disembodied voice. The carriage filled with fog. Perhaps she was fainting. But her eyes stung. Passengers coughed. There was an acrid smell.

The train slowed through a station. The platform was thick with smoke. She glimpsed a few figures stumbling along through the shadows, but instead of stopping the sealed train insidiously speeded up again and hurled itself into the tunnel, poured itself on and on, past another station, they were locked in it forever.

But at the next station the doors opened again. Crystal was hot, shaking. Passengers shot out onto another dark platform where crowds hurried through the smoke, handkerchiefs pressed to mouths. What had happened? No announcement.

She didn't move – too late to get off the train. She would miss her flight if she tried to escape now. The mechanical doors snapped off her chance.

The train moved forward, but then in the darkness it slowed, hiccoughed, stopped, the pulse of its mechanical circulation throbbing, its panting laboured, then it ceased to breathe at all. Conversation was hastily brought down to a whisper. In the silence all sat becalmed. The air was thick with smoke. There was stifled coughing. Her eyes smarted, tears caught on her lashes.

It was a terrorist bombing; a coup d'état; the third world war . . . It was an accident – senseless, she would be buried alive – die with strangers –

The train regained consciousness, heaved, wrenched itself forward once more. By the next station the smoke had cleared. Flocks of office workers crowded in. And soon the train reached the upper air and set the secretaries down among the flower gardens of west London as if nothing had happened. And nothing *had* happened. Only the glass between her and reality had softened, wrinkled like a veil, dissolved. . . .

When the carriage doors slid apart she heard bird song. Then, as the train caterpillared towards Heathrow, there was only the whistle of jets coming in, she saw them float downwards, miraculously near, flying turkeys that touched the runway in a shimmer of heat, amazing grace for such clumsy birds.

Now they were locked in the carriage together, the ones who were travelling to the end of the line. They snatched furtive glances at one another, avoiding eye contact. Wax-work strangers, their polyester clothing was uncrushed, their faces preserved with make-up or suntan or artificial hormones, smoothing out all difference to uniform orange, the smell of their bodies masked with aftershave, deodorant: airport dolls from all over the world, with eyes that moved, heads that turned from side to side, arms that moved up and down, embedded in each one the battery of ego and desire, the motivator, the chip that made them human.

Soon another airport tilted up beneath her. The long alleys and light halls were thronged with the same glazed earth-lings. She, a stranger from the past in this future, came out, looked around, took the bus to the centre of the city. There, she turned into the side streets and walked along and across the canals. Noise flooded from the cafés, crowds sat at tables outside, a tram rattled across a bridge. In between there were glassy stretches of peace.

She reached the house of her friends. Soon she was gossiping with them over glasses of red wine. Oh yes, I'm relating to men again too . . . I'm afraid . . . Philip's a sweet guy, really, nothing heavy you know – and the smiles, the conniving smiles. It's another turn, times have changed, they all are. And Hanneke's pregnant, at thirty-nine.

Music came faintly from the square. Now in the warm May evening she was caught in this future – but where is the present, she and some lover holed up together, locked in a little hotel room in a city silenced by snow: Ian, her first real lover – and she's old, a woman of the world, she's twenty-three.

In the morning she walked to the university. The woman met her, took her to the right room, gave her coffee.

She'd done so many talks since her book – *The Doubled Image: Women and Narcissism*.

Eileen had liked it. Crystal had been surprised, she'd expected her to disapprove.

It's rather introverted, she'd said, it's you looking into a pool . . . but it's good, I like it, she'd said loyally.

She could tell from these upturned faces that they were waiting for her certainties. Because she wrote a book they thought she had the answers.

But times had changed. She wasn't in that mood, the daring activist – she'd turned away from all those shattered certainties –

Back to the Freudian mirror, the consulting room, the hushed hour, the inner world –

The mirror cracked from side to side –

She recognized a face in the front row – who was it? It was a woman she knew – from that time before *this* time, this living in the future –

She spoke calmly, drily, in a measured, intellectual way. Almost a rebuke to these women for being such enthusiasts, for demanding the moon. Her almost mocking irony caused a gloom to settle on the women in the lofty, half-filled hall. Afterwards they asked her carping, dissatisfied questions. They wanted affirmation, they wanted solutions, they wanted hope, excitement, energy. But living in this future she was arid, dry.

There was a big group for lunch, a photographer clicked and flashed. She smiled, answered questions. A young woman escorted her to her next engagement. Clouds of dust rose from a building site where the Waterloo Plein had once been. Beyond the scaffolding and the rubble the market had moved, changed. Turks and Surinamese bargained over piles of rubber tyres, ex-hippies peddled high-priced junk, tourists loitered along.

In another hall she was giving her seminar. Then she was whirled on again, was moving through the glassy light of the publisher's party, and the half-familiar language was a pane of glass between her and everyone else, this future.

It was good to be alone at last, in the late afternoon, the moment between afternoon and evening. The café was empty. It was a long, dim room with the pool of a big mirror at the back. There were worn tables and bentwood chairs and tattered theatrical posters.

She stirred her coffee, lit a cigarette. The young woman behind the bar disappeared into the back somewhere. Crystal was alone. Then the door swung open. It was a man with a large leather satchel; a noble head and shoulders, and flowing grey curly hair sat top-heavy on his dwindling torso; his face was marked, pitted and eroded with life's disappointments, he was an antique Roman bust, weather-beaten, crumbling. He cast her a single, disappointed glance, and, like her, waited. Except that she wasn't waiting; she was just sitting in the future.

The door swung again and two young women, wearing little jackets, baggy trousers and espadrilles, greeted him with coos of delight. He rose. There was too much embracing. He kissed the dark one very tenderly: 'You're nice. You're so *nice*.'

Laughter.

'So are you!'

Her friend, with hennaed hair, kissed him too.

He held onto the dark one's shoulders: 'Your hair – it looks American.'

'Well – I suppose I *am* American now.'

She spoke English with a London accent. The friend with hennaed hair went to the bar to order drinks.

The dark woman's nose turned up too far, and she had darkened her face with chipmunk streaks of brown blusher. Her eyes were circled with black, her eyebrows darkened.

173

They spoke with the freedom of those who converse in a foreign language, sure of not being overheard.

'Yes . . . I am living with him. In fact . . . well – we're married! Neither of us believes in marriage. We don't believe in it at *all*. So we don't tell *anyone* we're married! You're very privileged I've told you my big secret!'

'Ah . . .' The smile on his ravaged face didn't change, but it glazed a little.

'It's only that – if we weren't married I wouldn't be able to stay with him there, and he couldn't live with me in England either.'

'So you're married,' he said.

'It gets so cold there – it's forty below in winter, you know, you can't stay out for very long at all. And there's no transport. My studio is thirty miles from the house. I cycle over there, or sometimes I take the car – but in any case, everyone's so *kind*, if the car's broken down or something, they say, 'Borrow ours, it's yours' – because everyone knows that otherwise you simply couldn't get there, get anywhere . . . it's quite near the White Mountains; you can get up into the hills – '

When she went out to the WC at the back of the bar her two friends discussed her in their own language. Their laughter was low and gleeful as they bitched about her behind her back. She returned, and the man stood up: 'Let's meet again *very* soon.'

'Oh yes – *soon.*'

They kissed. He stood back, gazed at her, limped away, was gone. The door swung softly to.

'It's such a pity – he – ' The two women giggled and murmured. The London woman with the secret marriage was full of sympathy: 'Yes, it's a problem when you don't see someone often enough, and it's a problem if you see them too much . . . I *know!*' The cigarette smoke curled upwards.

The two women paid, and left the café. She was alone again, time to go. She went to the WC, where, scrawled on the wall, was a sentence from her book: ' "The mirror cracked from side to side" – the woman immured in her turret was fatally punished for daring even to look out on the real world. But we have to take the risk.' Pretentious rubbish! With a sudden spurt of angry self-hatred she tried to rub it off with a paper hanky; then, when this failed, blacked it out, feverishly, with a biro.

Dinner with the women. The vaguely familiar woman from the front row was with them: Blanche.

She remembered now – Blanche dressed in white from her enveloping shawl to her boots, her bleached hair spread out over her shoulders like a second shawl. She had burst in on Karen's dinner party all those years ago.

'I remember that evening so well – you were helping that Russian dissident – '

(Blanche's clear voice: 'Andrei Andreyev is dying, you know. He has to finish his last book before he dies – his great work. Day after day we go through the notes and the notebooks, boxes and boxes of them, in his study, all those cardboard boxes, disintegrating – '

The dinner guests stared at this angel.

'He needs me – I'm the only thread between him and – ')

'Poor Andrei Andreyev! He never finished his great work, you know.'

She'd left the dinner party as suddenly as she'd appeared.

Afterwards Karen had astonished them with tales of Blanche's life: a lover in the PLO, killed of course, another fiancé who died in a car crash, as a young woman at university she'd done nothing but play poker all night, daughter of the richest man in –

Now, in this future, Blanche still spoke for an audience: 'I want to have a child – but there aren't any men.'

A terrible, mournful reproach.

They were in the café again, the crowds of friends, Blanche too. The man with the grey lion's mane and his women companions had reappeared as well. And Shelley – Shelley was there.

She turned towards Shelley, bathed in the most intense desire – and Shelley had promised that they'd be together. Only now she'd gone off with some other woman, they were behind closed doors, and she was left outside, outside the white painted door in an empty corridor. It was five in the morning. It was too late –

She woke, still burning with desire, suffused with erotic longing. A strange visitation. She lay in the darkness. A clock chimed. For some women who'd tried it – Karen, for example – it had been too little, the love of women; for others, for herself, it had been too much, no holds barred, no careful, civil distance between the sexes, no rules to the game.

The woman in yellow paused in the doorway of the coffee lounge. Then she waved, and strode across to Crystal.

'I'm late! I'm Selma. Come.'

They crossed the city on Selma's bike, wobbling and swerving at every junction in a chorus of bells and motor horns.

Reflections from the canal trembled on the walls of Selma's flat. On every ledge and shelf plants grew and trailed.

Selma asked her questions – about life, about women. Crystal was supposed to have the answers, to open up a vision of female power, to represent in her own person the strength of womanhood. She was to take up arms on behalf of her sex, to challenge the oppressor male, to exist in a realm of purity unsullied by the bloody stain of vulnerability, or cracked with the fissures of ambivalence.

But she rejected this steely public self. She would only speak of difficulties, of contradictions.

The interview was also supposed to be suffused with women's intimacy – women together, an exchange of confidences, like the two women, heads close together, in the café, murmuring and laughing. But she could not be intimate. So, thwarted of the confessions of a fellow feminist, Selma herself began to talk: 'What is this love?

You say you are training as a therapist now, you again concern yourself with psychoanalysis, but – what is this love? Did not Freud himself say that being in love is an illusion, a neurosis, even? We have all struggled so hard against it, and yet . . . I and my lover, we were in love. It was a great passion. Then: there came a time when we were not in love. We had affairs; he first, then I too. Really – we were estranged.

'But now – we have returned to each other. Once again we are in love. There is no other. It is once more a great passion. And yet . . . sometimes I feel that we have to invent quarrels, anger, in order to build up this passion afterwards – as if it's a story we're telling each other, as if we are inventing it, making it up. It's willed. We *decided* it.'

'Yes, Freud did say – '

'You know,' said Selma, 'sometimes I think that romantic love is something we invent for ourselves, a kind of mental drug – like giving yourself an injection.'

The drug's been withdrawn.

Wind ruffled the surface of a backstreet canal. She crossed an iron footbridge. *Now* was New Year's Eve. Fireworks, gunshot in the distance, died like bloodstains on the snow.

In this future the porn shops with their lights and jukeboxes lined the canalside. The prostitutes seated in the windows looked like dummies, like bulging dolls. She was a ghost in this future, insubstantial beside them, unnoticed by the loitering men intent on pneumatic giantesses, plastic vaginas for sale.

She was glad to reach the airport once more. In the marble lounge, like the hall of a bank or some great emporium, she stood by the bar and ordered a double vermouth. A woman in high heels and a slit skirt teetered beside a beefy man in blue. Both of them had the orange suntan skin.

177

'Yes, I used to live here,' he was saying, 'this used to be my country. But now I've made the big time – I've been lucky – I live in Jeddah.' He drank. 'Europe's finished,' he said.

An ancient Surinamese man pushed a mop around the already spotless marble floor. He dragged a little cart behind him and into its rubbish he emptied the one stub from an ashtray, wiped a clean glass table, picked up from where Crystal had dropped it the stub of her tram card, with one ride left, studied it intently, pocketed it. He shuffled round a sofa, paused, stared with stunned venom at the woman in the slit skirt as she ground out her cigarette on the marble pavement.

She heard her flight called. Willed by the disembodied voice towards the gates, she would pass beyond them into that limbo between worlds; hushed vacuum of the final departure lounge.

She walked across the concourse, drawn forward, will-less. Then beyond the shops she caught sight of a sign: 'Meditation Room'. She pushed open the door. It was a room with carpet on the walls and seats like egg cups clamped to the floor in rows; like a small art cinema. At the end a table with an all-purpose symbol on the wall; the light was discreet, subdued peach.

The room was empty. She sat down to wait. The light dimmed a little.

Waiting for the fix to appear.

She would stay here forever, in this limbo within the limbo of the airport – no-man's land. Yet it was a horrible room, false as the whole airport structure, this encapsulated world.

Unbearable to be in here. Padded walls – insane . . . locked in self-pity, her ivory tower. . . .

I must move on –

Paralysed, caught in the trap of her own internment, interned. . . .

'Last call – ' The disembodied voice relayed all over the airport, inescapable –

She grabbed her bag, fled from the room, rushed across the concourse, colliding with other travellers, hurled herself along the moving passage and towards the exit to the sky.

Do You Like Poetry?

They walked down the hill in the heat, two white-faced red-heads, whiter than ever in the glare, two versions of the same design, one bony and violent with the clarity of youth, the other softening, smudged, becoming indecisive with impending middle age.

Venice said, 'That doctor asked me stupid questions. I could see what he was getting at all the time. Not very subtle.'

'Do you want to go back?'

'There's nothing wrong with me. Dad said so.'

'But he was the one who started all this – going on about your school work. And then when we were having those rows – he wanted you to see someone.'

'We don't have to do *everything* Dad says.'

The doctor had given no verdict, just, 'We'd like to see you again.' The interview had been like a tea party gone wrong. They'd all sat on easy chairs, but the psychiatrist and social worker, host and hostess as it were, had failed to offer tea or cucumber sandwiches, or even make conversation. They'd just sat there in sphinx-like silence. Karen had tried to be a good guest, to please, to entertain, but all her efforts had fallen flat, and now she was left unfairly feeling it was all her fault.

At the bus stop Venice swerved away: 'I'm going for a swim.'

'But I'll be gone when you get back!'

'Have a nice weekend.'

'Sure you'll get over to Dad's all right? He doesn't like it if you're late – '

Venice laughed indulgently at the old worry-guts: 'Don't *worry* – I'll be *fine*.'

'Your clothes are still in the machine, I shan't have time to iron them – '

'Oh Mum, I'm old enough – '

'But you never do – '

'I *promise*.'

'See you late Sunday then.'

Venice turned along the forecourt towards the baths.

'Do you like poetry? Do you like poetry?' came the mournful chant from the man who always stood outside the library. He was American, with a leather stetson hat and singsong voice. She shied away from his pleading eyes and the urgently offered leaflets with a poem stencilled, smudged and furry, on each side. They were strewn along the pavement further down, by the bus stop, across the forecourt, as far afield as the steps of the baths. He trapped the unwary into conversation – the kindly ones who held out a hand for his poems found themselves sucked into his soft, urgent monologue, trying vainly to escape through a chink in the seamless web of words.

She ran up the steps, already hearing the call of the pool, the jungle parrot-shrieks echoing in the glass roof. The attendant's whistle squealed and a shoal of skinny boy-tadpoles was emptied from the side of the pool as if an invisible hand had turned a basket of them into the water. The men who did the crawl sliced up and down the pool, machine-driven, relentless. Some were silent sharks with just a fin carving the surface, others sent up noisy whale fountains. Women swam breaststroke, their heads lifted above the surface with the dignity of dogs. On the high board a crowd of older boys jostled for their turn to plunge down and crash through the shuddering crazy pavement of blue marble. Two girls with elongated eyes and long black hair clutched the side and giggled. Above them young men with balls and biceps that bulged swaggered along the edge. An old woman crept down the steps into the water. A girl of ten shouted to her mate: 'Hey, you going on the high board? You 'ave ter 'ave the guts, and I just ain't got the guts today.' But her podgy friend scampered round and up the ladder. The smell of chlorine soured the air.

Venice let herself float like weightless seaweed, her body flowing into the water and it into her, so nearly naked it was like being in bed. A man and a woman played by the rim. He kissed her; they laughed; she splashed water in his face.

Their hands were hidden by the water, innocent above, exploratory below. Venice dived down, opened her eyes and saw limbs that waved like seaweed against wobbling, bent tiles. She saw the girl's leg and his gripped round each other, his bulge, his hand –

A muffled explosion, and a seal-like body sank and rose towards the surface. She came up for air too, and shook the water from her eyes. Solitary men positioned themselves round the edge. Some of those watchful ones gazed hungrily at her; some had eyes only for the boys. Quite cruisy, Jay called it.

The baths had become a new world to Venice since Jay had opened her eyes. No longer purely a temple to celibate muscular skill, it changed all through the day from hour to hour.

Dawn: from the sacred Roman spring that gushed hidden, deep below, the municipal naiad disported herself beneath the surface of the pure and silent pool. Early morning: the caretaker arrived and she withdrew to the invisible depths. The cleaners and attendants came rattling in like Shakespearean comics and banged about sacrilegiously in their behind-the-scenes world of broom cupboards, boiler rooms and gas rings, brewed tea, read the *Sun* and discussed the news. Eight am: and with the unlocking of the doors came a silent throng of early morning swimmers in dignified undress, incognito in tracksuits and old Burberrys. They queued for their tickets with clasped hands, a line of worshippers moving slowly towards the Host, their faces locked into the withdrawal of preparation for spiritual uplift and the sense of moral worth bestowed by their dedication of self to fitness and physical improvement. After that the schools, the giggling crocodiles of kids, and after lunch the mothers and their water babies; now in the late afternoon and early evening, the secular hours, crowded, worldly, fun, the hour of the boastful youths and licentious lovers.

But at night, after the doors were locked, it changed again. The thunderclap of the divers and the shrieks and splashing ceased. The light faded. Only a ripple of moonlight streaked the wavering darkness of the pool; only the drip of a tap broke the stillness. And then – at last – Jay must walk out from the dressing rooms, lean and white, with slicked-back black hair and strong, strong body. A single splash shattered the silence. And then they were alone in the water, the two of them, locked together in its black embrace.

Karen swam slowly against the heat. The far end of her street was lost in a dusty shimmer. The tights she had worn in honour of the clinic clung to her legs and crotch. She would sink into a cool bath, then lie becalmed in the shadows of the bedroom, with the blind half drawn and the trains rattling by.

The flat smelled of stale meals and dust, and clothes and newspapers strewed the floors. There was washing-up piled in the sink, the laundry basket oozed dirty linen. She hoped Charles wouldn't see it, wouldn't bring Venice home on Sunday.

Her tights had made a red weal round her waist. Her body, the clothes shucked off, emerged pale and puffy as if chemically altered by the heat, its blurred outlines merging into the reflections in the glass so that it seemed to melt and disintegrate. Or perhaps it was just that her eyesight was getting worse. She ran the bath and hoped Garth would be late.

Garth was early, she'd pinned up her damp hair in a hurry, and felt flustered and unrelaxed now that they were on the road. Garth looked handsome in profile as he drove, although his good looks were of an oddly old-fashioned kind: he looked like a 1930s matinée idol or lesbian novelist, Ivor Novello or Radclyffe Hall, but they would have been too gentlemanly to make smutty jokes, as Garth was doing now.

They'd met at Gloria's. Karen had taken Bob on that occasion, one of her fly-by-nights. There'd been talk of a threesome, but then Bob had gone to Australia. Karen stared out of the car window and wondered why she could not get into the mood for being with Garth. The wheatfields were greenish-gold. Nuclear silos crouched somewhere out of sight on this plain, but what she saw was an eighteenth-century landscape with cornfields and clusters of oaks and rich hedgerows, a zone of rustic peace between toiling London and the dream hotel set apart in the depopulated land, luxurious but abandoned, like the empty, floating ship, the legendary *Marie Celeste*.

The hotel was less grand than Garth ('It used to be a stately pile, you know') had led her to believe, just an ordinary country pub set back from the road. The bedroom was a between-the-wars survival, with satinwood furniture, cream paint, a black bath, no shower.

'*Pas trop mal*, I'd say.'

Karen pulled the beige curtains together to create an artificial twilight. She looked round the room, quaint, prudish somehow, and remembered other occasions, all those cheap hotels –

Venice smelled the chlorine on her body. With the heat at bay beyond the window the flat itself was very quiet, yet, since all the windows were open, the noises from the road on one side and the railway on the other blew through the rooms and breached the barrier between public and private, as her body had been breached, flooded in the pool. The voices and sound of shuffling feet filtered through the limp net curtains as the families dribbled back from the Heath towards the little knot of shops at the bottom of the hill.

She'd rung Dad, made her lame excuse ('Sandra's family's going to their country cottage – they want me to go'). He'd barked, got annoyed – he hated last-minute changes of plan. He was always right, of course, knew what was best for her, wanted to decide. And always harping on about school – do better, do better. Only – when he was pleased, the big smile, the hug that wrapped you up, enveloped you, then he hit you like a sunny day.

But this time – she'd a feeling he hadn't really minded. Didn't ask to speak to Mum, insist on coming over, argue, make a fuss, take her to Sandra's, anything like that. So now she was deflated, cheated of a row. And suppose after all this Jay didn't come.

Music, she needed music, a throb, atonal, dissonant, as she lolled on her bed and let memories into her mind, hearing those words, remembered words, as she reproduced the memory of Jay's hands and let her own drift across her nipples. A cord seemed to join them to the spot between her legs, and it tightened, tightened; her sex hung swollen, heavy, ready to burst. She kept herself on the edge, kept herself from going over, the torpid dreaminess focused into a throb, almost a pain, and then into satiation without pleasure.

The tape had long since stopped. A passer-by with a ghetto box sprayed the solitude with song:

> The Poetry of love
> Is pleasure and pain –
> Pay – hay – hain
> The poetry of love –
> Is pay – hain and pleasure –
> Yooo are my treasure –

Slowly the light changed. There was still brightness beyond the window, but the corners of the room grew shadowy. The bell rang. Venice shivered, sprang up, pulled on her tee shirt.

As the front door shut Jay already had her against the wall. They stared without kissing.

'Have you brought the book?'

'Maybe . . .'

'Have you brought it?'

'Who wants dirty books – '

Jay kissed her neck, pushed her towards the inner recesses of the flat.

'Your mum get off then?'

''Course – not here now, is she?'

'What about your dad?'

'Shsh, I fixed him.' Venice felt shy now, and wanted them

to be doing it, it was easier than talking. But Jay was looking at the poster-sized photograph above the bed.

'Who's that?'

'Them – and me.'

The seated couple, dressed in white, had luxuriantly flowing red-gold hair, he had a beard above his wide-lapelled white jacket, both had wide-brimmed hats; she, granny glasses. Blond replicas of John and Yoko, but with the solemn, white-robed baby propped up in front of them.

'When they got married.'

'Blimey.'

'They were hippies.'

'That why they give you your funny name?'

'It's where I was conceived.'

Jay choked: 'No one's called after a fucking *town*. Like being called – Birmingham or something.'

'I like it.'

'Suppose we all had to be called after where our mum and dad had a fuck. Suppose you had ten children and lived in the same place for fifty years, suppose – '

'Don't be stupid.'

They were on the bed now.

'Don't call me stupid – you didn't know nothing till I come along.'

But Jay's voice had changed, she was talking differently. Words began the ritual, words that pulled at their nerves, words that led to acts, and acts that turned to groans as dammed-up sensations burst through, to recede abruptly and leave them floating on a womblike sea.

It was almost dark when they strolled out to buy a takeaway. Pleased with themselves, they became part of the carnival atmosphere of the triangular green where buses turned at the railway station, lights sparkled against the sooty dusk and crowds still milled down from the Heath and into pubs and cafés. They did not think of rest, but when they returned to the flat, sleep caught them by surprise, so the pizzas stayed half-eaten, the porno book unread, they curled up like puppies and slept their freedom away.

* * *

Garth laboured doggedly. Apologetic but not too much abashed he puzzled away, baffled as if by a suddenly conked-out domestic appliance.

'Can't understand it – perfectly all right before – '

As at the clinic earlier that day, Karen felt in the position of the polite but somehow failing guest. He got up, rummaged in his weekend bag, produced some baby lotion and suggested a body massage. The sticky lotion felt like sweat, only slimier. The mattress was too soft. It was unbearably hot. She longed for a shower and a drink, while he made appreciative growly noises and pretended something was happening.

'We'll miss dinner – '

Garth wanted to go on trying. She lay on her back and stared with disbelief at his luxuriant waving hair, while his mouth nuzzled her breasts and his hand rubbed painfully between her legs. She would have to pretend. She tried to fantasize, and put her hand on his, to make it gentler, faster.

As she pulled on her dress she felt guilty. Garth's failure must have been her fault. Ball-breaker, castrator, Charles had said things like that, although never for a reason like this. That had never been the problem.

Was it just an unfair trick of fate, that some were sexually talented and others not? Was it that one just *felt* unattractive? Was it all in the mind? Could anyone be a wow in bed if only they loosened up, or did encounter, or went into therapy?

No good blaming yourself – or men. 'It is not you, my lord, it is the times.' Potency problems – effect of the recession.

Only one couple still sat in the dining room. They were holding hands across the table and glanced self-consciously at the new arrivals, then back at each other. Karen guessed they were in their early twenties, both wore spectacles and had prim, tight lips. Karen tried to picture them in transports of passion.

The wine was cold, earthy, greenish. Karen drank it

quickly. She found it difficult to read the menu without her glasses, for it was written in contorted Gothic script on vellum, but in any case she did not feel hungry. And anyway, Garth was the sort of man who wanted to choose for you.

Garth talked of his broken marriage. Why so much need for sympathy? At work, with Venice, at the clinic today – life constantly demanded that Karen should fit in, her role stage management, receptive acquiescence. Even with *Termagant* it had been the same, she'd always done the dreary jobs, never written the articles. Once, she'd had her needs, exposed desires, made demands – but Charles in the end had spurned them, rejected her, and needs rejected became shameful secrets.

Garth ordered more wine.

The Heath was hot and crowded. At tea time they'd finally crawled out of bed, suddenly moved by an urgent desire to escape the lassitude of indoors, to feel the sun instead of tousled sheets.

'We'll go round to Jill's mum tomorrow,' said Jay. 'Watch their video.'

'My father's got a video.'

'Wouldn't let you watch *I Spit on Your Grave* though.'

'Don't know if I want to.'

Now they were out with the weekend crowds Venice craved the dim, stale odour of the flat. There, washed up on the beach of a new country, they repeated their ritual again and again; better than any video. Why go round to Jill's, anyway, ever? Mutinous sulks and the beginnings of jealous suspicion curdled her mood.

'Let's go home.'

Karen walked through the empty landscape, only now she did not notice its emptiness, for hedgerows walled her into the winding country road. She heard a car and climbed onto the verge. The car slowed down. The farmer, in the country way, offered her a lift. He was young, had black hair and a blue shirt.

Sleep gripped the land. It was not yet six. To be awake at this prehistoric hour freed her from the tacky, baby-lotion slime of guilt, embarrassment and failure. That was all left behind with Garth, sleeping unsuspecting in the dream hotel.

Then the sun was less bright. The light changed. The sky darkened. Rain came, first in spots, then more definite, then lashing down. Water poured in runnels aslant the windscreen. The sweep of light disappeared behind a steam curtain.

'Have to be stopping for a while, till this slacks off.'

The drumming rain became part of the silence. They were lost; nowhere, washed out. They looked at each other, smiled, then laughed. In this waterlogged time pocket, reality somersaulted inside out.

The rain came later to London. Before they'd even heard it consciously, the sound of solid downpour drove them further down their burrowed bed. Past eleven and the tangle of two in a single bed became oppressive. But Venice kept quiet and still, in awe of Jay's deep breathing. At last, from the depths: 'Make us some tea.'

Released, Venice sprang up, put on a cardigan.

'Any chocolate biscuits?'

'For breakfast?' Pert.

In the kitchen Venice stared out of the window. Suddenly the rain depressed her. She wanted to do something different – wished, now, that she was over at Dad's, suddenly forlorn. Then the sound of voices outside the front door and of a key turning in the lock sent her flying through the flat, calling Jay to get up, grabbing her clothes.

'Must be Mum back early.'

But it was her father in the hall. There he stood, shaking water off his umbrella, and behind him a nervous woman with yellow curls.

Dad went on the offensive at once, as usual: 'Why aren't

you at Sandra's? You shouldn't be here on your own –
what's your mother thinking of?'

'I – came home early – didn't feel well – '

'Where *is* Karen?'

'Mum'll be back soon – '

Dad roamed the flat, inspecting everything, glaring at Jay.
Under his gaze the place became small, cramped, sordid.
Jay, slumped on the sofa behind a paper, looked sly. The
strange woman hovered by the door.

Karen sank into a taxi at Liverpool Street, speeding thank-
fully towards the haven of the empty flat. Thank God for
some solitude.

As the train had galloped across the flat lands she'd leaned
back and closed her eyes. The back of his van had been
spread with old carpet, there'd even been a cushion. Did
that mean – ? Not that she cared. He'd simply risen from
the landscape, then disappeared again, chugged off in his
rusty van with just a backward wave; an agri-industry Pan,
modern god of the rationalized, mechanized farms – or a
monster of the local headlines, sex maniac of the hedgerows
strikes again.

She unlocked the door of the flat and stopped at the
sound of voices –

Venice, paler than ever, came staring out, muttered and
gesticulated: 'Dad – the keys – '

'Why did he bring you back so early?'

Karen stalked into her invaded flat. That sulky girl on the
sofa, and David with a strange woman – all five of them
stared in silence. No one knew what to do. Jay grinned
behind her paper. There was a moment's gripping silence,
before the shouting began.

Well, they'd routed him. Karen, as soon as the front door
had banged, began to shake; but for once she'd won. That
set of keys he'd hung on to for so long lay on the coffee
table. For once the patriarch had slunk away, his tail
between his legs.

'Can I go over to Jill's place in a while?'

'You should have stayed with Dad.'

'I don't like it there, Marjorie's always so cross.'

'Poor Marjorie . . . but, look, we must talk about this seriously – you can't just – '

'Mum, can I go over to Jill's this evening?'

'I was going to go to Gloria's . . .'

At Gloria's the parties always went well. The flat was softly lit, and Gloria mixed wonderful cocktails. Gloria said monogamy screwed you up. She helped her guests off with their inhibitions, and after a few drinks it seemed quite natural to love everyone. At Gloria's every man and woman seemed attractive, and there were no tears, no tomorrows, no hang-ups, as ugliness and shame dissolved. Gloria made everyone equal. Karen always had a good time at Gloria's.

Venice was bored. Jay just slumped there, reading.

'Let's go over to Jill's now, then.'

The air was fresh and clean after the storm. Jay hummed a tune, clicked her fingers.

'I like Jill, she's all right,' she said.

Jealousy came to the aid of flagging romance. Did she fancy Jill? Did she – ?

They walked up the hill. Jay swaggered a little, hummed her tune:

> The poetry of love –
> The poetry of lo – huh – ove –

It all happens in the square mile between King's Cross and the British Museum. The main roads converge towards the railway terminal. Further north and east are the gentrified terraces with cleaned brick façades, but in the tenements round the station live prisoners' families and women in flight from violent men; squatters, refugees from mental hospitals. Fights and vandalism in the stony forecourts. Men batter babies, dogs savage children; pharoah ants infest a block, eat everything in their path; the young rob and rape old ladies.

Those old women – you see them in the supermarket, clutching the wire basket with its packet of tea, sliced bread, cheap sausages and catfood; they dig out the change from a shabby purse, keep everyone waiting while they squeeze out the last ½p. What must a boy feel to savage the wincing face, break the papery skin, bruise the stick-like arms and legs? Is it rage that stiffens his prick, a lust to shatter the whining, cringing weakness of the old, an act of revenge on a mother?

Young women loiter round the corners of the one-way traffic system at the back of the soot-stained cavern. The booming intercom, the shunting locomotives throb and echo as the girls hang in at the windows of the cars and bargain with the punters. In a sunny square further south toddlers play in the dust and women cluster along the railings. Now, in the late afternoon, they're waiting for men on their way home from work, who'll buy half an hour in a seedy hotel.

There was a death not long ago. Suffocation during bondage – he pulled her hood too tight. When he tried to burn her body the smell was indescribable, so he cut it up instead and buried the dismembered parts in the Hackney marshes.

Women have crowded into a dusty room. Rows of them face the speaker; more cluster in at the back, crouched on the parquet, leaning against the faded walls. The windows are opened on to the street, and the noise of traffic rises.

The hammer blows of a woman's voice ring out with confidence: 'Our sexual identity is created by men. Men construct us as sexual objects and our sexuality is defined as a response to men. Our bodies must conform to a stereotypic standard of perfection; woe betide the woman who deviates from the ideal 34–24–36. Daddy flirts with his little girl while Mummy tells her not to get dirty, not to be rough, to stay with Mummy indoors. This is how we learn to be feminine.

'In the fifties our sexual identity was still mixed up with virtue and with virginity. We were to develop our sexual attractiveness – yet we were to retain our purity as well. What kind of sexual identity is that! Purity as sexual identity – my *God*! That's some contradiction!

'Then came the permissive sixties – and we all know what they did for us. It was out with purity and virginity and in with compulsory sexual activity for women. The contradiction became a stranglehold.

'How could we cope with the incompatible demands being made on us? We were still to be passive – available, feminine, flirtatious – yet now we were to be active as well. We were chicks and dollies, as dehumanized as the inflatable rubber women of the sex shops. We thought we were liberated. We believed that liberation meant being fucked by a man and enjoying it. We learned to believe that the woman's rhythm is the same as the man's.

'For our sexual identity to be in order we had to conform to a standard measure of desire as well as to a standard measure of bodily perfection. Men set up the standard – your sex life was in order if you were doing it – say – three times a week. Three times a week was what it takes for you to be normal. And for a long time we believed what men told us.

'So what has happened in the liberated seventies? What has *feminism* to say about women's sexual identity? What awaits us as we cross the cusp of the eighties?

'Women have discovered that we have *no* sexual identity. It has been entirely constructed by men. Patriarchy defines

193

us. Patriarchal heterosexuality locates us at the wrong end of the male voyeuristic gaze. We have not yet even begun to carve out our own autonomy.

'What is happening now is the beginning of our resistance.

'Just a little anecdote about how women are beginning to question – simply to *question* – those male definitions of sexuality and sexual identity. I was in hospital recently, and – it's the custom, isn't it – the women in the ward started to talk about intimate things, things you feel safe to say to these other women you won't ever have to meet again. These are the secrets women share when they've been temporarily defined, so to speak, out of patriarchy. That's not to say that the average gynae. ward isn't every bit as patriarchal in its practices as everywhere else, only that when women are able to talk together, even within the limits of a patriarchal structure, they start to construct their own resistance.

'So what did these women say? They said things like:

'"I can't see what all the fuss is about myself."

'"I wouldn't be sorry if it never happened."

'"He seems to think I'm just there to be used if he wants to."

'"You'd think it was the bloody Eiffel Tower the fuss he makes about his."

'"More like the Leaning Tower of Pisa if you ask me."

'This set me thinking – these words from real women in the real world – and I began to ask myself: how do *we* – feminists – define sexuality? Quantitatively – male definitions, yes, but you have to start somewhere. And I think if men are saying that they regard three times a week as the norm, then women are saying something quite different.

'I've thought about it, and talked to women, and I think that frequency for a woman doesn't necessarily mean at all the same thing as it means for a man. Maybe once every six months is normal – or a lot – or *too much*.

'And qualitatively – men have identified the sexual act as *penetration* – all right, so now we can have compulsory foreplay moving from kissing to fondling the breasts to manual stimulation of the clitoris, but it's all leading up to the grand climax of penetration: *The Sexual Act!* That *is* "the sexual act": penetration.

'But I question whether penetration is where it's at for women. Penetration is not The Sexual Act for us.

'Now the feminism of the past ten years has only scratched the surface. It's true that individual women have found a space for renegotiation with individual men. Great! So now we don't sleep on the wet patch any more; *he* sleeps on the wet patch. But this process of individual negotiation still leaves women's sexual identity where it always was – nowhere.

'There's room for individual negotiation – he sleeps on the wet patch. But so long as we live under a patriarchal system the gains made from individual negotiation are limited. So he sleeps on the wet patch. That's the sole result of ten years' negotiation – *he sleeps on the wet patch*.

'But the question is not how individual women can wrest concessions from individual men by means of a debilitating and costly process of personal negotiation that drains our energy and concentrates it more than ever on an individual man.

'The question isn't: who sleeps on the wet patch? The question is: *How Can We Overthrow Patriarchy*?'

There's a moment's silence as she ends, then a rustle of approval and a low buzz of conversation. Eddie's rhetoric hasn't changed. Crystal looks round for friends, but there aren't many familiar faces. The women are strangers, they're young and their style is a new style. It's not a question of uniform exactly. All are highly decorated, although the decoration is trained on the extremities. Some wear earrings made of clusters of feathers or plastic fruit, or heavy metal and semi-precious stone; some wear boots hand-painted with flowers or landscapes or a multi-coloured sunburst; some have flashes in their hair – blue, green, magenta; some have fistfuls of rings; some blue or purple nail varnish. Some have short hair Eton-cropped like 1920s schoolboys; some still have long hair standing out in a mass of crimped waves;

some are full breasted in billowing harem robes; some are lanky and wear skin-tight jeans. The only point of unity is exaggeration.

The chairwoman calls the audience to order. Discussion begins. Or rather, women throw bald, anonymous comments into the silence. There's an atmosphere hard to define. The women do not look at one another.

'I can't understand why the speaker didn't even mention lesbianism – I find it hard to believe that after all this time there are women who have still only just discovered the tyranny of penetration and who still have nothing to say about lesbianism as a radical alternative. After all, it's lesbianism, isn't it, that marks the far parameter of patriarchy.'

'Yes – but I also feel you are making it very hard for any woman here to admit that she actually enjoys penetration. But actually I *do* enjoy penetration – '

A clear voice rises from the corner of the room, by the window: 'What you didn't say was that male sexuality is actually killing women. We are killed every day: by the birth control that is foisted on us, by the Pill, by the coil, by Depo-provera injections. And cancer statistics show us that sexual intercourse and penetration themselves kill us. Nuns don't get cervical cancer.'

'But there are class differences,' objects an older woman, 'and Jewish women – '

'No! No! I'm not talking about working-class men or circumcised penises. It has now been shown that it is sperm itself that causes cancer in women. *It is sperm that kills women.*'

'And we are not told!' screams her friend. 'We are told nothing.'

'But there are risks in everything – you run a higher risk of breast cancer if you don't have a baby – '

'Why are we talking about cancer? I thought this was a discussion about sexuality.'

'We're not talking about cancer. We're saying *sperm kills*!'

Crystal eases her way out. Steve calls to her from the terrace.

'As usual the women's meeting seems to be the most exciting.'

'You have to be *kidding*.'

He's sitting with Eileen, they sit at a white table on which stands a bottle of white wine. Crystal fetches a glass from the bar.

'It was *terrible*,' she says, 'not socialist at *all*. I mean Eddie always – you know, she exaggerated, but this was *so* over the top – Men are the Enemy with a vengeance.'

Eileen makes a face: 'Her trouble is she believes her own rhetoric.'

'I don't understand this Communist split,' says Steve, he's both curious and bored, loves the gossip of sectarian infighting, yet it's all tiring, debilitating even to hear about as well.

'We used to be good friends with Eddie,' says Crystal, wondering at the swiftness with which it all changed.

Eileen looks grim and changes the subject: 'These women all hate you Steve,' she says. 'Gay men, you're the worst of all, ripping off women, stealing our oppression.'

'I thought it was heterosexual men who hated women,' says Steve mildly, 'fucking as penile imperialism and all that.'

'Gay men are even worse because they won't.'

'I see,' he says, 'a no-win situation for men.'

Women drift onto the terrace from the workshop – they're talking about feminist erotica now, about desire, about fantasy –

More women crowd round their table. One of them talks about the Gaze. All contemporary images of women are organized, she asserts, around the Gaze, around the notion of looking, of voyeurism. As she talks the Gaze begins to take on a life of its own, like the Cheshire Cat's smile. Women are everywhere pinned down by the Gaze; it is omnipresent, like God.

'Anyone coming to the women's bop?'

Crystal walks with Eileen through the soft June evening to another dusty hall. The dust of Bloomsbury – would Virginia Woolf have liked these women? Would she have been a lesbian separatist? 'Women alone move me,' she said.

It's dark in the hall. Dust streams down the spotlights' rays. It's a cave of noise and shadows and the sour smell of beer and wine. Crystal leans against the wall and watches the band. She likes it here, but feels quite distanced from it.

Crystal, apart from the crowd of dancers, watches the all-women big-band band on the platform. They bend and sway like charmed snakes. Five singers lean intimately towards the mike as if whispering secrets; but they belt out 'Ain't Misbehavin'' in close harmony. The lead singer wears a long black dress and long white gloves, the others wear cocktail frocks; all have deep red lips and blacked-in eyes.

The trombone rises up with a sour wail; the five women click fingers, sway hips, purse lips. Feet stomp the floor. The music comes to a discordant, triumphant finish. Women clap and cheer.

'Better than the bloody Party,' says Eileen.

'I'm going to leave.'

But they don't even – for once – want to talk about it. It's all drowned in the music and the noise and the young women gyrating in the smoky hall.

They don't stay for long, either. Crystal has to prepare her paper for tomorrow; on women and psychoanalysis.

Faces look whiter, harder in the morning light. Crystal's paper is not too well received by this particular audience of women. It's the wrong constituency. A thundery silence thickens.

Then there's a film. It seems a pity to stay indoors on such a fine day, but Steve says they must, it's *Peeping Tom*, 'a classic study of voyeurism,' he says.

'You can come to this bit, they're allowing men in.'

It's an old print. Its flickering shadows hardly skim the surface of Crystal's mind, it seems remote, this story of a sick photographer, who impales his models on his tripod and photographs them as they die – the Gaze gone mad.

At the back of the hall the swing doors bounce to and fro. There's shuffling and whispering. Shadowy figures surge along the gangway: 'Take it off! Take it off! Women against pornography! This film shows violence against women! Take it off!' A rude awakening in the somnolent auditorium.

The lights go up. The film winds down. Young women climb onto the stage, defying the audience.

The women and men sitting in the chairs below the dais protest:

'Can't we all just be *people*?'

'I'm a woman and I want to see this film.'

'We're all oppressed by capitalism.'

But the women on the stage chant: 'Take it off! Take it off!'

'Men watch this film and then go home and rape their wives!'

'Men see porn and kill women.'

'Go on wankers with your wet crotches – get out of the hall!'

'But we don't want censorship do we?' comes plaintively from the rows of chairs.

'Tell the men to leave!'

'But the film's about a very *sick* man – can't you see – '

'Not mad: Male!'

The woman who organized the weekend goes up onto the stage and argues with them. She's a friend of Crystal, Crystal follows her up there, the women protestors surge about, but they're wavering and at last they stomp down and file out, still shouting, their clenched fists raised.

The lights are dimmed, the reel winds itself up and the crackling soundtrack and shadowy images return like a dream. At the end the men hurry sheepishly for the bar.

Crystal takes a bus to north London, to visit Philip. She brings wine. They sip restrainedly. Each time it must be negotiated anew.

'D'you want to stay,' he says. 'You can if you like.'

Often he says, we're *friends*, aren't we? It ought to be good that a man wants a woman as a friend, but he seems to want her body so little, while Crystal yearns only for his ivory neck, his ivory, strangely hairless body, wants only to plunge her hands in his black curls and gaze into his empty eyes, deeply recessed in their sockets, a hollow-faced saint, a Botticelli god. She doesn't care about friendship, but longs to kneel before him, longs to surrender to his will. But he has no will, he's indifferent. She longs for the Gaze to pin her down. But he's staring at himself in the pool of his thoughts.

The weekend seems to last forever. Now they are into the final session, a kind of revivalist meeting is going on.

One after another these women speak out. One tells how she used to watch blue movies with her husband. One tells how a friend was raped. One tells of the horror of violent films that masquerade as art.

'Lastly we want to talk about the part porn plays in causing and justifying male violence towards women. Porn is the theory: rape is the practice. Throughout the twentieth century the sex experts have been re-educating women to 'enjoy' sex. What they mean is enjoy the violation, humiliation and degradation of male sexual imperialism. Women are weakened by it, and men are made strong. Porn weakens us and strengthens them.

'But ordinary women know instinctively that porn destroys them – and what we have done is harness women's gut anger to fight back with acts of civil disobedience against the violence that is killing us. We don't argue for censorship. We argue for direct action.

'Women have actually succeeded in getting porn shops closed down in some parts of the country. There have been public campaigns in which local women have joined. Some sex shops have been damaged with paint or even fire bombs. Women have taken it into their own hands to fight this horror.

'Women are angry. We will no longer acquiesce in our own oppression. The anger of women has been aroused, and that makes us strong. Every march, every picket, every action rouses the anger of women and strikes a blow against male supremacy. That makes us strong. The Anger of Women!'

There is a storm of applause. In the interval they pass some soft porn magazines around, encouraging women to look, to react, to *realize* its full horror. Crystal flips through glossy coloured pages that seem to be all about naughty nighties, underwear and visible ejaculation in suburban lounges.

Two women near her: 'I don't see why one need fantasize at all. I can't see the necessity for it.'

'I *never* do. I just think about women's bodies.'

The chairwoman calls for discussion. Someone brave begins: 'It's difficult for me to speak – the experience of this afternoon for me has been rather like being an atheist at a revivalist meeting. I simply do not see the world in this way. I have felt unable to have an unequivocal feeling of sympathy because I feel that the way in which you have talked is so one-dimensional, and leaves so much out. I know we should understand the exploitative and vicious nature of some pornography and intervene politically. But you've left so much out, so much of our subjective experience.

'It can be very pleasurable to be passive sexually. And you don't take account of the pleasure some *men* may have in being passive and indeed in masochism. Men mostly go to prostitutes to engage in masochistic, not sadistic activities. Of course I know that it is the prostitute who is in danger of being killed when it does come to sadism and bondage enacted on her, while men, when they ask to be tied up or whipped, are still in control of the fantasy. Yet we ought nevertheless to explore the meaning of pleasure in passivity and even in submission and not simply dismiss it as false consciousness.'

'Yes – I agree with what the last speaker has just said, and I feel rather irritated and annoyed, actually, because I

201

feel I've been preached at. I don't know why this pornography has been produced and passed around. I feel we're just invited to have one reaction to it – shock horror – and that any other reaction would be unacceptable.'

'Yes – I'm sure many of us have had quite ambivalent reactions as we've looked at the porn – we may not like some of it, but on the other hand some of the images we may find quite a turn-on.'

'Are you saying it isn't violent? Have you looked at it? Are you saying it doesn't lead to violence? We know some murderers have read porn. We know that violence is daily legitimated by porn.'

'You say it's all so complicated. Well, I don't think it *is* that complicated. *Men are killing women*. That's quite simple, isn't it?'

'How dare you say that pictures and stories of women being raped and spanked and whipped and *enjoying* it isn't violence against women. Because that's what the stories are all about – about women *enjoying* it.'

An older woman speaks hesitantly: 'I'd like to talk about the place of fantasy in all this. Because it seems to me that simply to say it's used by men against women doesn't account for or explain our fantasies, whatever they are. It doesn't account for porn that's directed at gay men, either. Why, there's even lesbian sadomasochism. I don't see how that can all be explained as male violence.'

'Perhaps some women wouldn't need to get so worked up about porn if – '

Noisy sobbing breaks out. Women turn towards the one near the front who is wringing her hands and shaking her hair to and fro. She is gasping and choking out her words: 'I have never – *never* been so – offended in my life – women – are being *killed* and you – you say – we needn't get so *worked up* about – '

'All I was going to say if you'd let me finish – '

But there's another volley of shouting: 'There's nothing *to* say – all porn is violent – '

'I'm sick of academic wankers who try to turn violence

against women into some sort of intellectual debating point – '

'You're just like Mary Whitehouse – '

'How *dare* you say that – how dare you suggest – '

'You talk about male violence. But there's violence in this room now, now this minute.'

Exhausted, they loiter on the terrace, sit at the white tables, sip white wine again.

'The problem is at the end of the day men *are* violent,' says Eileen.

'Yes, but – '

There's an angry knot of women still arguing in the lavatories.

'It was you who spoilt the workshop.'

'Yes, you just shouted and stifled debate.'

'It's you academics who stifle debate by saying things in a way no one can understand.'

'But what's the point of just attacking other women?'

'*Us! We're* not attacking other women. We're unleashing women's anger – '

'Well, you certainly unleashed mine. I'm furious – you're undemocratic – '

'Do we have to talk about this in a toilet?'

Steve's waiting for Crystal and Eileen outside. They wander along the street, dejected, deflated.

The summer passes; winter comes on. Crystal meets Steve in the Reading Room of the British Museum. She's doing some work on Freud and anthropology. Steve tells her that the story went round that there was a knife fight that weekend in the summer; that women slashed the screen to prevent *Peeping Tom* from being shown. 'You're a heroine,' he says, 'threatened with a knife by screaming women.' Crystal laughs. It all seems a long time ago, a bit remote.

In the grey December afternoon, with the dusk already coming down like soot, Crystal walks home along the back streets of Bloomsbury south of King's Cross. The women still loiter in the square. There are more of them now, braced against the raw, gritty wind. They're so young, some of them aren't even sixteen. They're edging along the side streets right down towards the forecourt of the railway terminal itself, always closer to the bright lights and the traffic, prowling like the timid reindeer who circle down to frozen villages of the far north when there's no food on the steppes, when Siberia's covered with snow. The winter's biting now.

From the warmth of the bus Crystal sees them loitering round the back of the station as well, in the bleak one-way system with its orange lights. They wait on the corners, in ones, in twos, in threes. They call to one another across the street as they wait for the cars. You can see them there late at night, at one, at two in the morning, alone under the lamp, in a desert of railway wasteland – sidings, good yards, empty factories.

What do they talk about as they wait on the corners? Do they talk about the Gaze, about male violence, about the structure of their desires?

PART SIX: THE NINETEEN EIGHTIES

The airport was little more than a hangar in a field at the end of an empty road.

'You've come at the best time of year.'

The Professor led Eileen to his car. They drove through an ocean of boulders and scrub, dashed with blots of red. She'd expected the maple trees to flame, but they looked like Christmas decorations, or as if, enraged by its gloom, someone had flung red ink across the forbidding landscape. Before they even reached the town Eileen had a sense of it as small and lost, a settlement pinched between the cold Atlantic and the empty, grey sea of land that stretched away beneath the soft, grey sky.

Later Lorene from the Faculty women's group collected her from her hotel and drove her out into the countryside again. They came to a log cabin at the edge of a lake. The lake forked into the firs, an icy splinter of silver between the black spikes that crowded forward, mustered like a vegetable army against intrusion, their reflection painted on the glassy water. The silence and solitude pressed near to meet Eileen, to draw her away into the emptiness of the wilderness.

Madeleine owned the cabin and she was at the centre of this group of women gathered to welcome Eileen. They sat before a newly lit fire and drank wine. The others came and went; Madeleine stayed seated solidly in her armchair. Unlike the others, Madeleine smoked. Eileen felt she was being sized up.

She'd come as a lark, really, for the ride. They'd invited her to apply for the job – so why not?

And soon she was laughing and chatting to these boisterous, friendly women who dressed like Tory women but spoke of radicalism, threw themselves into the wildest ideas. Eileen threw herself in alongside; soon they were talking about demonstrations, meetings, campaigns, swopping tales of rebellion, women thumbing their noses at patriarchy. Eileen said nothing about being a Communist – here the

Party was wholly outside the parameters of normal radical life, better not to mention that secret identity.

Yet it acted as a slight brake on Eileen's high spirits.

They sat at a long table and ate lobsters. There was spinach salad with mushrooms and bacon. There was a platter of European cheeses. There were rich breads, flavoured with seeds. There were chocolate brownies and ice cream.

Afterwards they reassembled in a semicircle round the fire and drank crème de menthe and coffee. The exuberance and excess of the meal matched that of the women. But now, more serious, they turned to Eileen; this was the moment she had to show her paces. Madeleine watched her. Was she enough of a feminist for them, to teach on their women's studies programme?

Not fiery now – the Party had changed all that, wrought a subtle difference in perspective, presentation. More of a tactician, she'd lost her youthful madness.

Communist – a paranoid identity in a way, because it made others suspicious, hostile. And perhaps it was somehow a waste, Eileen thought, with sudden bitterness, now that the Party itself had fractured into contending factions, eating its heart out – Thankless it had all been.

So she talked about her teaching, then later she turned the conversation, asked them about the life out here. And it was interesting what they said, about this sparse dour land, interesting although in a way a familiar story. There were the same struggles, there was genocide, the persecution of minorities, the red-baiting, and always the victors were embattled and paranoid as they clutched at their spoils.

Madeleine enlarged on the conflicts in the Faculty – this group of women against the men – with a kind of fanaticism that was all too familiar. Eileen sensed also that Madeleine was 'difficult', one of those Cassandras, always in the right but never heeded, isolated, never on the winning side because some missed sense of proportion, some failure to charm, some bitterness from within drove her colleagues away. Eileen could see she herself had been cast as ally, big

208

new guns wheeled in in this battle for careers, status, recognition for women, but she hated all that. She couldn't care less about women professors. In that at least she hadn't changed.

She walked into campus. The sun shone on autumn leaves. 'You're seeing it at its best.' She passed through quiet streets with clapboard houses set in reassuring whiteness against the blue sky, the green lawns. At the next crossroads the campus rose – old-world grey stone and creepers.

She worked hard. Lectured – gave classes – met the Faculty. One by one they sought her out to show her their wares, diffident and defensive, assuming that the world she came from was politically and intellectually richer, more sophisticated, more advanced than theirs. She on the contrary felt that these men and women lived out their ideas with a sincerity and also a tolerance she and her friends had missed, with on the one hand the feverishness of their intellectual fashions, on the other the sectarianism of their political world.

Could she live here, with these courteous, friendly, serious women and men? Were their values hers? Theirs were the values of radical individualism, the values of the struggle against the Vietnam war and the student movement in the sixties, the values that, earlier, the McCarthy years had tried to batter down, and, going back earlier still, the values of anti-slavery and suffrage, ideals of equality and freedom. These values, though, had been changed by their translation to this rooted settlement which, so far from home, preserved the values of the past in a more certain, less changed form. She felt closer here to the radicals of nineteenth-century Manchester or Bradford than to the twentieth-century rebels of London or New York.

Where she came from, women could cry freedom, change partners, switch lifestyles, swop careers – and nothing had changed. The seething city swept it all away and carried on as before. Here, you risked losing a husband where no others were to be had, risked slipping out of your stable slot in a society in which each life was a visible knot in the social network, risked losing your job. Here it was really for real. Yet there was tolerance and good humour. They were gracious in the true sense of the word, with none of the snideness and brittle chic that could disfigure the world of left-wing radicals at home, in London. There was generosity too – in such a small community you couldn't always be knifing sisters and comrades in the back. You had to survive.

She sipped Manhattans with the Professor and his wife, a painter, and knew they would do things the right way, not because for them it was a matter of observing forms, but because they respected the spirit of it all. Seated at their dinner table she smiled across the bristling acres of linen and cut glass, and the Professor's wife described the difficulties they'd had at first. They'd come from Toronto – at first it had been strange – but now they liked the friendliness, the sense of community – they understood her hesitation, of course, they knew how difficult it was to make such a big move. But they hoped –

Did they understand, though, Eileen wondered. (Can't you see I'm a Communist, an enemy within?) She felt giddy as she floated in the free fall of leaving everything behind. A new life – well of course, it was an exciting idea.

Yet here the sparkling ideas, the theories that had once intoxicated, their bubbles pricking her mouth, would become the tap water of everyday life. No longer the heady, hedonistic joyride on the big dipper of ideas. Here those ideas had become workmanlike tools with which to forge an honourable house of life, tapping away to produce slow change. Here they would be for real, but the reality would dim their excitement. For Eileen the initial pull of those ideas had been that they'd made the world strange – she'd seen it through different lenses, the world turned upside down. Then in the Party they were for real too, of course, but the main buzz was the fight, the tactics – get the ball, dribble it down, run, a kick, a try – Here the solemnity of everyday life would shape those ideas into new and plodding forms, political pudding instead of political football, nourishing but dull. Equality became a sane and sober ideal, no longer a firebrand of revolution. The new life would be a trip into the past, for this was an old world, not the new.

Across the dinner table the other guest, head of a local women's college, described her fight for funds. She told them how she'd trudged the offices of big oil companies, vast corporations, had waited in ante-rooms lined with Impressionist paintings no one ever looked at, bought because they were good investments. It enraged her to stare at a Monet water lily garden melting like fondant into the canvas while she prepared her begging speech.

'Just *one* of those paintings would fund us twice over! Men! It's all male greed!'

Eileen tried politely to dissent. (It's not just men, it's class society too.) But the bony older woman flashed her a hurt look, a look of betrayal.

'You've worked so hard, Marion,' said the Professor's wife.

Eileen walked back to her hotel after midnight, feeling no fear in the empty streets. Yet somewhere there must be a poor part of town. Or perhaps the poverty was out in the countryside, in the mining villages, in the fishing communities that were scattered through the islands, or among the settlements of Indians towards the north.

She walked onto campus each morning, abstracted, thinking: can I? Can I? She was on the brink, toying with the idea of flinging herself into this void forever. If it hadn't been for the Party, the politics . . . The emptiness of the hinterland and the enormous half continent excited her. She liked the idea of it waiting in the silence of its huge spaces, flat under a flat sky.

And there was Lennie. Lennie was a frail woman, came up to Eileen after one of her talks and said straight out she was a Communist.

Lennie gave her weak coffee and carrot cake, and there was a smell of cinnamon in her crowded living room as she talked about her years in the Party. Yes, she'd done a lot of work on women's issues –

'You know how I joined the Communist Party? I was doing a summer job in a factory, before the war this was, and I thought, well I *knew* I could do the work quicker, and I thought that was the right thing to do, to work as fast as you could. So soon I was turning out twice as many skirts as everyone else. And then one day one of the workers came up to me and said, "Hey, you're busting the rate, Lennie." Well, and he sat down, and he explained to me about the rate and how if one worker went too fast the bosses would try to make you all do more work for the same money, speed up the rate, and how it was rough on the slower ones anyway – and then, what exploitation was, and how you couldn't talk about a fair day's work for a fair day's pay – and gradually it went on from there – '

In the fifties there'd been MacCarthyism . . . She and her little boy, they'd been stoned. Broke her son's arm –

Now Lennie was working with a women's writing group. That was so important, getting women to speak, to express themselves, to find a voice. . . .

Fragments of a life. In this bleak outpost of the Western world Lennie was vivid, full of life, full of hope. It didn't really matter, not being at the centre of things, wherever you were what counted was how you did it.

It was through Lennie that Eileen was invited, on her last evening but one, to meet a group of women peace campaigners. The white drawing room was all deepness, deep carpet, deep sofas, deep bow windows with deep white curtains. The hostess poured coffee in front of the fire.

Mrs Vermont Newsom belonged to an older generation. She'd campaigned right through the fifties, had an international reputation, had worked with peace groups all over the world, was regarded as a figure to be reckoned with by governmental circles here at home.

She and the other women were discussing a forthcoming peace march to present a petition to heads of governments due to assemble in the capital later in the month. While they sorted out organizational details they discussed the larger issues, engaging Eileen in their conversation.

Didn't she know that Reagan had plans for Europe? You British, you Europeans don't seem to realize – the Pentagon's preparing for a theatre war in Europe, a nuclear war. Europe was expendable, the United States had it all worked out.

Eileen could see that even these peace campaigners believed that they themselves might well survive a holocaust.

'It seems to be coming so close again,' she said, 'war. For a few years it seemed to recede – '

'It never really recedes,' said Mrs Vermont Newsom. 'The hands of the clock move forwards and sometimes they stand still – but they never move back.'

A woman of Eileen's age said suddenly, passionately, 'Women don't *do* these things. It's because we have children – we don't *want* war – and somehow we *have* to get these women's values across. It's so *terrible*, this male aggression.'

Eileen said nothing. (It's not just men, it's class society too.) But she was thinking of her visit to Hungary as CP delegate to a conference on women. Peace had come up, the same things had been said, with the difference that *there* those values were called socialist . . . Hungary, if anywhere, should understand that basic human longing for peace, its history seemed to have been a blood bath for hundreds of years.

There too they'd spoken of motherhood – it's values, how much it was to be prized, its role in the making of socialism, the safe-guarding of peace –

But what she remembered most clearly of all was their visit to the thermal baths. These were housed in an enormous Edwardian palace, replete with tessellated pavements, marble caryatids and Alma Tadema-type frescoes. They'd paid about 5p to get in, and in the dressing rooms two huge women in aprons had ordered them to undress; they'd trotted giggling, naked, to the communal women's pool and down its magnificent turquoise mosaic steps into the hot spa water. Half a dozen or so women of varying ages and shapes were standing or sitting in the water. It really was like some Edwardian rendering of a classical scene.

And naked, lolling in the healing waters in a corner of old Budapest, the idea of East and West, of power blocs, of Soviet and American 'ways of life' had seemed absurd and meaningless – or even more so than usual. There'd just been these women, soothed in the warmth of the mineralized water that gushed up from its source deep beneath this secular monument to the Austro-Hungarian empire.

You had a sense then of some other way of being.

On her last evening they left her to her own devices. They had all gone away for the weekend, the week's friendliness had ebbed away, the social network had let her slip through its mesh, and she had to make her decision about the future. She walked down to the harbour and round the shopping precinct – you could get from one side of town to the other in fifteen minutes – and felt lonely as she returned to the hotel.

Her thinking took a new turn. She imagined herself living in the town: the new life. A war has broken out in Europe. Everything she has known is destroyed: her family, her friends, the Party, her whole past.

She imagined London gone, Paris, Amsterdam, all burning. The places she loved, the lovers, the comrades, the struggles and passions, all have been buried beneath a pile of radioactive ash.

She imagined herself seated by the wireless, stunned, alone, isolated in her grief and her guilt for having survived, for having been the rat that left the sinking ship. She imagined herself silent as her new companions try tc comfort her. And she imagined that then the veil of radiation, driven by the winds, billowed across the Atlantic and slowly swelled above this new life of hers.

Would she with her new friends, who now more than ever would seem like strangers, would she set off with them on the flight across the stony countryside, towards the lakes, towards the plains, towards the ice-locked northwest territories? Would they trudge towards the north, find refuge in the forests and ice floes, some dying by the wayside, some surviving, a new generation of pioneers? In a new wilderness?

Perhaps, as in some of the old pioneer communities, there would be free love, communism, equality for women. Perhaps desolation and the fight for survival would drive them into authoritarianism. Would they move further west over the grain prairies and make for the Rocky mountains? Or would they live among the Indians, catch fish, kill bears?

How strange a twist it would be to end her life in Hudson Bay, or as a frontierswoman in some new wilderness, some new wild zone.

The alarm call woke her early for her plane. Once she was strapped inside the jumbo jet, floating through the upper air, she was nowhere, in transit, suspended between worlds. She was inside her chrysalis, Jonah inside his whale, trapped in some waiting room of life. Out of this ante-chamber she would come back into the real world, shake out her wings, and the dreams and nightmares of the New World, the other life, would melt away.

Only they cast their shadow forward, making her everyday, familiar world strange with their projection of that other, future reality. Loyally, she'd turned her back on it. Yet the shadow fell before her as she stepped from the plane.

Even at the height of the fashion Andrew had never worn his hair in the long greasy ringlets or dusty clumps that some of his friends had gone in for. He said he was a situationist and never dressed to prefigure an alternative society, but rather to caricature this one. So he wore wonderfully tailored suits of grouse moor tweed or crumpled linen, and his blond hair was brilliantined back from his widow's peak. Long, dark eyelashes shadowed his violet eyes with a smudge of melancholy. His style placed him halfway between the glamorous end of the underworld and a Vogue photographer. He transformed seedy academia into romance. In his own way, of course, he was an Entertainer, though when he spoke of 'doing a gig' he didn't mean music, just a guest lecture. On telly he talked about crime.

He defended criminals on the basis that crime was a rational activity 'in our society'. 'In our society' suggested the possibility of others, although he seldom mentioned socialism. He too much enjoyed the *film noir* world of the present, where the real crimes were the crimes of the rich and powerful, and the 'crim' (short for criminal) was a kind of latter-day Robin Hood, a Byron of the people, a dandy of danger, dicing with death; the working-class hero.

Which he was himself, in a way. He too had scrambled out of the mean streets. Grammar-school boy or borstal boy – either set you apart from the rest. The escape route from the sour air of the lounge was mapped out. Without a wrench of guilt he left behind parents whose hatchet-faced grimness came from false teeth and 'failed anger' rather than the puritan work ethic.

Years later they'd grown accustomed to his face on the TV set, and no longer boasted, bored by now with this stranger. Retired, they'd rather talk about their holiday in Portugal. He meanwhile spoke of his parents with unfailing warmth – a genuine working-class background was such an asset in the 1970s. At the same time he capitalized on the genetic accident that gave him an aura of public school and country house. It enabled him to slip in and out of roles – a whole range of identities that satisfied his need for secrecy, change of scene, escape.

It was part of his every persona, though, to be a fixer. One time, for example, he drove with a crowd from his department to some criminology conference in the Midlands. On the way they stopped off at a motorway caff, and Andrew, who was always hungry, led his party round the self service, piling their trays with more than they wanted, and then somehow ushered them away without passing the cashier. They settled in a far corner which overlooked the road. Below them vehicles glided, unreal and silent beyond the double glazing. Some members of the party were bewildered, not sure how they had managed not to pay, imagining perhaps that Andrew had treated them.

It was the same when they got to the conference. Andrew fixed them all up without having to pay. They found themselves packed four in a room, wedged down on the floor and even sharing sleeping bags. But at least it was free. Andrew, mind you, had a room to himself.

In those days the men thought it was cool to pull a chick at a conference. Andrew, aloof at the bar, made it seem vulgar. He played pool with someone from off campus. But on the Sunday, just as some of his mates were backtracking in the cold light of day after a sweaty night in a bed designed for one, not two, Andrew sauntered onto the steps in search of a lift, and immediately a woman six feet tall with a lion's mane of curls and a Lamborghini roared him away.

It was the era of the radicals. Andrew was a star. Moving in circles dedicated to the revolution of everyday life, the politicization of the personal, and the building of an alternative utopia, Andrew brought to this mighty task an enthusiasm for the pleasures of the bourgeois world he denounced, while prophesying imminent catastrophe.

'We are the froth on the daydream – seize the time!'

Riding the breakers of the decay of capitalism as they thundered towards the shore, he and his generation would wrest from the explosion as they crashed down the seeds of a new world. Rewriting Marx he ranged himself and the lumpen intelligentsia of higher education and alternative journalism alongside the very groups Marx had rejected – the prostitutes, the gangsters, the fixers, the victims whose heads were filled with thoughts of revenge. Together they would forge an army strong enough to defeat the forces of reaction, the trade union official, the petty bureaucrat, the men in power.

He denounced the consumer society, society of the spectacle, yet aimed in this society to be the most exciting spectacle of all: the revolutionary. He called himself the war correspondent of the ideological front line. He reported, he snapped, he recorded – and melted away as the forces of repression bore down. The Scarlet Pimpernel of the student unions and Prisoners' Aid (the organization he'd masterminded), he advocated silence, secrecy and cunning when he addressed the campuses of the provinces, or charmed his invisible audience from the television screen.

The book which had made his name was a series of interviews with convicted terrorists, mostly IRA, an example of the New Journalism. His friend Hugo wrote a similar, but more academic book, about murderers, lifers.

Those hard men, really, were their heroes. The lifers had realized that the world is a prison, they had ridden the breakers and seized the time. And now: in their top-security prisons they studied for degrees, painted, wrote, did press-ups, isometrics, yoga. It was an ascetic, dedicated preparation, a régime as disciplined as that of a novice monk or infant prodigy – as if they would come out fashioned, tempered into the stuff of which a revolution might be made: perfect bodies, steel minds – a world of purity.

But for what? They were there for good – virtually. They were in the room from which the only exit was death.

A world of purity – Andrew's north London flat looked out on a long, narrow, winding hill lined with junk shops. Every day he passed boxes of cracked saucers at 5p each, second-hand gas stoves with burnt-on grease, racks of musty clothes, bulging three-piece suites and disintegrating paper-backs in neglected rows – best-sellers from twenty years ago, now forgotten. One day he saw a copy of his own book in one of the trays. The lifers had banished bricolage from their régime, Andrew's life seemed like nothing but bricolage, a junk shop full of bits and pieces that didn't fit together.

There were the carelessly pursued encounters in all those different beds, the shoplifting adventures that had only once nearly gone fatally wrong; there were the words spinning off into theories, and the drinks spinning off into hangovers – One of the prisoners he'd most liked murdered a guard. A friend died in a plane crash. An ex-girlfriend committed suicide. Cancer and nuclear bombs threatened the body, senility the mind. He hated even to pass the gates of the hospice in the main road and, if forced to do so, crossed to the opposite side of the street, crossed his fingers too, a childish talisman against bad luck. And although he knew it was irrational to worry about both a plane crash *and* a horrible lingering illness, at best such fears acted as counter-irritants.

Somewhere along the way he fathered a child. She became his new, most secret romance. He wept sometimes when he thought of the angelic toddler, swept along by her mother in a different direction from his.

Politics ceased to be the froth on the daydream. The meetings he went to were no longer vivid street encounters or marches on the seats of state repression. Now it was the crossing of swords with the Dean at Faculty Board, while the caucus of the Revolutionary Party had somehow trans-mogrified itself into the constituency Labour Party GMC. Whatever his championship of the underdogs had done for them, it had propelled him along a familiar route. How he'd derided the previous generation for their sell-outs, those yesterday's reds in their comfortable berths on Boards and in Faculties, in business or the BBC, or alternatively their faded lives in some dusty corner of the Communist Party. But he did not see himself in that light at all. It was simply that the time had come to embrace reality. He was the Young Turk become mature, no longer a hothead romantic. Poltics *is* after all the art of the possible, even if it was a Tory who'd said it.

Andrew had a woman in the new style, a post-feminist who made him a drink when he came home and didn't nag him about petty domestic details. Once he'd had girlfriends who'd dragged their long skirts in the dust of demonstrations and vituperated their consciousness-raised insights from behind a cloud of pre-Raphaelite hair. The new New Woman mixed a mean dry Martini, but wore a punk outfit, had her own work but talked about his, was independent but didn't push it. After all, equality too is a matter of style, it depends how you approach things. A live-in lover wasn't such a bad idea after all, despite his fear of being tied: it gave you, he admitted, more space than all those your-place-or-mine relationships, when you ended up living out of a briefcase on the Northern Line.

Perhaps this new stability would allay the nightmares. For he'd never slept well. Yet still he found himself telling lies. He writhed smartly out of tricky corners at work and managed to keep in with the administration by going missing when there was a contentious union vote, broke appointments with students but never with management, had no time to write another book but always went on TV, slipped somehow into evasive dates with women who were never mentioned at home.

Fortunately he never felt tempted to shoplift these days. A handful of credit cards achieved effectively the same ends with considerably less risk.

So – nothing had changed, not really. He was still a political person. He could still pull an audience or a chick.

And yet . . . was it that the women were too young? There was a kind of boredom, a sense of *déja vu*. The girls seemed never quite to live up to the promise of seduction, the meals were never quite worth the money – particularly as, with increasing salary, he discovered he was rather mean

– at least towards others, if not towards himself. His post-punk woman laughed about it: 'Do you *believe* Andrew – both spendthrift *and* mean!'

She was so good-humoured about everything that it was rather a shock when she left him. No big deal – she simply got a job in Paris, out of the blue. He'd always thought of the stuff she did for magazines as a hobby, dilettante stuff. There was another child by now, a boy this time. He disappeared too, along with the Clairol canisters and the boiler suits.

'Paris! You can't take him to Paris! What about his education!'

He fought a rather squalid custody battle, and lost. Some of the feminists in his department refused to speak to him.

His nightmares got worse. He'd never been able to sleep alone. A succession of women came to ward off bad dreams.

'Why don't you see a therapist?' one of them said.

The idea was laughable of course. It was society that was sick, not the individual. Of course, individuals get *smashed* by the system. Internalized oppression. The women's movement had taught us all *so much* about that. Feelings – men have real problems *expressing* their *feelings*.

They'd all thought that everything could be changed from without. What they hadn't understood was the depths of the unconscious, the grip of the great fear. Now – look around – it was everywhere. Thatcherism – the Id calling – the Return of the Repressed. It was much harder than they'd ever dreamed to change. They'd all thought revolution was a change of socks.

The therapist was a woman; long curly hair, long fashionable skirts, little boots, discreet make-up. She was so sympathetic. He had no trouble talking – on the contrary. The only rule – to free associate, to say whatever came into his head – unleashed a saga of incidents and jokes, a flood of entertaining charm they could neither of them stem. The only trouble was that he lied even when he was free associating, and as the weeks passed he found himself caught in a tangle of deceit. He simply could not bring himself to admit that some of the more lurid anecdotes were invented, or had happened to someone else, or were, at the very least, well – embellished. For one thing she'd be so disappointed, when she'd responded with such subtle interpretations. She'd brought order to a chaos that did not actually exist.

Yet – did it really matter? Fantasy, after all, also tells the truth about the Unconscious. Did it matter that his mother was still alive, when so many of her interpretations had hinged upon the fact that he'd been orphaned at the age of two? Did it matter that it was not his step-aunt who'd seduced him? He must have unconsciously wanted his mother to die, or he wouldn't have thought of saying it, would he? And what if he'd lied about his degree? The lie had appeared so often in his cv that by now it had achieved a kind of truth, and anyway many of his contemporaries who *had* got Firsts now languished in obscurity. It was the thought that counted, in therapy above all.

Sometimes he panicked, wondered if she knew. Suppose she saw right into him, suppose she really *knew*.

He played the familiar card of seduction. Tried, as usual, to charm his way out of a corner. When he got nowhere, he turned against her, resented her because she hadn't fallen for it. Therapy had been a stupid idea in the first place, anyway. All this verbiage – talk, talk, talk, that had been the trouble all his life, the gift of the gab – that was his job, after all, talking, presenting a persuasive argument, how could a so-called cure that was all talk change *him*?

He missed a few appointments, neglected to pay bills. In the end she terminated the treatment, which merely reinforced his cynicism. At the end of the day they cared about the money. That was their bottom line.

But he sometimes remembered, though he tried to forget, those times, early on, when his flood of words dried up and the consulting room went silent and very tense. Those moments he'd been terrified, stammered out anything to end it. And once, she'd said, 'You know, sometimes I feel these silences are the only time you are being at all truthful.'

But in any case he'd moved on. Landed a high-powered advisory job at the Home Office – solutions to the crisis in the prisons, privatization maybe. He was interviewed for a Sunday colour supplement. 'We can't just *ignore* law and order,' he said. 'It's always been the *property* of the Right. The Left has to *own* the problem – it's *our* kids that get nicked, sure, but they're mugging *our* old ladies.'

He didn't need an analyst any more. For, by the way, he'd married one. Marriage, of course, was part of the new eighties realism, a rather cynical adoption, almost in parody, of conventional forms – post-modernist marriage, if you like. For which he didn't need a younger woman, glamorous and nubile, but an older one, professional, perceptive, intelligent – he wouldn't have used the word motherly. But a woman who could be part of the performance –

And, as she said, he can be awfully kind, you know. I think he must have changed . . . I know he does silly things sometimes, but he's a sweet guy really.

The weather turns nasty while the builders are in. Sleet
batters the windows and the wind whips round Crystal as
she dashes out to the dustbins.

Today the electrician's due. Crystal tries to get dressed,
looking for the nail scissors. Like the cats and everything
else, they've no settled place to be. Life in slow motion –
every normal activity takes three times as long. When she
goes to wash there's the awkwardness of the door with no
lock, and it doesn't even shut properly, she sits uneasily on
the bowl, ready to spring up in case Micky the builder
comes storming in; he's removed the towels, she has to look
for them, the talcum powder's in the bedroom, miles away,
but her clothes in a heap under the basement stairs. Even to
get dressed involves three trips up and down three flights.
The mirror's propped against a box in what will be the
kitchen but which is now a kind of garage, icy cold, with
bags of cement spilling out over the concrete floor. And in a
solid mass it will be impossible ever to unclench, are all
their worldly goods – the removal men have created a giant
Chinese puzzle that fills the room.

Must have some more coffee. She switches on the
machine. It starts to bubble and burp; this remnant, at least,
remains of civilization. But there's no newspaper delivery.
No table or chairs, nowhere to sit. She paces up and down
with her coffee cup. The cats scurry for the flap, spitting
reproachful looks at her as they slink by.

Now the trek out for the shopping. Her umbrella's disappeared. She wraps her old fur coat round her and pulls on a
woollen hat to face the wind. At least the hail has melted
down to a drizzle. Her body bent in the wind, her collar
clutched round her face, she soon creates a warm wet zone
between her mouth and the outside world.

She trudges from shop to shop. The bags grow heavier.
There are the tiles, there are picture hooks (but she forgets
the wire), there's paint, light bulbs and, of course, food.
And she'll have to go straight out again.

Back at the house Micky arrives. He climbs into his work clothes, a pair of dungarees in which he looks like a giant contented baby. And of course, she's forgotten his money. She leaves the house again, out into the cruel wind.

In the bank a cloud of smoke rises above the restive queue. Someone is having a row with the manager: a student. The queue moves forward at a snail's pace, it's paying-in day, and then they'll take forever to phone through to her branch.

'We'll have to clear the amount.'

'I know – but can you be quick?'

'We'll do our best madam – if you'd like to take a seat.'

'There aren't any.'

She leans against a shelf and waits. The student is upping the aggro, shouting for his overdraft to be restored. His shabby coat clings round his ankles: 'My dad's allowance will come through any moment.'

An anxious Asian woman slips bag after bag of coins into a basket, looking round to see if she's going to be mugged before she's even got out of the bank. An ancient pensioner quavers on about his balance. The young man behind the counter beckons her at last. He counts out the large green notes. There are a lot of them – surely too many. But she grabs the bundle and thrusts it down her trouser pocket. She hurries along the street, pushes her way through the dawdling throng of pensioners, unemployed punks and single mothers festooned with children, trips over the dragging baskets and lopsided buggies, hating the human race, fearing the X-ray eyes of the thief, holding onto her bundle, secret, deep down in her pocket. If only people would move quicker, walk briskly, buck up their ideas. Instead they trudge, they dawdle, dither and hesitate, unable to make up their minds or embark on a trajectory through life. Idiots, idiots. She ploughs through them, bruising shins, knocking arms and shoulders, ricochets through the throng. There's a huge queue outside the post office – surely not a giro day, must be the Christmas rush –

'The money, Mick,' she calls out with false cheer.

Better count it. As she half knew there's far too much. The clerk has given her twice what she asked for, there must have been a mistake, and the fifty-pound notes slip and flutter all round her on the floor. Where have they come from? How could they give you so much over the counter, just like that? It's so easy, appears from nowhere, bits of paper, with no weight or value, lying on the ground like faded leaves. The notes themselves, even, look unfamiliar, foreign, wide, pale notes that might be, for all she knows, pesetas, roubles, lire, anything.

'There's too much.'

Micky laughs: 'You'll never find they'll give you too much – I doubt that.'

'They have really – look.'

Micky giggles. Is it a windfall? Could the bank have made an error of a thousand pounds? The unspoken question between them: will she take it back?

Micky tells her about the farmers in Ireland. They carried large sums of money about on occasion, buying and selling cattle. Once he'd found a great wad of money on the ground. Instead of taking it to the police, and getting five pence in the pound reward, he'd taken it back to a local shop, knowing that the farmer, whoever it was, would be making enquiries. Might get more of a handsome reward like that, you see.

'But you know what he gave me for my trouble?' Micky laughs. 'A florin. 10p.'

They stare at the money. Crystal gathers it up.

'A florin. That's all he gave me.'

She hands him his money, folds the rest away. It's spend, spend, spend. She swings onto a bus, it stops and starts down the shabby, congested high streets and then sweeps more rapidly on into the West End.

She pays for everything with plastic cards. The parcels bump against her legs, drag her arms into orang-utan limbs, stretched out unnaturally from their sockets. Families and above all couples clot the furniture shop. The place gives her claustrophobia as her domestic obsessions mingle with theirs and the display rooms are electric with tension, bored children whimper, partners nag and bicker – anxieties about measurements exact, colours just matching, styles to fit the lives they lead, as if the life can't start until they have the setting, always becoming, never quite achieved.

Will Micky do the floor just right? Can we afford new curtains? I'm left to do it all myself – all right for Andrew, his work takes him to Europe, an absentee husband –

Worse with him here, though – he spends it like water –

Blasts of central heating are making her sweat. The hot flush of shopping mania threatens to get out of control. Christmas is coming, the glut's on. Outside it's snowing again now, but the snow like frozen grit on her face comes as a momentary cool relief.

It's still snowing when she returns to the grimy streets with their pockets of smartness, old sweet shops jostling with new boutiques.

'I'm sorry to say, Crystal, that I broke your coffee jug. The machine was burning hot, d'you see, when I went to lift it up, I wasn't expecting it, it just dropped from my hand.'

'Oh.' Now she'll have to get a new one – at the special shop, it's miles away. She pouts. 'That really is a drag.'

Now for a sortie to a more distant shopping mecca; this is Chelsea on a Saturday afternoon. She's been looking forward to the trip, but now she just feels tired, irritable, depressed. An ageing hippie in a moth-eaten fur coat, she grouches along through the chic crowds. Not even an elderly hippie, with her straggling hair and thrift clothes, more like an eccentric old lady, that's the image that blinks back from the boutique windows, a mangey creature, a leftover from a different Chelsea, fifteen years ago.

Her mother sits near the door, another fur-coated old woman.

'Oh *there* you are!' She looks so small, thinner.

'Am I late? I'm sorry – are you all right?'

'All these people – they frightened me – they look so odd – ugly I call it. Dyed hair and such queer clothes.'

227

'Well, I'm here now.'

But she's not, not really.

'Let's choose your present.'

But the fun of spending has gone. She is weary, weary of it all. She flings things into a basket. Her mother stutters along behind, eyelids drooping. She shrinks into her shell like an old tortoise.

'The rates are going up again, you know – '

Don't make me feel guilty. I mustn't spend too much. But it all comes to more than expected.

'Shall we have a cup of coffee?'

But the café upstairs is crowded with Chelsea clones, a long queue stretches far beyond the tea room, not a woman in sight. It's all gay men.

'Oh, let's go somewhere else, Ma.'

'But I like it here.'

'Look – we'll have to queue for hours.'

It's too depressing, to be stuck among the smart gays with your old mother. So they go to a new place, further along the road.

The ambience is fake American. Everyone dresses in the latest style, trilby hats, greased hair, angular, metallic clothes – although already the smart new styles are tired old clichés, as boring as Crystal's fur. But her mother looks round and preens as the pianist starts to play a Noël Coward tune.

'It's rather good fun this place, isn't it? And they don't mind your just having a coffee here.'

'I expect they charge for the privilege.'

Her mother sinks back – tired? – on the velvet banquette. Lights a cigarette with a gesture from the thirties, holds it raised, cocked sideways, sophisticated.

There's so much money around. These young men and women in their twenties, they're loaded, and knocking back cocktails and smoked salmon at half past three in the afternoon, scrambled eggs, coq au vin, bacon sandwiches, chocolate éclairs, croissants, kiwi fruit salad; smoking and drinking like crazy. Crystal asks for freshly squeezed orange juice and a Perrier.

'I'd like one of those Cappu-thing-a-me-jigs, you know,' says her mother.

'A white coffee?' The old-Etonian waiter flings his black forelock back with a sneer.

Here men and women dress alike, as men and men dressed alike in the other café. The boyish must be the pinnacle of everyone's desire.

She wants to escape into this world, a world she's forgotten, sunk as she is in the sliding morass of matter that is moving house, a quicksand of material objects out of place, a life of their own. Once she roamed the King's Road. There were parties. She wore her mother's long ivory beads. 'Mummy's beads!' a strange woman had jeered. Yet despite the spiky words she fingered the beads, slipped an arm round Crystal's shoulder, perhaps it had been a stifled pass. Her mother must have worried – with Crystal out till all hours, up to no good, no husband in sight, at drunken parties, not working for her degree –

Now they sit together in fur coats, apart from hedonistic youth. But aren't these young women and men boringly respectable beneath the façade – headed for the Surrey hinterland?

Her mother reddens when she sees the bill: 'That's nearly three pounds. A cheek I call it.'

'Oh Ma – *I'll* pay.'

'No – I said I'd take you.' Her mother snatches the bill, and holds it away from her in a parody of childish play.

She has so many garments to get on and round her, so many oddments to gather up, as soon as one is in place another falls to the ground. Down the steps in the raw grey air she still chunters on: 'It's all the fault of the rates – these places charge such a lot – it's that man Ken Livingstone – he's responsible for all this – the GLC – he's *doubled* our rates, you know – '

'Oh don't be *ridiculous* – this is Chelsea – – it's got nothing to do with Livingstone. You spend too much time with those silly old Tory friends of yours, those Tory ladies don't know what they're talking about – '

'Oh, don't be so cross with me – now you've spoilt it all – '

Well, they've been spoiling for a fight. Her mother only says these things to needle her, it's stupid to rise to the bait. A few tears roll down her mother's cheeks. You're horrible, you've hurt her, and she's old. So rough with her always, never kind – all your kindness saved for your patients, endless patience, endless attention, listening as you never listen to her. Crystal presses her lips together, hunches along in silence, twisted with remorse she can't express.

They part, grudgingly, at the Underground. In the tube are tired faces, more bulging parcels, swollen feet, an air of satiation. Spending money drains you, you're emptied, spent, evacuated. Her dreams have turned to these stones that weigh her down.

In Camden Town there are those who have no money to spend. They don't hurry like the Chelsea crowds, they shuffle past the window displays with heads down, or swig cider and British port on the corner. Money makes you hurry, hurry, always pressing on, avid for the next thing, it's always the next thing that'll solve it all, life's problems; penury's like age, slows you down.

Back at the house they're still at it, Micky and Pete, his mate the electrician, he's there now too, they've taken up the floorboards to expose the sinews of the house, and Pete lies flat, his arm plunged in the entrails, reaching for the nerve centre, the ganglion.

'We're nearly done now, Crystal, we shouldn't be much longer now, and that'll be the electrics finished completely.'

They wrestle with the cable, it's like some legend from antiquity, Laocoon and the Serpent, some life and death struggle for mastery, the domination of mind over matter. Crystal waits in the dark, her fur coat still wrapped round her. This is the secret economy, the underbelly of commerce, they struggle to make life work, to get the show rolling, the wad of money changes hands, the rest is a dream, the crowds, the bric-a-brac, the plastic cards.

Pete grapples with the cable, sweating blood. At last it's

done, and the house blazes suddenly with light. Pete phones his girlfriend. He'll go home, have a bath, spruce up for the evening down the revamped pub, the cocktail lounge.

'You know, Crystal, I really do apologize about your coffee pot.'

'Oh Micky, it wasn't your fault. I shouldn't have been so cross. It only happened because I forgot to switch the machine off. You really weren't to blame. I'm sorry.'

Somehow she's soothed. She telephones her mother, apologizes again.

'And thank you for the presents. They're *lovely*.'

'Oh, I'm so glad you like them – did you get home all right?' Her breathy, girlish voice comes down the line so eagerly.

'I'll come over soon and we'll see that film you wanted to – '

'Oh yes, that *would* be fun.'

Micky takes off his rompers, leaves his tools stacked tidily in what will be the downstairs shower. Crystal is left on her own for an evening of rest, of quiet, of work. Time to look at her case notes. She won't go out this evening, seeking new sensations, rushing about on the surface; she'll worm her way into the earthworks, the hidden underside of life, tap the vitality that gushes out, where Micky and Pete have exposed the root. She'll start to get things straight.

Never a good mother to her mother (who never knew quite how to mother her) she'll climb into her role as healer/mother, wrestle with those serpents that throttle the heart, squeeze the life out of her patients –

One of those women, her patients, said, 'Coming to see you, it was as if a light was turned on in a darkened room – '

She who saw too well, who watched, observed, but who found it so difficult fully to engage, she's found a way of turning that passivity to active use; a mirror to her patients she shows them themselves not only as they are but also as they could be.

She'll put her feet up on the sofa, read through her case notes, she'll focus her attention on them, she'll set aside the chaos of downstairs, she'll relax, she'll be calm.

The letter had come. Eileen tore at the envelope, unfolded the single sheet, tried to take in the words. 'We have pleasure in informing you – ' She'd got the job.

'It's too cold for a cotton dress – wear your nice dungarees.'

'Oh *no* – '

'Well . . . you must wear a cardy. And tights.'

'The red – '

'It's in the wash . . . how I hate these cold spring days.'

She dumped the cereal packet among the discussion documents and scribbled lecture notes, the book from which she was working propped against her mug of coffee.

'Come on darling, eat up your Weetabix, we have to get off early today.'

'Where's Vic?'

'He'll collect you this evening – I've got another meeting – '

'Want you to get me – '

'It's just today – '

The lecture wasn't finished. She'd have to ad-lib.

Rosie ran along the path, her ribbon was coming undone already. Eileen could never manage to make her look all tidy and sweet like the other little girls. Rosie hardly looked back. She was eager to begin her busy day.

A water main had burst at the junction. There was a long detour – time to plan the rest of her lecture. But the stopping and starting, the jerking crawl irritated her. And it was bad to be late. Slovenly.

The sky was bruised and dark. May blossom and lilac stood out in glimmering chalky pallor.

There was no picket outside the college. But the main hall was strewn with leaflets and a new poster had been pinned up: 'No Victimization – Reinstate the Ten.'

In the departmental office the typists talked about holidays and illnesses. Three of Eileen's male colleagues were leaning against the filing cabinets. They moved apart to include her.

'Have you heard? The Principal's resigned.'

'That's a bit heavy. How d'you know?'

'Read it in *The Times*.'

'That's how we find out what's happening around here these days.'

'It makes us seem even more unmanageable – '

'Oh yes, they're even more likely to try to close this department down now – '

'Don't you count on it. Don't you count on it – '

And Jack was off – the veteran of '68 in full flood, still manning the barricades long after everyone else had sloped off. That's why he annoyed everyone so much, he reminded them of their youthful selves. Where hadn't he been – Paris, Berlin, Berkeley – why had it all dwindled to this dismal aftermath?

She'd worked with these men for eight years – had known Simon for years before that, too, right the way back to LSE. Yet there was no *intimacy* with any of them, her relationship with them entirely public, not what she would call friendship, and certainly no workplace affairs for her, she was always too intent on other things even to think of it, never noticed that sort of thing, and who would want to now with these forty-year-olds, still in jeans with longish hair, pregnant with their beer bellies, or beginning to be stringy instead of youthfully thin. Simon was attractive of course –

They wouldn't fancy her either, she terrified them, apart from anything else –

Simon said, 'There's a meeting in the Old Lecture Hall at noon, an aggregate of the whole staff throughout the Polytechnic – to try to get support for the department – '

'But there's a union meeting then – '

'Oh, come on Eileen – the union exec. isn't supporting us, it's more important to gain mass support – '

'The union *would* support us if we took a sensible position, we can't just dig our heels in and say nothing can ever change. We have to find *some* points of compromise, otherwise – and there's absolutely no point anyway in having general aggregate meetings which don't represent anything except the people who happen to be there.'

'Well, of course, if you don't think the principle of democracy's important – '

'I *do* think it's important. I don't think these one-off meetings *are* democratic, that's all.'

'Ah-ah! *Ahah!* That's just it, isn't it? We all know where Stalinist definitions of bureaucracy lead, don't we – they lead to the betrayal of the students in '68, they lead to – '

'Look, we're all about to be *fired* because of your mate Barker – we've got to stick together – '

'Everyone keeps referring to Norman as "my mate" – do I have to say it again, I – '

Clive patted Eileen's arm: 'What you don't appreciate, my dear, are the strategic problems. You may be right tactically – but strategically we must have a clear line, not some muddled compromise that doesn't really satisfy anyone and that no one will wholeheartedly support.'

They all stuck together, always, just because they'd once been in the SRG –

'Look,' she said, 'we have to take the most progressive position that is capable of winning the most support. We can't go out on some limb – '

'On the contrary, my dear, what we must do is take a *principled* position – '

'What's principled about going on strike because Norman couldn't keep his hands off some student? That was your notion of a principled strategy – '

'Management allegations! Management allegations.'

'No it's *not* management allegations, Jack. A woman student has complained that she's been sexually harassed.'

Simon, always conciliatory, suggested they bring the union meeting forward by half an hour.

'I'll go and see if that's all right with Alan.'

Alan was on the phone. Eileen waited. When he'd finished he said, 'That was Roger Benthall at Box House. He's coming down at eleven. Can you be there? We need to meet to brief him, and then he'll address the whole union branch – '

'But there's this aggregate meeting – Simon wondered if we could bring the branch forward by half an hour to accommodate both meetings – '

'The aggregate's not an official meeting at all. It's not a union meeting, it's got no place in the polytechnic structure, though obviously the Trot lot would say that's all the better – '

'I know all that, but we must *have* the branch meeting, and if they're all off somewhere else – '

'Well, I suppose we could try to meet fairly swiftly with Benthall – You know what he just told me – looks pretty serious – this whole thing's going to blow up in our face, and then it'll be just a cover for redundancies – close down a whole department – marvellous way of getting a massive cut in one fell swoop. And we have to fight it. But we must fight in such a way that we at least have a *chance* to win, or win *something*. That lot want a general strike every time someone's rude to them – '

'You heard the Principal's resigned?'

'Heard at the weekend.' Typical of him not to bother to mention it to her. 'That makes it all worse, of course.'

'I must go – I'm due to teach.'

'Just before you do – is there any possibility that you might speak to the student union this afternoon? They want a member of staff – Jack or Clive are sure to volunteer – and you'd be more acceptable than me – '

'But we have to go down to Party HQ, don't you remember?'

'Oh damn – of course. And we ought to have had a branch meeting here to discuss the issue – hear the views of the other comrades – '

'Perhaps we should just say we can't get down to Geffrey Square today, why should we be at their beck and call, after all there's this crisis going on here – '

'Could you manage tomorrow instead?'

235

'Well – it's open day at the nursery. Parents are all supposed to go – '

'Afterwards? Early evening?'

'I'd have to bring Rosie with me – Vic's on a varying shift now, it's murder – '

'No look, let's go down as arranged. We'll just have to have the other meeting afterwards. Unfortunate, but there it is, with so much going on – '

'Oh, I forgot to tell you – I got the union job.'

Twenty or thirty students scattered around the lecture room. They looked pale in the neon lighting, and sat blankly indifferent to whatever she might be going to say.

'Today I want to talk about the family.'

Once she'd lectured not too badly, now she'd lost her touch; she was no longer the great radical, the latest thing, her words exciting because unfamiliar, her explanations for their angst and alienation meeting their frustration, their need, their anger. These days she felt their anger was a kind of anti-intellectualism more likely to be turned against her as a middle-class, white authority figure, her feminism a bit fuddy-duddy, remote from their raw, unfinished world, processed into an image of staid respectability, with mortgage, child-care problems, a dishwasher, dinner parties, an image of hypocrisy, speaking of oppression but living a bourgeois life.

At the end an Afro-Caribbean woman commented that the black family was a source of strength for black women, that black women weren't demanding the abolition of the family, that to assume they were was racist.

'Yes, but that wasn't what I was trying to say – '

Defensive, wounded, she tried to explain again. But it was too complicated –

'It was Marx and Engels who spoke of the abolition of the *bourgeois* family – '

It upset her to have another woman attack her; but why shouldn't they resent her, they didn't care if she'd once been in the vanguard, she could never be their vanguard.

236

You felt resentful and hurt all the same. But that was to personalize it too much, when really the antagonism came from outside, from what they were all caught up in –

'It's more like – the state – this society has a stereotype of what a family should be like, and it tries to pressure *all* kinds of families and households into that stereotype, and I believe that all women *are* oppressed by that stereotype, but in different ways – '

The students had begun to shove their papers into their baskets and plastic shopping bags, chatting as they pushed back the chairs and drifted from the room.

'And how much do we care about them or our teaching – *really*?' said Susan, as they drank their coffee. 'It's a meal ticket, our relationship to this place, it's like two ugly people who get married – you know, we never really *wanted* each other – '

'Is it as bad as that – ?'

'*I* don't blame the students for griping about the Course. We tell them everything that's wrong with their lives and this society, and how nothing is going to change it except some sort of nebulous revolution – "transformation" as we all used to say – in which neither they nor we actually believe – to them that's total cynicism, and it just reinforces theirs.'

'There were only about twenty students in my lecture today.'

'They're all in the occupation in the Admin Block.'

'Oh . . . that's why there wasn't a picket. I suppose – '

'Sometimes I have this awful feeling the whole place is in process of disintegration – and nobody will really care. We all make a big fuss, but could you really honestly say our department is worth saving?'

'Well yes,' said Eileen stoutly, 'but even if it weren't it's such a moral victory for *them* if it goes down.'

Susan was in a depressed mood. But Eileen had to tell her she was leaving.

'I've got another job – with the union.'

Susan looked at her. Was she sorry? Did she feel deserted,

237

betrayed? Yet more depressed? Another rat leaving the sinking ship?

'I can't *imagine* ever getting another job. Most of us here, we're unemployable, middle-aged intellectuals. I suppose some people in this department could get management jobs . . . Clive, maybe. Simon will go into local government. Alan will go into union work, like you, won't he? I'll be left with Jack and all those women in Domestic Science who wear too much make-up and carry their handbags like the Queen.'

'You've got your writing – '

'I can't live off that. I used to want to freelance, but actually I'd just be a housewife then, stuck at home ferrying the kids about; I'd probably get agoraphobia and be too frightened to venture out into the main road where all those mad old ladies are blown about with the bits of newspaper and drunks huddle in doorways and shout on the corner – '

Then her mood changed, and she laughed: 'You know, I've just remembered, I dreamt about you last night – In my dream first of all you were dancing and I was watching, and then we were both dancing this tremendous, wild dance; crazy, wild, like gipsies, like flamenco – oh, I don't know, but it was very vivid, very exciting – '

'And then?'

'That was all.'

'But I'm so surly and uptight these days, just grinding about from meeting to meeting.'

Eileen put the compromise motion to the meeting, the one the comrades had discussed among themselves. Although everyone in the union branch knew that Eileen had done a major part of the work of organizing the campaign to save the department on two previous occasions, there was general disgruntlement about any compromise now. Jack denounced her, haranguing them all from the front of the room. Some of the right-wingers in turn tried to shout Jack down. Brenda, who was also ex-SRG, burst into tears and accused

Alan of insulting her. Alan retreated into procedural form and rule book.

'They hate the union,' Alan muttered afterwards, 'that's all that Trot stuff is, really, a middle-class attack on the union, it's their class position at the end of the day – '

'We'll have to go – we haven't time to get to the aggregate – '

Outside the rain came at them in little squally rushes. The pavements glistened. The sky was dark and wild. As they drove east the streets became more empty and desolate. Shabby regency houses along the Hackney Road were boarded up or gaping open and collapsing from within. Litter, like dead leaves in this spring, fluttered listlessly over the pavements, and posters peeled away from corrugated iron fencing. Two youths with shaven heads and heavy boots stood in the mouth of an alleyway. Further on a punk with a mohican haircut lurked in the shadows of a railway arch, a bedraggled garish parrot. Two women in saris called to their children from a bus stop where an old man also waited, his paper white face hollowed as a starving man.

'Vic said he might be at the Falcon and Glove – end of his shift.'

He was. Alan ordered drinks while Eileen went to sit with Vic in the polished mahogany depths of the bar. In a faded suit and unravelling sweater and with receding hair that still managed to frizz up wildly, Vic suggested the youthfulness of a bygone era, a tearaway of circa 1956, the postwar generation, a welfare state socialist, an adolescent from the Age of Austerity.

'Been hauled over the coals then?'

'Just on our way,' said Alan.

'Wonder who it'll be – Robespierre or Madam Defarge. Makes no difference of course, they've both got their hand on the guillotine. I shan't last much longer. I'm just waiting for the call. I'm the one's supposed to have fiddled the branch membership – old Madame D cooked that one up.'

'Poisonous woman – nose into everything – '

'Now her *nose* – that's very significant. Eileen's friend,

Crystal, she was on about Freud that time she came round. Well, I went and read some of the stuff. Now *he* goes on about noses. What was it? *Displacement upwards*. That's it. Well, that figures. Her sniffing all the time, what Freud says, that means you can't get a leg over – '

Alan munched his sandwiches gloomily. He and she had regularly sat in here in the early evenings, enjoying a drink between college and some Party meeting. Now was the last time, a whole part of her life about to break off and slip away.

In the States, and in Canada that time, she'd always thought: thank God for the Party. It gave you a political perspective, took you beyond feminism or the union to a wider view of things. Without it, how quickly feminism drifted into a cry of sectional privilege, how quickly union work narrowed to the immediate issues, how easily radicals – like at the college – became just anti-authoritarian. But the Party was over.

'Time to go,' said Alan. 'Let's just think for a moment what we're going to say.'

He went through it again, as he'd done in the car.

'They won't let us say all that, you know.'

'But we have to get it right.'

'Oh, sure, but – '

Don't let's have any illusions.

The building had not changed since the 1930s, the pale green and cream paint was unrenovated, the brown lino on the stairs had worn through on the treads. She went to the wc, but the lid of the lavatory basin was closed, and on it was propped a piece of card:

> This toilet is out of order. For further information see the Treasurer.

Did that mean she had to obtain permission from the Party Treasurer to use the gents? She went in there anyway.

She and Alan passed the main Committee room with its bust of Lenin and the ceremonial axe presented to the British Party by – Dimitrov, was it? She couldn't remember.

But Lenin himself had sat in that room, had lived and worked in this very building. . . .

She tried to imagine Lenin sitting there, reading, writing, looking out of the window. It seemed impossible that someone so monumental, so central to twentieth-century history could ever have inhabited this zone of shabby marginality. In exile for years, though, sitting in a Zurich café, he'd thought the revolution wouldn't come in his lifetime. . . .

Lenin would turn in his grave. This lot that were in charge now hated Lenin. She remembered Eddie fulminating against Leninism at a *Termagant* meeting –

It wasn't Madame Defarge. Geoffrey Price stood behind the desk. He was just a polytechnic lecturer, like themselves.

And to one side of him sat the Eminence Grise – one of the Party old-timers, full-time Party workers who'd sacrificed their lives to the Party, worked for a Party wage, a pittance, trudged through the fifties, despised on all sides, even sneered at inside the Party itself as intellectuals, not real workers – now, after years of toeing the line, he and his like had twisted Party loyalty into a new, strange, rightward spiral. All those years some corrosive bitterness must have been eating him from within. What had it done to him, and those like him, to be Communists then, such a marginal existence –

Yet in another way they'd been at the centre of things.

The Eminence Grise himself had actually been at the Twentieth Congress of the Communist Party of the Soviet Union, when Krushchev had admitted that the purges and the labour camps had all been true. How had this grey man with his withered youthfulness felt? His ideals smashed in that moment? But then there was so much more the Eminence Grise had seen and heard, what he knew from those years in the Comintern, through the War, in the Cold War. He had secrets he'd take to his grave, that was for sure.

And all the while something had been working on him – was it the woodworm of some ultimate cynicism boring into him, until he was riddled and honeycombed with doubt, a secret destructiveness that hollowed him out from within, a loss of faith at the heart but silenced for years, held in? You could see from the lizard watchfulness of his long green eyes – He was a Miss Haversham of the Party, waiting twenty years too long among the ruins of the banquet –

So now he was orchestrating the Party's very own Purge.

The weird thing was, it had all been played through before. She'd read novels about it; there were several quite famous ones. Eileen had read those novels long before she'd joined the Party. In the novels Party apparatchiks behaved just like this: grey, mechanical automata who never listened but simply churned out some Party line. Or rather they listened, they heard, but nothing ever touched them, it would all just be turned against you.

The Party hadn't been like that at all when she'd joined. There'd been discussion, debate. . . .

Of course it was always a looking glass world, the Party, it was life turned inside out, the world turned upside down. What was bad out there was good in here. Perhaps in the end that Wonderland aspect of it, the constant strain of seeing the world inside out, had driven them crazy, the women and men, the old-timers. Or else the mirror had cracked when they'd looked out of the window at the real world –

Geoffrey Price sat behind a desk, moved papers around, gestured them towards ancient bentwood chairs.

The matters to be dealt with –

How could it be that he – and the old man in the corner – could act like this, could play out these caricatures, these clichéd roles? The whole scene was like something out of a Cold War movie or novel, unspeak, a trivial version of 1984, a purge in the name of democracy –

'There have been allegations that the Education Advisory not only did not promote discussion of the Party's Political Programme, but actively campaigned against it. In addition, its officers failed to abide by Party rules, and when instructed . . .'

At the first opportunity Alan launched into his prepared defence of their work.

242

'. . . of course I agree that intellectual openness and the relationship between Marxist theory and the political situation today are of fundamental importance, but surely what distinguishes the Communist Party from other Parties is that it does base its practice on a body of scientific thought, Marxism, and we can't simply jettison that as if the Party Programme replaced Marxism, instead of being, as it actually is, an application of it.'

'Marxism is a *method*, though, isn't it, Comrade?' said the Eminence Grise, making Eileen jump as his cheese-grater voice came unexpectedly from the corner, 'not a theological body of dogma – '

'I think it would be more accurate to say that – '

But Geoffrey Price interrupted, reading out the list of their offences; it was all being dealt with by administrative means, they simply ignored the real arguments, that was what made it such a stereotype, an outsider's nightmare of what the Party was like, so hackneyed as to be brain-numbingly boring, had it not been so insulting. . . .

The shelves behind Comrade Price's head were stacked with pamphlets and papers dating back to before the Second World War. It could not be the first time that scenes such as this had taken place here. The long and not always glorious history of which she had elected to become a part began to oppress Eileen, it was stifling her, she wanted to leave, and yet it gripped her, imprisoned her like a nightmare.

But abruptly Comrade Price drew matters to a close: 'The purpose of this meeting has simply been to inform you that the Executive Committee has decided to suspend your membership pending further investigations into the allegations that have been made, and to explore their basis by giving you an opportunity to respond to them.'

'This is hardly an adequate opportunity!' Eileen laughed, it was so ridiculous. 'It's unheard of to ask an individual to refute allegations without giving them an opportunity to study those allegations in detail and at leisure. You can't just read out bits of somebody's letter and expect us to respond on the spot. We have the right to see everything that's been said against us in written form and to have time to prepare our replies properly. Otherwise it's just innuendo and gossip. It's meaningless.'

'A very bourgeois legalistic view if I may say so, Comrade.'

'The Executive will consider your replies at its next meeting and will then decide what action to take in respect of these and other suspensions.'

The departmental secretary was almost running along the corridor with a pile of folders in her arms.

'The occupation's headed this way,' she called when she saw Eileen, as if referring to a hurricane, a force of nature rather than the outcome of human intentions. They emerged into the hallway together. Jack was arguing with two students and another member of staff, but when he saw the secretary he shouted: 'And as for you, you're just a management stooge – look at you, removing personal folders students have a right to see. Right to information is a basic principle of free and democratic – '

The secretary went red. The students giggled.

'You see, unlike *some* of my colleagues *I* believe in democratic socialism. That's why the meeting today was democratic. It's the same principle as the Soviets in 1905.'

'If I remember rightly,' said Eileen, 'Trotsky supported the Mensheviks in 1905 . . .'

'Ah! Ah!' Jack swung round, pointed his finger at her; 'What Trotsky did in 1905 – '

And he was off, careering through a brief history of the Russian Revolution before coming back to the present with the finger of guilt pointed directly at her: 'And so it's hardly surprising that all these Stalinists we have in our department, who are all in *favour* of what the Soviet Union did in 1956, in 1963, in 1968 and now in Poland and Afghanistan, actually don't *like* it when a *really* democratic meeting occurs: because it *prevents* them from *controlling* it. *That's* the difference between a reformist and a revolutionary. And *I'm* a revolutionary – '

The audience was drifting away, tearing themselves from the Ancient Mariner of the barricades, but Jack, becoming more and more excited, continued to stab his finger in the air and began to circle the hallway like a demented electric rabbit, shouting: 'I'm a revolutionary! I'm a revolutionary! I'm a revolutionary!'

Rain dashed against the bleak ten-foot windows.

Susan was seated with Crystal in the bar.

'Oh good, you found each other. What's all this about the occupation?'

'Oh, nothing – nothing.' Susan made a soothing, flapping gesture with her hand, and the smoke from her cigarette formed a momentary pattern in the stale air. 'Just the secretaries getting hysterical. Simon says it's only a rumour and that actually the students have all voted to stay in the Admin Block and not try to spread the occupation anywhere else.'

'I'm sorry I'm late – I've just been suspended from the Party.'

Susan smiled with constraint, as if Eileen had announced that she'd broken up with a lover everyone else had always loathed. Crystal looked guilty. She'd drifted away from the Party several years ago.

Susan said, 'Until I met you – well, I could never even begin to imagine why anyone would ever join the Party – like going to the Isle of Man for a holiday, or something – '

Crystal said quickly, 'Oh, but people do that – I even met a woman who wrote best-selling romances and she was a tax exile there. Can you imagine having all that money and having to live on the Isle of Man! Don't they still have the death penalty there – or is it only corporal punishment?'

'It's not funny!'

'Oh look – I'm sorry, I expect you're feeling pretty fed up about it – '

'What happened to that book you two were supposed to be writing?'

Eileen and Crystal looked at each other, and Crystal said, 'We've been awful – just let it lapse.'

'Our interests diverged – I've been so caught up in all these rows in the Party – and then there's Rosa – '

'And I've been finishing my analytic training.'

'It might be good fun to think about doing it again – '

Crystal said, 'I think perhaps we conceived of it wrongly . . . we always assumed that it'd be kind of sociological or journalistic – that we would talk to lots of women, collect hundreds of testimonies, you know, *evidence* about women's lives. But it might be better to talk to just a few women, but in depth. In fact, I feel that feminists haven't made enough use of the psychoanalytic *method* – '

'There is a lot of confessional writing, though,' said Susan.

'But that isn't what I mean either – the sort of book I had in mind would *interrogate* the confessional process, question the whole notion of recollection, of memory, of testimony – '

'But that's been done too, hasn't it?' Susan was being rather negative, but Eileen said, 'I'm quite into that idea – only how would it be *political*?'

'Well . . . it would explore the way women have had to live out cultural stereotypes, their inner resistance perhaps, their subversion of those stereotypes – And then it would also show how the same women change over time and become different people; and how what seems politically right at one time changes as well – there has to be a more multi-dimensional way of representing our lives than just different women saying the same thing – that's been the problem, that women's testimony has usually been used to prove the already-known truths of feminism . . . and it's more complicated than that – they're only half truths, often.'

'I still think it would be better to have more women, then the differences as well as the sameness would have more impact.'

'But this would be about the differences within the experience of each of us. The contradictions. Questioning the idea of some linear, one-dimensional narrative of a life, leading unproblematically forward – '

'Perhaps one could do both – '

Susan looked at her watch: 'We'd better go up.'

Eileen stayed for Crystal's talk to the evening degree students. At first Crystal spoke of sexual difference, of femininity, as if it were a kind of necessary fiction, unrelated to biology, yet inescapable both at a deep psychic level and at the level of performance, almost a kind of masquerade adopted to protect the human animal from the chaos of androgyny. And Eileen thought her appearance was consistent with this: a full skirt and black sweater, almost parodic, fifties style.

When she went on to talk about her work with women, though, she seemed to change, to grow less stilted, more warm, more energetic.

Afterwards they had another drink, this time in the pub. Eileen and Crystal decided that they must resurrect their work on the book.

'Now's a good time,' said Eileen; 'we're both more settled.'

Crystal smiled: 'Are we?'

Eileen waited for her to go on, and when she didn't, said, 'What d'you mean?'

'Well, one thing analysis has taught me – how romantic I am . . . you know, I always wanted to be in love – life wasn't worth living unless one was in love – but then being in love never worked, one's unconscious simply goes on propelling one towards the wrong person – '

Eileen looked at her, again expecting more, but Crystal only said, 'I think you may have been right, really, there is something awfully *straight* about married life. I'm going to spend more time with women, I've decided.'

'Yes.'

That was how they'd drifted apart. It was the women's movement that had brought them together, without it they diverged, living with such different kinds of men, caught up in different spheres. . . .

'The book will be fun,' said Eileen.

'You know – I know what's happened in the Party is

247

awful, but perhaps for you personally – well, maybe it's not so bad. I always felt – working in the Party, it made you a bit staid – more cautious – you used to be so fiery, it would be terrible if you lost that fire.'

'She wouldn't go to bed till you came in.'

'You're late Mummy.'

'Let's get this little girl to bed.'

'I'm not tired. Vic and I played chess.'

'Chess! My goodness.'

'I won.'

Vic winked.

Such a pretty little girl, so pleased with herself and with life, in her silly, frilly nightdress. They had a big kiss and hug: 'You smell like newly baked bread, my fat little loaf, you've risen – look at it, your tummy's risen – '

The fat little loaf gurgled and giggled, wriggled, was getting excited. Calm her down, a little read of a book, look at the pictures, drowsy girl.

Goodnight my darling, my little angel.

Vic and Eileen sat on the sofa. The telly was on, but they weren't watching.

'Without the Party we'll both just be union hacks if we're not careful.'

'There's some comrades you know, think we should form a new party. But I'm against breakaways. Never get anywhere. Just leads to more splinter groups and factionalism.'

'What about the Labour Party?' said Eileen. 'We ought to discuss it at least – '

'I'm not going to join the Labour Party. Not after the way those councillors railroaded the union. It's not on; definite.'

'Something new will emerge – it just can't happen at once, I suppose – but things can't *not* change either – '

They knew they'd go on, that this wasn't the end. But for a while they sat, sad about the Party.

'At least I'll have more time with Rosie. That's really the most important thing – '

Yet it was wrong to set the private life against the public. That was what women had not to do. Women had to claim both.

'I'm going to work on that book idea again, with Crystal.'

'You'll have your hands full when the new job starts, you know – '

'I mustn't lose touch completely with feminism though – I must hang on to that somehow.'

Eileen got out of the car with Susan and Crystal at the top of the hill. The hot, empty landscape drew them on. Everything was still, yet the madrone trees rustled as if in a breeze.

'I'm sure Willow will be here soon.'

They looked round, expecting Willow to appear from among the trees. Susan and Crystal wore long skirts, but although at first Eileen had felt hot and awkward in her old jeans, now the sense of discomfort and unease slipped away. They drifted on, Rosie danced ahead.

'Be careful of the rattlesnakes! Be careful darling.'

They came to lower ground and were walking forward across a long lawn that stretched towards some woodland in the distance. The sun slanted across the lawn. They were picking blackberries; her mother had a stick with a crook on the end, to hook down the ones that were too high to reach. Dad had made it for her. They dropped the glistening fruit into the wicker basket, and it formed a mound of shiny black beads. An aeroplane droned across the empty blue sky, a gnat buzzing from some other world beyond this universe of a summer afternoon.

They meet again at a party. They sit in a renovated conservatory, secluded by palm trees and panes of glass from the chattering familiar people and the gossip, which bores them – Labour Party gossip, gossip of the highbrow media, academic gossip.

And everywhere these days, in the houses of friends, there's the new race, the nine- and twelve-year-olds, the fourteen- and sixteen-year-olds, strangers, they live in a separate world.

We saw motherhood in relation to ourselves, what it did to *our* lives, *our* personalities. But now it's them, into something new and different.

It's not so different, they have their movements too.

They're so precocious – so grown up – little Martians with their deadpan chic, their cults, their private obsessions.

They're beautiful too.

Yes, they're much more beautiful than we were.

It's claustrophobic in this glassed-in space. But there are French windows that open onto a garden, and they walk out into the soft, cool darkness, you can hear the traffic, distant, waves beating a far-off shore.

How shall we do it then?

You know, I thought, it's not about women's lives exactly, and it's not really about feminism either – really it's about the Movement, isn't it? What it was. How we experienced it.

Not just that, but – yes – I suppose –

I had a letter from Willow. She has a new girlfriend, she's very happy – well, and I thought, on her land, she's like – she's like the pioneer women really, isn't she? They went into the wilderness, into the wilds – new territory that would be theirs –

But then it's the reverse of that – *those* women stamped their image on the wilderness, they conquered it with what they called their civilization, the civilizing influence of women, nineteenth-century womanhood. Whereas we're the mirror image, we wanted to get into the wild territory. . . .

Some place where there'd be no mediating mirror of civilization, just the truth of experience, all the time, we wanted the place, the zone where the veil of banality is torn away, where there's no more discontinuity, no more dead time. . . .

The mirror of civilization catches fire, the glass is melting, ourselves as spectacle, appearances, performances, the deadly boredom of our face in the mirror, day after day . . . the image melts, the ego dissolves. . . .

We were all in it together.

Also available in Methuen Paperbacks

Julia Voznesenskaya

The Women's Decameron

'Ten women, who ... have all just given birth in a Leningrad clinic, are unexpectedly quarantined together for ten days. Each night each woman undertakes to tell a story on some previously chosen subject: first love, rape, revenge, jealousy, money, betrayal, happiness, noble deeds or sex in absurd situations ... It is an intimate world, startlingly frank about personal and social relationships and, as such, reveals more about Soviet life than anything to be read in a newspaper.'
  Sheila MacLeod, *New Statesman*

'Now here is a robust, spicy saga of adultery, jealousy and betrayal ... a sharp and savage review of Soviet life'
  Sunday Telegraph

'Vigorous, funny, appealing and appalling tales'
  Books & Bookmen

'Lively tales about women getting by, even getting some fun, however grim, out of life in the Soviet Union'
  Hilary Spurling, *Guardian*

'A remarkable book'
  London Review of Books

Nawal El Saadawi

Death of an Ex-Minister

Translated by Shirley Eber

In his mother's arms, a government minister describes an encounter with a junior employee, a woman, who would not lower her eyes in his presence, would not submit. This incident, which shatters his preconceived notions of acceptable behaviour, ultimately leads to his breakdown, dismissal and death.

This cunning tale of how fear of authority, instilled in childhood, becomes authority over those perceived to be weaker – men over women – and blind subservience towards those perceived to be stronger is the first in this subtle collection by Egypt's best known woman writer. While writing of Arab society, her themes are universal – the meaning of life and love in *A Modern Love Letter*; female sexuality in *The Veil*; repressed emotions in *Masculine Confession*.

Nawal El Saadawi's, sympathetic and powerful stories of sexual politics in today's society offer a fresh and moving perception that will touch many readers.

Gloria Naylor

The Women of Brewster Place

Brewster Place is a godforsaken street in a rundown area in small town America. The black women who live there have admitted different kinds of defeat by being there at all, but there is no air of submission in this last stand place, full of courage and resilience.

Through the beautifully wrought stories of seven black women who occupy a condemned neighbourhood, this remarkable work of fiction evokes intimately and powerfully the lives of underprivileged women in an urban ghetto – a world in which the women fight against, survive, and sometimes transcend, the implacable desolation of their surroundings.

Winner of the American Book Award.

Methuen Modern Fiction

While every effort is made to keep prices low, it is sometimes necessary to increase prices at short notice. Methuen Paperbacks reserves the right to show new retail prices on covers which may differ from those previously advertised in the text or elsewhere.

The prices shown below were correct at the time of going to press.

All these books are available at your bookshop or newsagent, or can be ordered direct from the publisher. Just tick the titles you want and fill in the form below.

Methuen Paperbacks, Cash Sales Department, PO Box 11, Falmouth, Cornwall TR10 109EN.

Please send cheque or postal order, no currency, for purchase price quoted and allow the following for postage and packing:

UK   60p for the first book, 25p for the second book and 15p for each additional book ordered to a maximum charge of £1.90.

BFPO and Eire   60p for the first book, 25p for the second book and 15p for each next seven books, thereafter 9p per book.

Overseas Customers   £1.25 for the first book, 75p for the second book and 28p for each subsequent title ordered.

NAME (Blcck Letters) ....

ADDRESS..

....